Praise for Christian Baines

For *The Arcadia Trust* series

"Baines' brave new underworld is well devised, multi-layered, and dense with political and personal agendas—and it's frightening: so much so that I found myself looking over my shoulder more than once at night." FELICE PICANO, author of *Like People in History*

"Baines has a gift for twisted psyches, playing the supernatural to expose the human evils at play, and a talent for turns of phrases that leave you shuddering even as you turn the page." 'NATHAN BURGOINE, author of *Light*

"I love the world created here. It has the same feel as Laurel K. Hamilton's Anita Blake Series, with a little more grit, and of course, the added m/m element. There is plenty of paranormal elements involved, some more gruesome than others, but it is a very colorful and interesting story." JUSTJEN, *The Blogger Girls*

"Just fantastic! I'm just amazed by the imagination the author put into this, from the culprit to the resolution I just couldn't put it down." SARINA, *Love Bytes Reviews*

"A wickedly subversive wit." JEFFERY ROUND, author of *The Dan Sharp Mysteries*

"I really enjoyed this book and have great admiration for Baines' literary skill. My reaction to *The Orchard of Flesh* is that it's something of a mashup of Clive Barker and Noel Coward." ULYSSES, *Prism Book Alliance*

For other works

"Christian Baines is a writer with a bold, original vision, a vision not beholden to the limits of conventional genre tropes. This is a writer who knows his own voice, and a writer to watch." MICHAEL ROWE, author of *Enter, Night*

BY CHRISTIAN BAINES

THE ARCADIA TRUST *series:*
The Beast Without
The Orchard of Flesh
Sins of the Son

Other books:
Puppet Boy

E-Books:
Skin

CHRISTIAN BAINES

SINS OF THE SON

Christian Baines has written on travel, theatre, film, television, and various aspects of gay life, factual and fictional. Some of his stranger thoughts have spawned novels, including queer urban fantasy series *The Arcadia Trust*, the horror novella *Skin*, and *Puppet Boy*, which was a finalist for the 2016 Saints and Sinners Emerging Writer Award.

Born in Australia, he now travels the world whenever possible, living, writing, and shivering in Toronto, Canada on those odd occasions he can't find his passport.

SINS OF THE SON

ISBN 13: 978-1-9995708-0-4

FIRST EDITION: JANUARY 2019

EDITOR: L E DANIELS
COVER DESIGN BY JEANINE HENNING

Acknowledgements

Thank you to all who have supported my writing and this series, and to those calling for a broader range of both LGBTQ and speculative fiction. We're getting there.

Special thanks to my editor, Lauren Daniels for your tireless patience, support, and tough love, and to cover artist Jeanine Henning for making us look sexy.

Thank you to author colleagues 'Nathan Burgoine, Eric Andrews-Katz, and Brey Willows for all your support during events, and to Avylinn Winter, for your patient ear during those 'head pounds desk' moments.

Thanks to friends and family who've supported me for your inspiration, love, signal boosting, and occasional reminders to get back to work

Last by not least, thank you Dean, my partner, soulmate, biggest fan, and favourite grumpy cat.

SINS OF THE SON

By Christian Baines

CHAPTER ONE

I ducked in time to avoid the stake that shattered the glass cabinet behind me. When I looked up, my young attacker was already closing in, a shining blade in each hand. Balancing my weight on the kitchen counter, I pushed my feet hard into his chest. A blade nicked my ankle. I leapt upon my target and pushed him to the floor, gripping his chin and pinning his right shoulder.

He blindsided me across the jaw with the dull edge of the other blade, breaking my hold.

I staggered, sizing up the left-handed assassin. Narrowly avoiding his weapon as he lunged again, I grabbed hold of his hair and threw him into my dining table with a crash.

I clapped a firm hand over his mouth, muffling his cries as I slammed his left wrist against the table, forcing him to drop the knife. The blade in his opposite hand flashed as he struck out with it.

I yanked him off his feet and dragged him across the floor before he could find his mark. Ignoring muffled roars of protest, I buried my teeth in his shoulder, puncturing through his flimsy mesh vest. His youth, his anger, his alarmingly good health, all brought such a warmth and sweetness to…

The foul taste of bitter roots spoiled the stream. Poison. I shoved the boy away, spitting rancid blood over his face. When he came at me again, I used his momentum to topple him into the living room. I snatched up the knife he'd left on the kitchen table and trained it on him as he regained his feet.

The boy had to have known the true nature of his prey. Why else would he lead with a wooden stake, knowing he was far outclassed for natural speed and strength? Or was he?

He lunged again, this time happily using his right hand. Was he ambidextrous? I couldn't tell, not while ducking his blows. He kicked me in the gut before pivoting his back foot up and into my chest.

I dropped to the floor just in time to sweep his legs out from under him. His forehead glanced off one of the side tables, though this didn't stop him from grabbing the lamp and throwing it at me with a force that plunged the room into darkness. I caught his weight as he came at me again, spinning him into the living room, bound for a set of shelves which splintered and collapsed, spilling their contents and my attacker to the floor. He sprang to his feet and snatched up a piece of broken wood.

Contrary to the myths of horror fiction, it would take more than a splinter of wood through the heart to kill me outright. I was not, however, in a rush to be paralysed, nor left unconscious at the mercy of whatever lethal objects remained in the boy's backpack. The one he'd collected from the club's cloakroom, that he'd so adamantly held onto when I'd offered to carry it. The one he'd taken with him, when he'd retreated to my bathroom to change.

Did I have to start bag checking my trade now?

He sliced the air before me with his knife, following it up with a staking attempt. I grabbed his knife-wielding hand, but he twisted his arm out of reach, nicking my hand in the process. I licked the wound as I backed off, kicking away a broken cat figurine from the rubble that had once been my bookshelves.

"All right, you little bastard," I muttered under my breath. "Are we going to talk, or does this get nasty?"

"Maledetto." He raised the stake once more.

"Excuse me?"

"*Maledetto!*" He cried, striking out at me.

I ducked to avoid it only to have the hand holding the knife slam into my jaw. I barely realised I'd been faked out before the stake plunged into my chest, missing my heart by inches. Choking down the pain that shot through my entire body, I caught the boy's arm before he could slice my throat. Not that that would have killed me either, but to quote a wise and much underrated human expression, that which does not kill me still stings like a bitch.

I pressed my long fingernail into his wrist, ignoring his futile effort to drive the stake deeper toward my heart. He had no momentum, and I wasn't about to let him go. Yet even as he cried out through gritted teeth, he refused to drop the knife. I pressed harder and forced his wrist back against itself until I heard bones snap.

This time, the boy let his scream go. He dropped the knife and clutched his wrist before looking up at me, eyes full of fury.

I wrenched the splinter from my chest and ducked another punch.

The kid simply refused to quit. I caught his arm as it swung wide of my head and lifted it sharply, forcing the shoulder out of its socket.

The kid screamed again, only to fall silent, slumping to the floor as the broken lamp came down on his head. With one limb broken and the other dislocated, he lay motionless as Brett, my Mannequin and loyal live-in servant, prodded the unconscious form with his foot.

"Nice work." Leaning against the wall, I let myself slide to the floor as my body worked its sorcery on the chest wound. Remarkable as it was, I'd have to feed soon and drinking from the boy was out of the question. Whatever he'd done to his blood had sickened me to my stomach. "When did you get in?"

"Just now," Brett answered, replacing what remained of the lamp on the side table. "Dude, what the fuck happened?"

I shook my head, too tired to go into details. "Picked up the wrong trade," I said, tossing off the explanation as if having a companion try to kill me were a weekly occurrence. I must have winced again, since Brett pulled away my jacket before I could wave him off.

"Holy hell! What did he do to your chest?"

"It's nothing. He..."

Brett picked up the fragment of shelf and grimaced. "I get it. Why's it taking so long to heal?"

"Can you grab my phone?" I said, before realising the absurdity of what I was about to do. While my handsome 'twenty-four-year-old' online profile would quickly entice a suitor, a gaping chest wound hardly showed me in the sexiest light. "It'll heal. It just takes longer without blood."

"Understood." Brett tossed his jacket onto the couch and offered his wrist. My sweet, loyal boy.

I rarely fed from Brett. He was my Mannequin, after all, meaning he sustained his life through drinking my blood, not the other way around. It enhanced his senses, abilities, mental acuity, and just occasionally, skewed his sex-drive in my direction, which made for some awkward conversations. Taking a little of that blood back for myself didn't harm me any, but it was no substitute for a fresh supply.

Beggars, however, could not be choosers.

I bared my fangs, gently bringing Brett's wrist up to my mouth. It was hard to repress my satisfaction as a faint shiver went through him, the dark hairs on his forearm rising over gooseflesh at my touch. I watched his throat twitch in those few nervous seconds before I bit him, then relished a pang of wicked pleasure at his faint gasp. The blood wasn't ideal, being at least partly recycled, but it did its job. The fibres of skin and muscle around the wound burned as they hastened back together. Brett turned away, allowing the grisly healing to finish its work undisturbed.

"Thank you." I put a hand on his shoulder as he helped me to my feet.

"Don't mention it. Who the hell is he?"

I heard the sickening sound of splintered bone as Brett tried to roll the boy over.

"Just leave him. I'll take care of it. Can you fetch me his bag, please? It should be in the bathroom."

Brett gave my wounded guest one last wary look before doing as he was told.

I tilted the boy's face to get a closer look at the features that had so charmed me in the club. The smooth black hair, the studded leather collar, the strong, pronounced Roman nose and high cheekbones. He even retained a hint of that cocky smile through his unconsciousness. I tried not to look at his sinewy arms, displaced as they were. But we'd done him no permanent harm, and I was in no hurry to go another round with him.

I quickly replayed our meeting in my mind. He approached me. Called me sexy and asked to dance. I was struck by his resemblance to... The boy's visage was an unwelcome reminder I tried to dismiss as he pulled me closer.

The scent of his blood was intoxicating, even now, which meant he was bleeding into my carpet. But this seemed a trivial complaint as I surveyed my shattered living room. The boy was trained. Otherwise, he'd barely have lasted seconds against me. Indeed, had I been any less vigilant, might he have accomplished his mission? Why the hell was *I* anyone's mission? One of the things I treasured about living in Sydney, my chosen home for the past forty odd years, was the relative anonymity it afforded me from the rest of the Blood Shade world.

Yes, Blood Shade. That is the term I used and I appreciate others who follow suit. Try calling one of us the 'v' word if you'd care to discover its origins.

Sydney is, and has in my experience always been the ideal hangout for those seeking to leave the politics of the old supernatural world behind. The elders who'd laid wager on the games of ancient Greece and Rome. The witches—oh, all right, Shapers—who traced their skill in the arcane arts through centuries of mentors before them. All those who proclaimed themselves older, wiser, and more qualified to act as lord and master over the rest of us.

Those who, to my mind, could bugger right off, as my current Australian neighbours liked to say.

Brett returned with the backpack and I pulled out a turtle neck sweater to reveal... Holy shit!

Two more stakes, an ornately sheathed dagger, two vials of clear liquid I absolutely did not want to open, and a small crucifix, harmless to me, but blatantly symbolic. I turned the bag on its head and tipped the remaining contents onto the floor.

"What are you looking for?" Brett asked.

I shook the bag a couple more times before my fingers closed around something firm in the front pocket. I claimed my prize. An Italian passport. I barely needed to turn to the photo page.

Luca Depuratore.

A soldier of the Scimitar of Light, a hate-driven organisation of religious warriors from supernatural family lines, dedicated to hunting down and honour-killing their inhuman brethren. But not just any soldier. My grip tightened around his passport as I swallowed my rage, comparing the photo to my would-be assassin's handsome features.

There was no mistaking the face of my fallen protégé and closest friend.

Depuratore? This boy had to be a relation, here in violation of the uneasy but longstanding truce that had—until now, at least—kept the Scimitars off our shores.

Did they even know Ross was dead?

I tucked the passport away inside my bloodied pocket. "I need to make a call."

CHAPTER TWO

In the not too distant past, the idea of bringing my wounded assailant to the Arcadia Trust would have repulsed me. Not long before that, it wouldn't have even occurred to me. The Trust, a loose association of supernatural beings from throughout inner Sydney, kept its existence a secret, at least from me, until some months ago when it enlisted my help in tracking and capturing a young werewolf wanted for a series of grisly murders.

That modest favour opened a virtual Pandora's Box of complications, most of which I didn't care to revisit. Now, here I was, asking for their help.

Help, of course would be at the discretion of Patricia Bakker, the human who ensconced herself at the head of this curious organisation. A self-proclaimed daemonologist—and former nun, no less—she had negotiated the Scimitar's expulsion from Sydney after their failed attempt on Ross's life. Such influence, power and confidence earned Patricia at least some respect. And where did I, an independent Blood Shade with no interest in the political manoeuvrings of the night fit into all this? I had agreed to serve as her liaison to the city's Blood Shades and their allies. The House of Blood. Those beings touched by immortality. I'd held the job for less than two weeks, with little to no idea what it would entail.

Was I simply to keep Patricia and the city's Blood Shades from killing one another? I could probably do that. Right now, I was more concerned with keeping Ross's estranged kin from killing me.

The cab driver, for his part, was not the brightest or most cooperative specimen of his profession. Only a sizeable tip had persuaded him that no, our young friend did not need a hospital and that it was no business of his.

The Arcadia Trust occupied a sizeable house on a leafy street in Paddington, one that stood out against the endlessly renovated terrace houses that surrounded it, like a queen bee commanding its workers to keep its hipster residents busy, and not bother mother under any circumstance.

Brett carried Luca's 150 odd pounds of lean muscle up the stairs with ease, though I doubted if, just a few months into his service with me, he expected his duties to include carrying wounded assassins. Striding up the aged stairs, I rang the doorbell. The only response was a somewhat anticlimactic buzzing from inside. We waited a moment, then tried again.

"Nobody home?"

I frowned. With the recent deaths of two of her resident Shapers, who remained under Patricia's roof? Did she even reside there herself? It also disturbed me to recall that many, if not most of my visits to the Arcadia Trust had begun with waking up from some painful and near-lethal misadventure or other, usually with Ross staring down at me, ready to lecture me on my foolish risks.

He took just one risk to save me, and died for it.

In residence or not, I was sure Patricia would at least leave the house under the watchful eye of Kelvin, her resident Cloak Walker and attack dog, unseen and impossible. If Brett and I had spent more than a minute on the premises without his accosting us, there was something wrong. We could have attempted to break the door down, but given her past collaborations with Shapers, I didn't put it past Patricia to have magickal protections in place, waiting for an unwary twist of a doorknob or—

I jumped as Brett broke open the door with a solid kick, his human strength augmented by my blood. I glared at him.

"What? This guy's heavy."

Another crash came from inside. Then another, from the darkened hall.

"Wait here," I instructed Brett, advancing along the Victorian passageway to the source of the noises, which by this point, included another loud bump and a dull roar. I recognised Kelvin's bellow of frustration before a harried looking Patricia threw the door shut behind her, eyes widening as she saw me.

"Reylan! Don't come any clo—"

The door's abrupt splintering sent the woman sprawling to the floor. I dashed to her side, scooping her up just in time to avoid the door's remains as they blistered off their joints. I caught sight of something that looked like a giant rat's tail on the other side, just as Patricia shoved me out of the way of a gigantic...

What. In. The. Name. Of. Hell?

I could only stare at the enormous beak snapping at us from the shattered doorway, dripping a sickly green gel onto the floor. I didn't want to know what was on the other end of that beak.

"Out of the way!"

I turned to face the familiar voice, only to see a shotgun cock itself in mid-air, then fire with a boom that reverberated around the hall, sending two portraits crashing to the floor. Though I'd not yet gotten a look at the creature, it bellowed in agony as it pulled away. The childlike forms of Sophia and

Giorgios, the two Premature Blood Shades who guarded the Trust's ancient library, came scrambling through the door's remains.

"I said you'd wake it up, silly!" the girl snapped, hauling her pouting brother through the wreckage, leaving the beast behind.

"I just wanted a closer look at it!" he grumbled, pulling a piece of gore out of his sister's uncharacteristically tussled red hair.

"Well, you made it very—"

Another bang silenced them both as the thing crashed its way around the Arcadia Trust's ballroom-come-emergency ward on what looked like thick, spindly legs. The girth of tree trunks, they were covered in a down of black hairs. Its body remained out of sight, which drew no complaints from me.

"What the hell is it?"

"An extremely pissed off abomination," Patricia answered. "Kelvin?"

"One that's now blind, for which you're welcome!"

"What time is it?" Sophia asked.

"Pardon?" I replied. "What are you talking about?"

"Just answer."

Patricia tossed a glance at the ornate clock on the mantle. "Nearly half past five. Sophia, what are you—"

"It's at least part Blood Shade. If we can open the curtains, it won't last long."

"You hope," said Giorgios.

I'd no idea what the thing was, but if it did, as Sophia claimed, contain some element of Blood Shade—

A thunderous kick sent what was left of the door sailing into the room. Kelvin swore as Patricia shot me a look I didn't like one bit.

"You're joking," I said.

"With me on three," she answered. "One, two..."

Without slowing to think, we dashed through the broken doorway that was now wide enough for both of us. The creature screamed its indignation somewhere off to my right, but I didn't stop. Not until I'd seized a handful of curtain and pulled it back as far as I could, wrapping it around me to keep out the cursed rays. Only once the morning's light streamed into the room did I stop to catch a look at our enemy.

Had I known its composition beforehand, I probably would have bolted home. I'd no decisive word for what I now saw. A patchwork composed of an enormous black and white bird's head, a filthy long rat's tail, and black wings, which beat in a panic atop eight long, spindly, hairy black legs. All of it smouldered as daylight did its deadly work.

Patricia and I ducked as the creature overturned the piano in the corner of the room with its great, burning wings. It let out a ghastly screech as two of its legs gave way, sending it crashing to the floor, where it fitted out its death throws in the toxic sunlight. It seemed a good deal more susceptible to the sun than I. A few stray rays across a Blood Shade's skin would do little more than leave a nasty burn, one that would heal within minutes of returning to the shadows. But small fires now erupted all over the creature as it shrank.

I watched in amazement as the remaining six legs, wings, and tail retracted into its inky black abdomen, which seemed to bleach paler with each new fire. The beak too seemed smaller and less pronounced as it and the feathers fell away into ash, leaving behind only the distorted, ruined head of a man who'd taken a shotgun blast to the face. Then a body, followed by four charred limbs that I assumed once ended in hands and feet.

Patricia and I slid the curtains shut as the thing stopped twitching. Sophia stepped inside, making sure the body had stopped moving before kneeling to collect a sample of the ash, and scraping a patch of the corpse's charred skin—if the word 'corpse' even applied. It could no longer be described as humanoid.

"Patricia," I murmured.

"Yes, yes, I know. What is it? Where did it come from? What is it doing here? Reylan, we can talk about it later."

"I told you, you couldn't control it," Giorgios said, sulking.

"You're the one who woke it up!"

"Enough!" Patricia snapped. "Reylan, why are you here?"

Leaving the Prematures to their dead monstrosity, I led Patricia out to the front porch, where Brett waited with the unconscious Luca laid out on a bench.

"Everything okay?" he asked.

* * *

"Get him up on the table," Patricia said, clearing space.

I glanced around at the jars and bottles filled with liquids and preserved solids I was happy to leave unidentified. The dimly lit walls confounded me further with their strange runes and sigils. Even if they were occasionally willing to share the benefits, the Shapers were not much inclined to share the specifics of their 'magick' with outsiders.

"I take it you've good reason for not admitting him to the nearest hosp…" Patricia's face blanched as I showed her Luca's passport. Without a word, she stalked away from the table, only to return with a vicious looking blade.

I grabbed her wrist as she raised the knife high above the boy. "What are you doing?"

"Unhand me. I won't ask you twice."

"He's a child!"

"Reylan, I appreciate your compassion, I do. But the Scimitar stole any childhood he had long ago. This boy's entire remembered life has seen him trained to kill. I told his organisation that if any one of them *ever* came within striking distance of this city again, they'd be destroyed. I don't make empty threats. Now, which body part do you think will send the strongest message? As this is a repeat offence, I'm inclined to go straight for the head."

"He's Ross's family!"

"Meaning what? Ross is dead, Reylan. For all we know, this one was sent to make another attempt on his life, then decided to pick off his associates when he realised his primary target was already gone."

"Conjecture!"

"Prove me wrong. From the beginning, tell me exactly how he came to attack you."

"He never said the kid attacked him," Brett pointed out.

"Then why is 'the kid' injured? If you're going to presume I'm stupid, you can keep quiet."

Doing my best to keep my words brief and my temper steady, I relayed events, starting at Blaze, my feeding ground for the evening. Luca's wiry frame had certainly stood out amid the dance floor's usual array of muscle-bound gym addicts. He'd been the one to make eye contact, luring me across the room with a faint smile and more than a passing resemblance to my late friend. A resemblance that now made perfect sense, of course. As a Blood Shade, I'd all manner of tricks and deceptions at my disposal to draw his eye, but I'd used none of them. He'd come to me.

But had he also come for me? I'd mentored Ross, which in the Scimitar's narrow view made me culpable in his damnation—to say nothing of what I'd done to the first of their rank who'd tried to kill him. Yet it seemed ridiculous that they would send a lone assassin—*any* lone assassin—to the ends of the earth to target me.

"Unless of course," Patricia said, "he's been watching you for months."

I shook my head. "Why would he? I doubt in any case that he'd be able to spend months in the city without Ross noticing."

"So, he came for Ross. Then, realising his target was dead, he decided you were the next best thing."

"Are you ready now?" Sophia chirped from the doorway.

Patricia stepped away from Luca. "You're sure you know how to do this?"

"Everything Elspeth knew about it, I know. I haven't yet had a chance to practice of course."

Despite her abrasiveness, my respect for Elspeth had only grown in the few days I'd known her. Knowing their mission would be fatal, the Shaper and her colleague had transferred their collective knowledge to the Premature Blood Shades—an unorthodox decision, but a resourceful one. Elspeth in particular had been a gifted Life Shaper. A medic. A shaman. Whatever the chosen name, her surgeon's hand had spoken for itself. But the transfer offered no guarantee that Sophia would inherit her skill.

Having surveyed Luca's broken arm, the Premature began picking out jars and bottles from the shelves. I shifted my gaze between the girl and Luca as Patricia helped her reach a jar on the top shelf.

The girl nodded her thanks. "You may leave now."

"I'm sorry?"

"I can't have the energies of three onlookers buzzing around the room while I'm trying to work. I'm nervous enough about this as it is."

"Reylan," Patricia gestured toward the door. "Please?"

* * *

Little more than a greasy black shell remained of the creature when we returned to the ballroom. Giorgios kneeled beside it, a clean specimen bottle open in his hand.

"I wouldn't get too close to that," I said. "Can you be sure it's dead?"

"If it's not, it won't get far, pretty boy," said Kelvin.

That, I didn't doubt. Giorgios stared at the corpse.

"Hey," I whispered, forgetting for a moment that this 'child' was probably at least a century old. "Everything okay?"

The boy nodded, scraping some of the black gelatinous goo off the corpse and dropping it into the bottle.

I peered closer at the wound left behind, a repugnant black mess of charred flesh, oozing equally dark fluid. "Why didn't the sunlight destroy the rest of it?"

"Don't know." The boy shrugged. "This is how it looked when we found it."

Kelvin gave a loud snort. "Only you two would want to pick up and study a giant dead cockroach."

"And where did you find it?" I asked.

A great scream erupted through the house before anyone could answer.

*   *   *

Luca appeared to be in the throws of a violent fit when we rushed back into the room. Blood spurted from his mouth and his arm flopped loose at a sickening angle as Sophia kept hold of his wrist.

"What the hell?" Patricia asked.

"It was only a sedative!" the girl said.

Luca howled as he tried to put his weight on the dislocated shoulder.

16

An unseen force slammed him back down on the table and turned him roughly on his side. "Are you just going to stand there until he chokes on his own blood?"

I signalled Brett, urging Sophia to step aside as we helped Kelvin pin the boy down. Patricia simply folded her arms. Even if Kelvin was prepared to help us, I'd clearly not convinced her that the Scimitar was worth saving. I wasn't sure I'd convinced myself.

"What happened?" I asked.

"I don't know," Sophia said. "My best guess is something reacted to the sedative in his bloodstream and—"

Another scream cut her off as Luca vomited up more blood.

"Sophia?"

"His organs are liquefying. I don't know what to do."

I shot a glance from her, to Patricia, to Luca's shaking form. Whatever error Sophia had made, was killing him.

"There's got to be something we can use in here!" Brett snatched one of the unlabelled bottles off the shelf to discern its dubious contents.

"Even if there is," Kelvin said, "Sophia's only been a Shaper for three weeks! What's she supposed to—"

"Reylan," Patricia's tone was kind but firm. "End it."

I knew she was right. Every second we stood arguing left Luca in agony. What should have been a simple injury now threatened to destroy him, thanks to the ill-conceived magicks of a novice Shaper. His only chance now was a little 'magick' of my own. I held his body firm and lifted my wrist to my mouth.

Brett's eyes locked with mine over the boy's convulsing body. "No."

I sank my teeth into my wrist, letting several drops of warm, fresh blood hit Luca's face.

"No!" Brett threw himself at me, driven by mad instinct to protect his sole ownership of my blood.

I shoved him away with my free hand, turning up my nose as the jar he'd been holding smashed on the floor, emitting a foul odour like rotting meat. Or perhaps it was Luca, vomiting over himself as he tried to clamp his mouth over my wrist. I jammed it into place before he could scream again. And so he drank, with not a trace of consciousness in his eyes. No sign of thought or reason beyond an animal need to survive. After several seconds, I pulled away, sealing my wrist with a lick, lest he lunge for it again.

The blood steadied him immediately. He sat up, staring at me as his breathing slowed, bony fingers gripping the edge of the table as Sophia stepped away.

"Interesting," said Patricia.

That was an understatement. By this point, Luca's insides should have been tearing themselves apart, preparing themselves for a new existence in service to my blood. But he neither screamed, nor writhed in agony. None of the horrors Brett had endured during his transfor—

Luca's eyes bulged. He clutched his stomach and turned away, vomiting a violent stream of blood over the other side of the table.

"Oh, lovely!" said Kelvin. "That's just great!"

I reached for Luca only for him spew forth another river of red. I put an arm around his waist. He was shaking all over in between coughing and vomiting fits.

"What the hell's wrong with him?" Kelvin asked.

Patricia remained unmoved. "It's the price he pays, isn't it?"

"*Così malato!*" the boy cried. "*Sto morendo!*"

"Shhh." I tried to hold him steady as he threw up again. I didn't have an answer. Nothing about this was normal. His body should have fitted out its trauma and stabilised in less than a minute. "It's going to be okay."

"Why isn't your blood healing him?" asked Sophia.

Luca released another stream over the edge of the table, coughing up the last of it as I laid a hand on his back.

"Sophia," I said. "What happened when you tried to heal him?"

"His body rejected the sedative immediately, as if it were poison."

During our encounter at home, I'd attempted to feed from him, only to feel instantly sickened. Had the same poison threatened his life when exposed to Sophia's magick, and was it now reacting to mine? In any case, his rapidly transforming body wanted none of it. The touch of my hand running through his hair seemed to calm him down.

"Did you take a blood sample?" I asked.

"Of course."

"Analyse it."

"Pardon?"

"There's a distinct bitterness to his blood. I'll wager he's had an inoculation of some sort."

"You might have mentioned that!"

"Just run the tests. Also, see if you find a higher concentration in what he's been coughing up. If my blood's doing its job, his body will be doing everything it can to get rid of anything harmful."

"He seems to have sorted himself out."

Kelvin was right. Luca didn't seem to be in any pain now. Besides the vomiting, his transformation was oddly calm. He wasn't even moving, just breathing steadily, his eyes watering, the sour waft of bile rising from his bloodstained mouth.

I exchanged a cautious glance with Patricia, who watched with interest. There was no way to know for sure what was happening inside him. No measure of what his body had endured.

Brett sat on the floor, dark eyes piercing me with undisguised rage. Why had I pushed him? I'd more than enough strength to hold him in place while Luca lapped at my blood. Blood that would soon infuse the boy with the disarming strength of his—

I gasped as Luca threw me against the sideboard. The boy's elbow then cracked loudly against what sounded like Kelvin's jaw. Before anyone else could move, Luca was off the table, howling and digging fingers into the mesh vest that clung to his lean, muscular body.

Brett rose to restrain the boy, but I held him back. Whatever Luca was going through, I didn't want any of us near him in this state. He tore the vest away from his body, only to continue clawing at his flesh, clutching now at the leather collar around his neck, agile fingers fumbling with its clasp.

"Help," he choked as his movements became panicked. He murmured more words in Italian before screaming. *"Aiutatemi!"*

"All right!" I kept my hands raised where he could see them. "We're not going to hurt you, understand? Just let us help." Though I still wasn't game to get close, my words, or perhaps my tone seemed to do the trick as he found the clasp on the collar and lifted it. The leather and metal slipped to the floor, revealing an ugly red scar that marked his throat from ear to ear. It was the last thing I noticed before his legs buckled and he slumped to the floor.

"Brett, his feet, please." I gently lifted Luca under his arms.

My Mannequin did as he was told. Still, his eyes burned with jealousy.

"Bloody hell," Kelvin muttered. "His neck."

"Well, there's not a lot we can do about that now." Patricia turned the boy's chin in her hands. "He's alive. I assume that pleases you?"

I was in no mood to argue. "You'd have him die?"

The former nun just raised an eyebrow at me. "There's at least another nine hours before sunset. I trust you'll be staying?"

"I trust we're welcome?"

"Our rooms aren't luxurious, but yours should keep out the light." She turned her attention back to Luca. "This one should find the cellar relatively comfortable."

'Comfortable' wasn't the first word I would have applied to the wine cellar beneath Patricia's backyard. Still, it was secure enough to hold a potential threat, be it Luca, or Jorgas, the young werewolf we'd been forced to detain several months prior. I just had to keep the memory of Jorgas's exhausted, drugged form far from my mind, just as I'd tried to do with my other memories of Jorgas since his disappearance. No matter what I'd come to feel for him, I wasn't about to let someone who didn't want to be found consume my thoughts.

* * *

True to Patricia's warning, the room would not have looked out of place in one of her former convents. An unremarkable wooden desk, a dark chest of drawers, a dusty armchair covered in dark red velvet, not a single window, and a small, sad looking double bed covered in linens that looked crisp enough to provide structural support to a multi-level car park.

"We put Brett in Elspeth's old room, since it has windows. Make yourself at home. Matthias wasn't much one for material possessions. He believed the mind and body to be one's only true home."

"A minimalist philosophy, you no doubt appreciate?"

Her mouth formed what could charitably be called a smile. "I haven't been a nun in over twenty years."

"Though you continue in the spirit of Saint Francis? Succour to beasts and all?"

"Succour to beasts doesn't extend to beasts with human faces."

Beasts, indeed. Blood Shades, Flesh Masters, as many werewolves preferred to be known, Shapers, Cloak Walkers like Kelvin, the Mutilated, the returned dead, or...

"What was it, then?" I asked. "The creature you destroyed in the ballroom?"

She nodded sagely. "I think it's best your servant doesn't know. So, strictly between us, that husk in the ballroom is what remains of Sklav."

The room suddenly seemed smaller and mustier. More than that, it seemed to be shrinking. Or perhaps I'd just stopped breathing. Sklav? The creature we'd destroyed in the disused tunnels of Redfern train station? The one that through assimilation of biological matter had been able to bend and change its shape at will?

"And you kept it in your house... why?"

"That creature consumed two of the most loyal and capable colleagues I have ever known before it was destroyed. Part of me dared hope that some of who they were remained."

"You thought you could bring them back?"

"We recovered what we could. We knew it would be a stretch to separate their genetic material from the flotsam flowing through that creature. It would seem—"

"It would seem being dead didn't inhibit its shape-shifting ability!" Not that I'd seen Sklav assume the hideous form we'd just witnessed.

"We miscalculated which of its genetic elements would come to the surface. That was why you saw what you saw."

"Who miscalculated this, exactly?"

The nun shook her head, looking tired all of a sudden as she leaned against the doorway. "Sophia knows it all, Reylan. All of Elspeth's memories, just as Giorgios holds all those of Matthias."

"Not enough though, is it? They aren't capable of practicing. They're not Shapers. Sophia's working from theory, alone. You've turned your librarians into living libraries, nothing more."

"*I* did no such thing! Matthias and Elspeth asked them directly. They consented. I approved it."

"And now you wish you hadn't?"

"Then Sklav would have continued to grow until it destroyed us."

"Then your decision was the right one."

She turned to leave.

"So," I said quietly, watching a tiny spider tumble its way down from the corner of the ceiling and disappear behind the velvet chair. "Are you going to tell her you need her, or should I?"

Patricia knew full well who I meant. Her face offered neither anger, nor condescension, and her voice was quiet when she finally spoke. "Out of the question. Sleep well."

I lay down on the bed as she took her leave, arms crossed over my chest, waiting for sleep. While I'd strived over the years to avoid the decadent excesses that cursed many of my species, Matthias's mattress was so dense and firm, I was starting to suspect that sleep, in any form, would be an elusive prospect at best. I don't know why it surprised me. The Shaper had carried six foot of finely tuned muscle as if it should be honoured to cling to his bones. In fact, he'd seemed oddly physical for a man whose powers lay in mental discipline and intellect.

A quiet creaking outside my door broke my train of thought. I eased myself off the cunningly disguised stone slab of a 'bed' and opened it, only to see Brett.

"Shouldn't you be asleep?"

"Couldn't." He shuffled.

I stepped aside and let him in. "Cosy, isn't it?"

He barely seemed to notice, giving the place a disinterested once over before turning back to me with a scowl. "Why'd you do it?"

There he was again, the old Brett. Besides the natural kinship his reliance on my blood compelled between us, Brett's attitude had improved immeasurably since the night we'd first met at the Black Soul. But every so often, I saw flashes of his initial coolness, along with the undisguised contempt he'd directed at Suzette, the young emo girl who'd mistaken us for a couple.

As for Suzette, I'd last seen the poor girl right before Ross, typical of his nature, had rushed her to hospital with what he'd led me to believe were serious injuries. Some people were just not meant to cross paths with the supernatural world.

I shut the door silently. "You know why."

"You should have let him die."

"Not appreciating the tone, Brett."

"He tried to kill you!"

"So did you," I reminded him. "Did you think I'd forgotten?"

Brett's lips curled into a faint snarl as the memory of his slashing my throat with a common street blade returned to him. "It's not the same."

"What's not?"

"I didn't know what you were!"

"So, thinking I was human and mortal, you dragged a knife across my throat without a second thought."

"I was scared!"

"Scared?" I edged closer to him, firmly holding his gaze in mine. "How do you think Luca is feeling now? What do you think he's going through? How do you—"

"I didn't hunt you down!" Brett protested. "I didn't stalk you, find you at one of your favourite clubs and pretend to be into you... He's a glorified contract killer!"

Fair point. I'd made a loyal Mannequin of a trained assassin. One with access to the Scimitar of Light. One who, with the enhancement my blood provided him, could easily destroy any number of their brethren without... I banished that train of thought. Was Brett right? Had I approached this with blind selfishness? No, I had not. Given the opportunity to let Luca die, I'd instead saved him. Taken responsibility for him. All because...

"Ross. He's part of Ross's family. He has to be."

"Yeah, but he's *not* Ross. For all you know, he was sent here to kill Ross, found out he was already dead and decided you were the next best thing."

"That's speculation."

He knitted his eyebrows with a sneer. "Right. Total speculation that this freak tried to kill you."

"You know that's not what I meant. You do understand, there's not been a single day in that boy's life where he's been free to make his own choices?"

Brett shook his head. "Fine. But one of these days you're going to have to stop making them for the rest of us."

My fists momentarily tightened, along with my back teeth. "Go to bed."

"I'm not tired. I... I'm going out."

"Home?"

"I don't know!"

I resisted the urge to fight him. Better to let him release some steam. "Meet me at Valia's tonight. Eight o'clock." Luca would need food, and Deborah, the evening server at Valia's was the only human I trusted with knowledge of our true nature. Of course, if the boy couldn't behave himself, he could bloody well stay with Patricia Bakker until he could think of nothing else but my blood. I would never have done *that* to Brett.

"All right," Brett said. "I hope you know what you're doing."

CHAPTER THREE

Luca didn't fight me when I fetched him from the cellar and cleaned him up. Having Kelvin stand guard made me feel better than it probably should have. Bakker excused herself, having made her thoughts plain. Changed into fresh clothes, a pallid, grey skin tone remained the only sign of Luca's violent turn in Patricia's lab. Was that it, then? Was he now my indentured servant, needing only nurture, food, and discipline?

Joy.

I didn't waste the cab ride trying to explain, instead keeping conversation to a minimum. Most of it centred on food, which he understood. Even reliant on blood to survive, a Mannequin was not a Blood Shade. Like Brett, he still needed solids.

"Speak of the devil." Deborah smiled as we arrived at Valia's.

Brett stood at the end of the counter, doing a poor job of hiding his disdain for Luca. Even Deborah's smile faded upon glimpsing his face. To be fair, I didn't have the best track record of bringing guests into her establishment, much less trained assassins.

"Is he all right?" she asked, not taking her eyes off the boy.

"He will be." I said, plonking Luca down into a booth and taking a seat beside him. "Can we see a menu? Actually, whatever you'd recommend will be fine. Something filling."

Luca spat out a short stream of Italian curses, too rapid for me to understand.

"*Stai attento a quello che dici!*" Deborah scolded him in Italian that far outclassed mine—a talent she'd hidden for years before sharing her vocational beginnings in Leichhardt, an area of Sydney claimed decades ago by Italian immigrants and miraculously never quite released to the hands of greedy developers or hipsters.

The boy seemed stunned to cop the rebuke in his mother tongue. He sank into his seat, avoiding Deborah's gaze.

"Just one meal, I assume?"

"And my usual, if you'd be so kind."

She stalked away to fix whatever she had in mind for Luca, plus my usual pot of loose-leaf tea, spiced with just a few drops of her own blood. With the unusual distinction of being the only non-Mannequin human I trusted with our secrets, Deborah had never once betrayed me, even in moments that had brought her frighteningly close to the darker side of our existence. A human like that deserved respect, as well as my confidence.

Brett inhaled one last forkful of what looked like cheesecake from his plate on the counter and sauntered over to us.

"Are you still hungry?" I asked.

"Just had dinner."

"I saw. Looked nutritious."

He didn't rise to my attempted humour, refusing to take his eyes off my new acquisition.

"What?" the boy finally said, sneering at him through a heavy accent.

"You know what."

Luca sank deeper into his chair.

"He hasn't given us any more trouble," I said, anticipating the question.

Brett nodded, though the threat in his eyes was plain. Nothing more was said during what might have been the longest four minutes of my life, until Deborah returned.

"Here we are," she said, setting the tea down in front of me. "And there's a pretty amazing chorizo penne on the way, if I do say so myself."

Luca gave an ugly grimace.

"Really?" Deborah poked out her tongue. "We're going to do this all night?"

I gently glowered at my new servant, exerting just a little of my power over him until his olive skin blushed bright pink.

"Thank you," he mumbled.

Deborah allowed herself a faint smile before putting a hand on Brett's shoulder. "Anything else for you, love? Coffee? Wine? Beer? On the house."

"Thanks, but I'm stuffed," said Brett, unable to keep the smile from his face.

"Stuffed, indeed?" I asked.

"Told you the penne's good," Deborah answered.

"Whatever will we do without you?"

She shrugged. "You've got three weeks to work it out."

"Three weeks?" I blurted.

"Reylan, it's like I told you. We're the only place open on the strip at night. Too many crazies, not enough customers. Now the boss is starting to lose money on nights because of those crazies and she's not going to hire any extra help. If I'm lucky, she'll put me back on days. I know that doesn't help you any. I'm sorry."

"Yes, but... Deborah! I'll miss you. If you need someone else to work nights with you, my offer to pay their wage still holds, and I'll make sure they know how to see off your 'crazies.' Your boss doesn't even need to know."

Her smile was sympathetic, if incomplete. "She'd know. She's owned the place for ten years. She knows its rhythms. Besides, even you're not coming in like you used to, and I haven't seen Ross in yonks. Is he off visiting family or something?"

My hesitation betrayed me before I could think of a convincing excuse, and Deborah's bullshit detector was impeccable.

"What is it?" she asked. "Reylan?"

"I'm afraid Ross won't be joining us for tea anymore."

She took a slow, unsteady step back. "What happened?"

I saw no point in lying, but nor did Deborah need to know the gory details. After all, no supernatural evil had caused Ross's death. The killer had been human. Just one arrogant human man.

"We have enemies, Deborah. Others like ourselves. Humans who get too close."

Luca stared at me, his face quivering. He turned away as I caught him, but his agitation said plenty. He really hadn't known of Ross's death.

"Who was it?" Deborah asked. "Or what? Don't think you can surprise me now."

"They met with swift justice, I promise you."

"You know what?" she said. "Ross was your friend. To me, he was just a good customer. Let's leave it at that. In fact, I don't think I need to know any more about you, or vam... Blood Shades, or whatever you call yourselves, or werewolves, or any of it."

"Deborah—"

"And since I won't be on nights any more, it's not going to be my problem, is it? You're a sweetheart, Reylan, and so is your new friend." She nodded at Brett. "But I think this relationship's run its course." She closed her bill pad and retreated to the counter, not waiting for me to respond.

"You want a hand with anything?" Brett called.

"Suit yourself."

My Mannequin got up and followed her, mostly, I suspected, to give Luca and I some space. Brett could be awfully perceptive.

Luca, on the other hand, just glowered at me.

"Go on then," I said in Italian. "Say it."

"You lie!" he hissed in English.

"He was my friend. I should think you'd be pleased. Had you been smart enough to leave me alone, you could have pissed off back to Rome already and stayed out of my hair."

Luca pounded his fists on the table and stood up, breathing heavily as he snatched up a butter knife—the only cutlery on the table—and brandished it at me.

"And what do you think you're going to do with that?"

"*Maledetto.*"

"Oh, for god's sake! Yes, yes, *maledetto.* 'Daemon.' Accursed. The damned. You've used that one already. It's getting tedious, particularly since you currently owe your pathetic life to the very same. Now, we can either talk about what that means, or you can sit there, quietly, until the food arrives, which you *will* eat."

His hand flexed around the knife and his lips tightened into a snarl.

"*Sit the fuck down!*" I barked, compelling him to obey with the aid of just a little Blood Shade trickery that went straight for his nerves. I tossed a conciliatory glance at Deborah, who'd rushed in to check on the commotion. She slank back into the kitchen without a word, though the look in her eyes said plenty.

Luca, meanwhile, was too afraid to meet mine.

"Look at me. I won't ask twice."

A faint tremble hung on his face when he finally did, hiding the knowledge that I'd just used aspects of his darkest fears and insecurities to control him.

"Who was your primary target, then? Ross? Me? Both of us?"

Silence.

"*Answer*," I compelled him again.

He dropped the knife on the table wincing as the word seared his nerves. "You are the reason he is damned! Your death would have bought him to me. He would want to avenge you."

"Not now, he won't."

"Because you killed him!"

"Now, we both know that's not true, don't we? And let me make another thing clear. Had you succeeded in killing Ross, I would have personally ensured you a death far slower and more painful than any you, Patricia, or anyone else might imagine. Consider that before you lament your failure."

He turned away. Did he really see me as the architect of Ross's damnation, just because I'd saved Ross all those years ago, sparing him the honour killing so favoured by the Scimitar of Light? Or was it my fault that Ross had rejected that fate? Either way, I'd not been wrong.

"So, what now?" I asked. "You can't go home. You'll die without a little of my blood every few days."

"I'm not your dog!" he snapped as Brett and Deborah returned from the kitchen.

"Come here and say that, you little—"

I cautioned Brett with a raised hand, not taking my eyes off Luca. "Let's be clear on one thing. I'll keep you alive, because that's the choice I made. But I didn't make it for you. You'll have to earn what Brett has. Until then, you are little more to me than an annoying obligation. Is that understood?"

The kid frowned, crossing his arms and looking at Deborah, who stood holding a plate of fresh pasta.

"Ah, you're welcome?" she said.

"He is paying you, yes?" Luca sneered.

"*He* can find something far less appetising to sustain you, if you don't fix your attitude." I watched closely as Deborah set the plate down.

She backed away slowly, not taking her eyes off the angry youth as he sniffed at it.

"Well?" I asked.

He raised a fork, tossing the penne around the plate. "There's sausage in it."

"That's the point, and it's awesome. Now, eat it." Brett remained at my side, just a holstered gun short of being the perfect bodyguard cliché.

The boy stabbed a piece of penne and made a show of shovelling it in. Then another, with no less sarcasm. But just as I expected him to drop his fork with contempt, he slowed his chewing. A thoughtful look crossed his face as he skewered a piece of chorizo and stared at it.

"Told you," murmured Brett.

The plate's contents soon disappeared with speed. Within minutes, nothing remained but a slick layer of red oil.

"I'll take that as a rave review," said Deborah as she refreshed my tea.

Luca shrugged. "Was okay."

My gaze drifted to an election poster past Luca's shoulder. "Adrian Tseng? I never took you for the political type, Deborah."

"I'm not. Adrian's a good friend. Jen, who does mornings, says he's been holding meetings in here at least twice a week."

"You want to start charging rent," Brett added.

"No, he's a good bloke. We've known each other since uni. I wasn't so big on student politics, but it was Adrian's world. He ran the Queer Collective for... three years, I guess?"

"The Queer Collective?"

She raised a good-natured grimace. "They weren't too keen on straight girls in the joint. I didn't mind. Their group. Their rules."

"Their loss," I offered her a smile, peering closer at the slight, almost elfin features of the man looking back at me with a confident, and just slightly too accommodating smile. The smile of a politician.

"With Gallagher stepping down, he's got a good shot. He's got the gay vote, and I don't think there's a business owner in Chinatown who doesn't know who he is."

"Way to racial profile," said Brett.

"Way to win votes." Her smile returned. "Adrian knows where his bread's buttered."

I nodded, not that I paid any real attention to human politics. I had, I was sure, brushed by the name Gallagher once or twice in the media in recent years, but I'd be damned if I remembered the context. Something about three prostitutes, a hotel in Wollongong, and not at all medicinal amounts of cocaine flashed to memory, though I could have been mistaken.

Luca's head tilted sharply in the direction of the front door right before its bell sounded. In walked a man wearing a soiled khaki jacket. Long, greying hair fell over his collar in greasy waves, and his gait carried a distinct nervousness.

"Get you something?" Deborah asked, returning to her spot behind the counter.

"Yeah, I guess." The fellow unzipped his jacket. "I'll get a cap'."

"Cappuccino? Sure."

"Thanks. And whatever you've got in the till thanks, love."

The man had barely pulled his gun before a teapot sailed through the air, finding its mark on the man's cheekbone and shattering, drenching his face with steaming hot blood tea.

My peripheral vision caught Deborah ducking behind the counter as the man screamed, right before Luca leapt onto the table, then bounded in the man's direction. I hadn't even seen him throw the pot. Sending the would-be thief stumbling back with a kick to the face, Luca landed, only to latch onto his prey again, forcing him down with a clatter as the gun skidded across the floor. Not missing a beat, Luca raised a butter knife and plunged it into the man's throat with no more difficulty than if he'd been wielding a sharpened dagger.

Blood spurted from the wound. Brett snatched up the gun and held it on the two of them. Our hostess, meanwhile, had procured her own, wisely keeping the counter between herself and the battle unfolding on the floor. Still, two loaded and cocked guns in the room was two more than I would have liked. What's more, the bitter scent of the man's blood distracted me. One of the crack-heads Deborah had told us about, who'd made her night shift so unbearable.

"All right!" I said, calm and collected as I could manage. "Let's put the guns down. Everything's all right."

"Jesus fuck, Reylan! There's a dead guy on my floor. This is *not* all right!"

Brett moved swiftly to the front door and locked it, pulling the blinds closed. "Lights?"

"In the back, on your left," Deborah murmured, not taking her aim off Luca and the dying crack-head. "What are you going to do about this?"

"We'll take care of it."

"Oh, that's a given! You are definitely taking care of this, because I..."

I watched the colour drain from her face as her voice trailed off. "Deborah, what's wrong?"

"What... What's happening to him?"

I put a cautious foot forward. "Luca, can you—"

The face that whipped around was near unrecognisable, its pallor now bone-white, save for lips the colour of darkened, congealed blood. That was to say nothing of the crack-head's blood staining the thing's mouth. Catching my attention though, were the teeth, two brutal incisors, longer than those on any Blood Shade I'd seen, dripping with the saliva of a predator's hunger.

"Luca," I whispered, right before Brett turned the lights out, leaving the room illuminated only by what little street light crept through the blinds.

The boy creature's head whipped around again as it resumed feasting. I could barely make out the whimpers of the dying man under Luca's snarls and Deborah's shrill cry of alarm.

"Reylan? Reylan, do something or I will shoot this fucker, I swear!" The silhouette of the gun shook in her hand.

"Don't move! Brett, turn the light back on!"

As soon as my Mannequin obeyed, the hideous creature that had once been Luca shrieked, covering its face. It leapt off its prey and barrelled toward me, hitting with a force like a speeding car. Unable to stop it, I instead rolled with it to the floor, using the thing's momentum to push it away. It smashed through the front door in a splintering of broken blinds and glass before disappearing up the street. I forced the door open and looked out after it, barely glimpsing a shadow before it rounded the end of the block. Only then did I look back at Deborah and Brett.

"I'll deal with this." My Mannequin pointed to the body. "Go!"

I bolted up the street with all the speed my Blood Shade nature afforded me. I rounded the corner, swiftly covering another block before realising the boy creature was nowhere to be seen. I swallowed, trying to stay calm. If Luca attacked a passer-by, we'd have a far more serious problem. On the other hand, if he was merely frightened, wanting more than anything to find some haven from the world, that gave me far more time to resolve this without a body count.

And there would be no body count. I'd make sure of it.

The boy had failed to leave anything so convenient as a blood trail. I instead sniffed the air for the scent of the crack-head's blood, but even that eluded me under a much stronger odour. Blood, certainly. But fresh blood, still flowing.

Oh, Christ. I could hear the poor fool whimpering around the corner.

"Please? P-please help?"

I looked over the man's rough clothing, which included a faded black nylon jacket, a soiled grey t-shirt with a couple of small holes, jeans that had seen better days, and black sneakers that were almost worn through. A mess of pitch-black hair topped his unshaven face, and he was bleeding from the neck.

"Please? It hurts."

"Hold still." Leaning in to get a look at his wound, I tilted his head to one side. Fang marks. Two of them, perfectly even and carelessly left to bleed into his clothes. Luca? But the wounds seemed so deliberate. The creature I'd seen attack the crack-head had behaved like a monster in frenzy, rending flesh from his victim's wounds. But not here. Was this the work of Luca's more human side, struggling to regain control?

"Are you just going to stand there?"

"You'll be all right," I said, truthfully. If the man hadn't fainted from his wounds, he wasn't about to now. That meant Luca had either known when to stop or had been chased off, possibly by something scarier. Not relishing that possibility at all, I cast my eye over the street, only turning back to the wounded man once I was satisfied we were alone. The guy would have been… thirty-two? Thirty-five, at most. It was hard to tell with his dark eyes dulled from blood loss.

"Where is he? Is he still... Oh my god! My god!"

"He's gone." I took the man in my arms and let him breathe into my jacket. It took several minutes for him to calm down enough to sit upright, his eyes glazed over with fear and confusion as his mind no doubt replayed the ordeal. I had to get him cleaned up before anyone else saw his wounds. Perhaps against better sense, I put an arm around him, firmly grasping his shoulders. "Whoever he was, you're safe." I dabbed my fingertips with my tongue and used them to seal the tiny punctures on his neck. I then took his chin in my hands, turning his gaze to my face. The fear in his eyes surrendered to dumb vacancy as he stared into mine. I had him. My gaze slid down the length of his straight nose, soft lips and high cheekbones. Probably not homeless, I reasoned. He'd shaved at least once within the last few days, but clumsily, leaving some patches of stubble longer than others. Dark bags weighed down his eyes, though like his clumsy grooming, they detracted little from his handsome face. In other circumstances, I might have taken him home to feed myself. "What's your name?"

"Iain. Two I's."

"Two eyes? Unusual nickname."

"*I's*. I-a-i-n."

"Ah." Feeling dense, I smiled at his precise clarification, no doubt a product of habit. My eyes remained locked to his as I reached into his mind and began rearranging his memory. "Do you have somewhere to sleep tonight, Iain?"

He stared right back at me, swallowing uncomfortably as I worked. "Please, just stop."

I did, so abruptly in fact, I feared damaging his brain. "Stop what?" Skilled as I am at lying, I'm lousy at playing dumb.

"Please," he said, clutching his repaired neck and trying without success to get to his feet. "Just let me go."

"Go? You've been hurt."

"Look, *please*? What am I? Catnip for you people? What do you want from me?"

"What are you talking about? What people?"

"Quit it! I know what you are." He backed away until he finally regained his balance and stood upright. "Just get away from me. Find someone else to bother."

"Hey!" I barked, hoping the shock would stop him if nothing else. I was tempted to try hypnosis again, but I'd no reason to believe I'd be any more successful a second time. "I just stopped blood from gushing out your neck. Why are you afraid of me?"

He backed into a doorway as if anticipating some unseen attack from behind. Paranoid, to the last. But he knew what I was. How was that even possible? I supposed Luca's transformation had made up his mind. But that beast resembled no Blood Shade I'd ever seen.

"Can I walk you home?" I asked, partly to make it abundantly clear that if I couldn't erase his memory, I would at least know where he slept if he caused trouble.

He grimaced, shaking his head. "I don't live close. Look, don't worry about me. Thanks for your help. I'll be—"

"No, you won't." I slid an arm around him and eased him to his feet. "You've lost a lot of blood. You need rest, and my home isn't far."

"I..." He staggered a little, eyeing me warily. "I don't think that's a good idea."

I gave him a moment to look me over, making no attempt to hide who I was. I was taking a risk, inviting this oddly resilient mortal into my home with no idea how to wipe his memory. But I couldn't allow such a man to slip into the night unsupervised, nor was I about to kill him outright over an ability clearly beyond his control. All I could do was clean and feed him, earn his trust, and buy myself time. Hopefully enough time to find a 'correction' to his little talent. "Are you sure I can't help you?"

Iain eyed me a moment longer, but I could see his scepticism fading. Homeless or not, the promise of a safe bed, and a little care from a man who obviously meant him no harm surely looked good from where he was standing. Ordinarily, I would have taken him back to Valia's, though tonight, that was out of the question.

"You're not..." He trailed off, plainly terrified to ask. Had I been cursed with immunity to a Blood Shade's gifts, only to be invited into the home of such a being, I'd have had fears of my own.

"Not what?"

"You're not... hungry, are you?"

I tossed him a sympathetic, if ever so slightly condescending smile. "Iain, really? What are those two eyes telling you now?" I caught him just in time as he tried to take a step and staggered, supporting his arm over my shoulder. "Come on. It's no distance at all."

CHAPTER FOUR

By Blood Shade standards, and certainly by the outlandish standards of romantic literature, I keep a modest house. The lower floor of a classic Darlinghurst townhouse, distinguished by the stairway leading to my upstairs tenant's private apartment. Generous storage space in the basement for a vast collection gleaned over my years of travelling had sealed the deal. My furniture, on the other hand, smacked of a modernity that bordered on cliché. All the better for keeping a low profile when you looked to be a man of twenty-four.

In my haste and worry over Luca's transformation, the commotion at Valia's, and now this mortal with uncanny resistance to Blood Shade hypnosis, I'd forgotten that much of my furniture was now in ruins.

"Caught you redecorating?" murmured Iain as I tossed a piece of broken shelf off the couch. He shuddered as he caught my eye. "Sorry. I didn't mean to—"

"The place could probably use it in any case," I pulled a rug over the blood stain Luca had left on the carpet.

The man sat down, still scrutinising the war zone that was my living room. Though I'd dimmed the lights, I could now make out the details of his face. It didn't seem as hollow as it had on the street, though it retained its blood-deficient pallor.

A light scar marked his left cheek, creating a faint break in the uneven smattering of stubble that shrouded his sharp jawline. His ears extended just a fraction too high to be classically handsome, yet they made him all the more endearing. Then there were those eyes, almost as black as his hair, their terror contained behind a curiosity that would ordinarily have irked me. On Iain, it seemed strangely genuine. Innocent, though far from naive.

"I'll get you some food," I said, retreating to my fridge and hoping to god... Damn. Poppers were not going to cut it.

"Don't let me put you out."

"It's no trouble." Grimacing at the paltry frozen meals Brett had stocked in the freezer, I finally took out my phone and looked up the nearest pizzeria. "You're not vegetarian, I hope?"

"No," he said as I re-entered the room. "Nor vegan. Though if I was vegan—"

"You would have told me by now." I smirked at the familiar joke.

He finally smiled, dimpling the scar on his cheek and revealing flawless white teeth.

"Glad to see you still have your sense of humour."

"It's just that, first this thing attacks me, and now... It's kind of surreal." He touched the points on his neck where I'd healed the bite, shaking his head. "How do you do that?"

"I hope you won't be offended if I ask a few questions first? Specifically, about how you knew what it was that attacked you. How did you know what I was?"

The man shrugged. "He bit my neck. That could only mean—"

"Stories," I interrupted him. "Superstition. There are crazy people all over this town and every other. What makes you think—"

"Blood Shade," he said with quiet excitement. "That's the correct term, isn't it?"

I slowly circled him, watching the twitch of his Adam's apple as he fought to keep his nerve. "Who told you that?"

"I... I read it. After that first time, I searched like mad."

"First time?"

"I never thought another one would feed on me though. Not in a million years! It's like... No, it's stupid."

"Go on," I said, careful to leave my voice not entirely without menace.

"I don't know. I thought it might be a territorial thing. I thought it might be, once one of you feeds off a human, it's fangs off for the others. Wishful thinking, right?"

Fangs off? Cute. There didn't seem to be any point 'correcting' him further. After meeting Patricia, and Isaac O'Baer, the priest at Saint Barnabas parish, both humans with knowledge of our existence, I couldn't feign surprise at finding others. Best they stayed where we could see them, and in that moment, I could see Iain quite clearly.

"This has happened to you before?"

He nodded. "When I was a kid."

"A kid? How can you be sure you remember?" My question was sincere. Any half-educated Blood Shade knew, firstly, that feeding from children was the detestable act of a coward, and secondly, to wipe the memory of *any* companion after the deed was done.

"What's your name?"

"Thomas," I lied.

"No, it isn't."

No, and the pseudonym was ridiculous. Why was I overcomplicating this? "Reylan."

Iain's lips curled into a nervous smile that was gone in an instant. "I appreciate you being cautious. I'm not exactly presenting as myself either, right now."

"Don't tell me, you're a werewolf?"

He laughed, again letting go of the nervousness that had dogged him since his arrival. "No. Hey, are they real as—"

"No." My answer came almost too quickly. But I wasn't about to fill any gaps in the man's knowledge. I was also in no mood to discuss werewolves.

"They said the parish priest at one of the churches in Sydney knew something about what I remembered from back then. So, here I am."

"So, you're a good Catholic boy?" I would have preferred a werewolf.

"I'm a bit more than that. My background is in youth ministry. So, since they put me onto Father O'Baer, I've been helping him—"

"Wait... Youth ministry? You're a priest?"

"Father Iain Grieg. Sorry about the lack of garb. I've been trying to step up our street operation. That means civvies. These kids open up a lot more if they don't feel you're about to bible bash them."

"That comes later?"

"Right!" He laughed. "Tonight... I guess one of them decided I looked tasty."

'Street kid,' indeed! Where was Luca spending the night? Had he forced his way into some unfortunate mortal's home and... I dismissed the thought. It wasn't as if I could do anything about it. "I'm sorry you had to experience that. Twice, no less. I don't want you to think... That is, I appreciate you trusting me enough to help you."

He smiled, sheepishly. "When the first one didn't kill me and this one didn't kill me, it seemed pretty clear that whatever you are in God's plan, you're not monsters. I mean, Jesus wandered the desert in the company of Satan himself."

I let the unflattering comparison slide. "Did you see his face? The boy who attacked you?"

"He looked strung out on something. Really not in good shape. But it would have been less than a second before... No, I don't know, sorry."

"It's fine." I took a seat on the opposite couch. "Please, relax. Lie down if you'd like. Pizza's about twenty minutes away."

A small, whiskered face peered at us from the darkened hall leading to my bedroom.

"Hey, hey kitty." Iain made several soft tutting noises, leaning forward to lower an inviting hand.

Demetrius hissed at him before disappearing the way he'd come.

"Nice cat."

"Don't take it personally. Demetrius has the worst taste in people." I took a moment to stare into the eyes of this man whose mind I couldn't compel. This man who'd had the misfortune to know of Blood Shades since childhood, even going so far as to describe himself as Blood Shade 'catnip.' I wasn't even sure what that meant. It might have amused me if it weren't so sad.

"You know who he is, don't you?" Iain touched his neck. "You didn't stumble on me by accident. You were chasing him."

"I'm afraid so. We'll find him though. Don't worry."

"I've just never... Are they often fucked up like that?"

Language, Padre? "It all depends on how they've handled the change. I imagine most of what you think you know about us is questionable, at best."

"Maybe. But I was thirteen when the first one bit me. I didn't exactly spend all that time sitting back thinking 'Wow, vampires are real. Better be careful,' you know? I found some things out."

I grimaced. There'd be time to determine the extent of those things later. "What exactly happened to you tonight? How did you wind up—"

"He seemed nervous, trying to hide in the hollow of this fire door. I didn't say anything at first. Even when you work with them, you learn not to grab the attention of some random kid in the street. But then he looked up. There was no way he couldn't have seen me, so I asked if he needed help. Next thing I know, that was that."

Oh, overflowing cup of Catholic virtue.

"Caught me totally by surprise. It was nothing like the first one. I remember her. I remember that first sting. How it hurt so much, I thought I was dying, just for a second. But it felt incredible. Like every muscle in me had doubled in sensitivity. I had my first... well, what teenage boys start to—"

"I understand. What happened then?"

"She put her hand on the back of my head and looked at me. Just stared into my eyes. She mumbled something about not remembering who she was or what had happened. But I knew! After she'd gone, I remembered everything."

"Her name?" I asked.

He shook his head. "I tried to tell someone, but who was going to believe a story like that? So, I started looking to the church, just hoping, praying they'd have something that could help. Some half-substantiated fable or explanation."

"There isn't one," I said, finishing his thought. "You'll find Blood Shade history and the Christian church follow decidedly different paths."

"Don't I know it? No offence, but there are things I've learned about your people that I've prayed to unlearn."

I caught myself stroking my lower lip. "Perhaps you can."

He swallowed again, nerves fired up as I approached him.

"Would you like me to try?"

He shook his head. "It won't work. Even if it did, I feel like I've been put on this path and given this knowledge for a reason. I know how that must sound to you."

"Or maybe *I've* been put in your path for a reason. This knowledge can't have been easy to live with, and nature has given us the tools to relieve you of it. Call it a duty to our companions. Isn't there some part of you that wants to let go?"

He didn't even flinch. Had he considered this? Probably not. In fact, I was willing to bet he'd never been made such an offer. How many others had he met? With that said, a wise man with Iain's gifts wouldn't be out advertising them, to Blood Shades or anyone else.

"It would make life a lot safer for you," I pointed out.

"Yeah, I worked that out pretty quick. Can I think about it?"

"It's your decision to make," I assured him, meaning every word. For now, anyway.

*　　*　　*

I hushed Brett as he let the door slam behind him. It was pushing five in the morning. I was tired, and low on blood. Once Iain had finally slipped from consciousness, I'd given thought to turning in myself, except for…

"Reylan?" Brett asked, nodding at Iain's sleeping form. "What the hell, man?"

…that.

I took Brett into the kitchen and summarised our encounter as best I could, explaining that with no hope of keeping up with a panicked Luca, I at least had a duty to the man he'd attacked.

Brett sipped his way through a beer as he listened. His rapid evolution from a surly, resentful man-child to a capable aide who took such things in his stride had impressed me. For this, I thanked Peter, first Mannequin to my former mentor, Colin. It hadn't occurred to me at first how Brett too might benefit from the experience of someone who knew first-hand what this new life was doing to his body and mind.

"So, once you're sure he's okay, you're going to wipe his memory and send him home, right?"

I paused, unsure of just how to describe our dilemma. I *could* just send Iain home. After all, if I couldn't erase his memory, and he'd lived this long without causing trouble... But how did I know what trouble the man had caused up until now?

"Wow," Brett said, noting my hesitation. "That's umm... So, you're not going to... you know?"

"No!"

"Okay."

"I don't know yet." Maybe I was too soft when it came to humans who knew our secrets. Deborah, and now Iain. Hell, I barely knew Iain. What did I owe him, exactly? Still, I preferred not to execute humans just for discovering the wrong thing at the wrong time. "I also don't know how I'm going to find Luca."

"Wait for the bodies?" Brett suggested grimly.

"Not loving that option. There has to be some way to find him. The Trust took a blood sample, for god's sake."

"I can go and ask them."

It was tempting, and yet... "No. The last thing Patricia Bakker needs to know is that we've lost him, and I'd really prefer the Trust didn't know about Iain." It wouldn't surprise me if Bakker too, advocated a much more final remedy to our human friend's unusually resilient memory. In any case, priorities. Luca had attacked a man. I was prepared to trust Iain's discretion, at least while we handled our other little problem. "How's Deborah?"

"I'd stay out of her way for a bit if I were you, but she's fine. I can see why you like her. Easy to talk to. Knows her shit. But you might want to, ah—"

"If you're suggesting I hypnotise tonight's memory out of Deborah, my answer is a hard 'no,' and we will not be raising the question again. We either trust her, or we don't, and I do. Is that understood?"

"Sure thing. Do you trust him?"

I shot a glance at the lip of sunlight breaking under the window shade. "If Iain wakes up before I do, please introduce yourself and take him to get some breakfast. Don't overshare. He doesn't need to know the exact nature of our relationship. Keep it casual. Maybe avoid talking religion. If you want to grab a few hours' sleep—"

"Sleep? What if he bolts?"

"He won't. He's too curious about us now."

No more curious than I was about him, though I didn't express the thought aloud.

Brett shifted his weight uncomfortably. "I'm setting an alarm for ten."

I smiled, putting a hand on my faithful Mannequin's shoulder. "Thank you."

With that, we said our goodnights. With Patricia out of the question, that left one person I could turn to for answers, and she definitely would not want Patricia intruding on her business.

CHAPTER FIVE

"I'd begun to wonder if you were still alive."

I paused. Only now, as my first Blood Shade protégé and oldest friend refused to look up from her work or turn around, did I stop to think my visit might be unwelcome. "I thought you'd want space."

"You might think that." Isobel scribbled something down under the dim light. "If you recall, it was Patricia who asked for space, from me."

I nodded, ignoring the fact that she probably couldn't see me.

"It doesn't matter." She lifted her head and peered over the back of her chair at me. "She's right. I'm perfectly capable of continuing my work elsewhere."

"Is that what you want?"

"Why are you now so concerned?" she asked. "Besides needing my help."

I rubbed the back of my neck, feeling sheepish. "Is it that obvious?"

"Not a word, Reylan?" She rose to her feet, rounding on me. "No shared hunts? Not so much as a phone call or the contrivance of a text message?"

"I thought you hated them."

"I would have appreciated the gesture. I thought it was Patricia who'd distanced herself from me. Not you."

"And did you not once think to call on me? After what happened to Ross, or with Jorgas? I could have used a friendly face, or voice."

"Fine." She folded her arms and stalked back to her desk. "We're both terrible friends. Now, what do you want?"

I pushed my shoulders back as I approached her, trying to ease my anger. "I want to start this conversation over."

She regarded me with uncertainty, before at last accepting my embrace. "It's good to see you. Now, what do you really want?"

"What I really want, Prickly Spice, is to find a particular someone."

"You need a Sensory Portal, then?"

I nodded, hoping the items in my pocket would be enough to not just track Luca down, but secure a remote lock on his senses, allowing us to see the world through his eyes until we could find him ourselves. "Can you do it?"

"Of course. Who's the target? And why not ask Sophia? It's a simple spell, and she has genuine Shaper knowhow."

I suppressed a cough.

"I see. And just who is this person you don't want them to know you've lost? Human?"

"Not so much, anymore."

"That's ambiguous, unhelpful, and more than a bit unsettling."

I took Luca's passport from my jacket and handed it to her.

She briefly examined it, then stared at me as though I'd just confessed to starting World War Three.

"We met at a club. I brought him home, where he—"

She smacked me hard across the face before I could finish. "You were attacked by Scimitars and you didn't tell me?"

I was sure the sting of nails had been deliberate. "I haven't had time! And how did you know he was—"

"Don't you think I looked into Ross's family and background when I discovered you two were friends? Do you really think I trust the Scimitar to keep their word to Patricia about not violating this city?"

"Fair point. Anyway, he's now run off. Can you find him?"

She examined the passport again. "The arcane forces aren't exactly big on human identity documents. They prefer something biological and primary."

"I hope this is enough." I said, taking out the comb I'd fished from Luca's bag. "I'm sure blood would be easier, and he was wounded, but…"

Isobel's eyes widened. "You didn't?"

"Cursed sentiment. He'll need me, and soon. You don't approve?"

"Let's just say I'm not in love with this habit of adopting men after they've tried to kill you."

"You're saying I've terrible taste in both friends and pets?"

She met my eyes with a dry smile before leading me out to the kitchen. "Not in friends."

*   *   *

Moments later, I found myself staring into the shallow waters of a large pan Isobel had retrieved from her kitchen. I was almost disappointed.

"Ready?" she asked, examining the comb for necessary stray hairs. "I'm not promising this'll work."

"I'm not entirely convinced myself," I said, nodding at the pan. My dear friend had spent the better part of the twentieth century studying the arcane, the supernatural, and all things occult, and she'd no better device through which to conjure our gateway to Luca than a cake tin?

"You need a straightforward Sensory Portal, correct? That means no fancy tricks. No arcane twists. If you prefer, I could run upstairs and dust off the one genuine Seer's Bowl I own, though gods know what else has been through it. The blood of Shapers, used in gods know how many spells? It leaves a residue, you know. Unless you have an innate power to clean—"

"Point made, thank you. The cake tin will be fine."

To be fair, only the most dogmatic Blood Shades of the modern era favoured conspicuously antiquated possessions. I was hardly in a place to criticise, since my own furnishings leaned towards the cheap, undistinguished, and replaceable. Not a bad idea, if I was adopting men who'd tried to kill me.

"Ready?"

I nodded.

She dropped the comb in the water without another word... or any result.

"Oh well. Worth a shot."

"Wait. The spell has to isolate his DNA. Here's hoping there's enough of it. You don't have a pair of his socks or underwear, do you?"

"Now you're just getting creepy."

"We need his DNA. That's all there is to it. Unless..."

I could almost hear the gears turning behind her eyes before she took hold of my hands and lowered them into the water. "What are you doing?"

"Trust me."

Bubbles formed under them as the temperature of the water rose, slowly at first, then more rapidly as the bubbles swirled around my hands.

"Isobel?"

"Just a few more seconds."

"Isobel!" I pulled my burned hands from the water with a gasp, only to find them as dry, soft, and whole as they might have been after any satisfying feed. Nothing burned. Not even the residual heat of what I'd just seen and felt. Only the bubbles in the tray remained.

"If he needs your blood, there'll be an arcane connection between the two of you. If it reacts with the hairs on the comb, which it should..." Her voice trailed off as the bubbles cleared to reveal an odd, flesh coloured bulge sprinkled with fine, brown hairs which spread out from a thicker central trail. The whole package seemed to contract and expand in a steady, organic rhythm, accompanied by faint, appreciative sighs. "Umm..."

"Yes?"

"Looks like it worked."

"Yes, and he..."

"You do meet the most interesting people." Isobel held back a laugh.

I couldn't resist a smile of my own. Luca Depuratore. So pious, so dangerous, so ready to lose the innocent... My smile faded.

"Maybe he wasn't entirely faking it when he hit on you?"

"Not exactly the time for flattery." I focused on the image, ignoring the murmurs and moans of the man enjoying Luca's tongue. How long did he have? How long did *we* have to find them? "We need to find out where they are, *now*."

"Why? His friend seems to be enjoying himself."

"He won't be for much longer. Think, Isobel. There's got to be a way."

"The only way would be a Scrying. That'd show you where they are on a physical map. But you'd need an actual Sorcerer to do it."

"Why not you? You know how it's done."

"I've tried. You've got to understand, there is a massive gap between Shaper science and conventional science. When I learn this stuff, it's like trying to decipher a foreign language on top of learning the spell itself. We're talking months of practice with no guaranteed result."

"Hey, ease up there, mate," came a voice from the bowl. "Ow! Hey, what are you…? Stop! Get off! Oh my god! Help! Somebody help—" The words dissolved into screams as Luca's point of view closed in on the man's throat. When it pulled away again, there were deep gashes in the man's neck, shoulders, and chest. Blood ran from the wounds. The man's carotid artery had been torn open, spraying blood across the bed and walls of what I only now recognised as a dingy hotel room, strewn with clothes. Luca's lay scattered over an unremarkable business suit I had to assume belonged to the poor bastard torn open on the bed. Our view tilted away from the body, wobbling as Luca stumbled around the room, all the while emitting faint, angry moans between low growls. When his gaze eventually chanced upon a mirror, he stopped, staring at his own blood-soaked reflection. His complexion was paler than I'd seen, a sickly blue tinting its otherwise ashen white. Blood covered his face and chest, as I'd known it would. But his eyes, those endless black pits that denied any shred of his former humanity, were now wide with horror, then disgust, then rage. A piercing shriek filled the room, just as the figure attacked the mirror, cracking it with one strong blow, then reducing it to pieces with repeated strikes. A half dozen copies of the ghastly apparition stared back at us from the broken shards, all screaming rage and fear at their own repugnant image. The shrieking grew louder, until Isobel snatched up the pan and upended it into the sink.

She turned to me, eyes blazing. "Reylan, that was a Death Shade."

"Sorry, a what?"

"You didn't tell me your little friend was a Death Shade!"

"Death Shade. Noun. Explain?"

She raised her hands, curling her fingers into claws. "God, I wish you would crack a book sometime!"

"Excuse me? The last time I 'cracked a book' with you, it sent me to—"

"Only in your mind!"

"…to some mixed werewolf and Blood Shade settlement in who only knows where, Bulgaria, where I saw…" I trailed off. The connection seemed impossible. The book of Temporal Echoes was filled with memories and stories one could relive by feeding it blood. On my first encounter with the godforsaken artefact, the creatures I'd seen during that encounter—creatures born to Blood Shade and werewolf—had seemed like… "Luca."

"You saw baby versions of your new pet?" Isobel asked. "Yes, I remember. That's one theory surrounding their origin, but there are several others that are more credible. I'd say whoever sent you the book just wanted to scare you away from Jorgas."

Right. As if my liaison with Jorgas would be producing offspring, daemonic or otherwise, any time soon.

"Death Shades? That's seriously what they're called? Why have I not heard of this?"

"They're practically extinct. The last recorded attack was November 12, 1832."

"Well in that case, it's no wonder!"

"Over fifty Blood Shades were killed in one night before it could be destroyed."

I sat back on my hands, staring at the space between my feet. "More than fifty?"

"That's right. And now we've got one running around Sydney. Oh, this is going to be fun! You can forget about keeping it out of sight. We can worry about that fallout later. He needs to be destroyed as quickly as possible."

"We're not killing him!" The force in my voice surprised me. I never yelled at Isobel. "I'm sorry, but no. He's Ross's family."

"He would have killed Ross without a second thought."

"He's a child!

"What he's turned into is most decidedly not a child! Reylan, this is going to be hard enough without tying yourself up in moral knots over the little beast's lineage. I can tell you plenty about what a Death Shade is, but above all, you need to understand, any sort of heart, conscience, or humanity? Forget about it. It's gone! They're not like us. Once that change takes hold, there's nothing 'human' left in them to negotiate or reason with. He'll barely even understand you. The best kindness you can offer him is death, assuming you even survived."

"That fills me with confidence, thank you."

"Or else, we wait until he kills a hundred people. Or a thousand. I'm assuming you don't like those—"

A loud crash from above interrupted us. We powered upstairs and pulled back the beaded curtain to survey Isobel's dimly lit study. Nothing seemed out of place, except for her chair, which lay shattered and broken in front of her desk. Then, there was the smell. A faint, musky odour, not altogether unpleasant, but definitely not of the house.

"Reylan," Isobel whispered, backing away. "Get out. Now."

The werewolf was on me before I could take two steps, tackling me to the floor, snapping at my throat with its long snout and cruel incisors. I strained to push it away, but it was all I could manage to keep its jaws inches from their target. The beast's hot breath broke over my face, nauseating me with its faintly sulphuric odour.

A great crack echoed through the room before the beast released me with a howl. I sprang to my feet, grabbing Isobel's hand as she pulled me out of the room. She brandished a heavy golf club in the other.

"Nice shot." I turned to catch a look at our foe.

It seemed leaner than most werewolves I'd seen, though it was packed with wiry muscle. It turned its hateful yellow eyes on us with a canine snarl. Isobel brought the club down again, only to have the beast duck out of its way and grab hold of the shaft, snapping it like it was kindling. My friend had just enough time to pull the heavy wooden door closed behind her before the creature threw itself against it with another loud crash.

"Isobel—"

"Go! I'll handle this."

"I'm not leaving you!"

She held the door firm as the creature shook the handle, then swiftly turned a solid metal key below the knob, locking the door with a heavy clunk.

"Okay. What now?" I leaped back as the beast's head, leg, arm, shoulder, and a good portion of its chest passed through the door as if it weren't even there. The creature gave a faint choking sound, and in what must barely have been a second, its head, arm, leg, shoulder, and half-chest slid to the floor in a bloody heap.

"I guess it works," Isobel said.

I was still catching my breath. "What works, exactly?"

She eased open the door and surveyed the bloody mess inside. "This room has more arcane energy in it than any other room in the house. It needs protection. The Shapers helped me with that."

I wrinkled my nose, stepping over chunks of dismembered werewolf. They'd already begun to revert to human form as I surveyed the carnage.

"The key alters the temporal signature of the door, leaving parts of it—"

"Turning it into a bloody death trap is what you're trying to tell me. I gathered that, thank you."

"I never thought I'd have to use it, much less from the outside to keep something in."

Which begged the question, how had the beast gotten in?

"She's left a mess." Isobel stepped inside with a stomach-turning squelch.

"She?" I looked down at what remained of the first female werewolf I'd encountered, not that I'd had the misfortune to run into many. I tried not to fix my gaze on the strips of head that had made it through Isobel's door, nor the frozen scream now forever etched on the thing's human face. It was easier to not think of it as having any sort of relatable identity.

"This'll take…"

I frowned as Isobel's voice trailed off. "Take what?"

She pointed to a small sports bag jutting out of the shadows in the corner.

"That's not yours?" I asked.

She shook her head, silently pulling the bag closer and easing it open.

"Where did she come from?" I peered behind the curtain that blacked out the room's sole window. It opened onto a what had to be a fifteen-foot drop. No ladder or ledge had aided the intruder's access. Only then did I notice that Isobel had stopped rummaging through the bag, having retrieved a small red passport. I swallowed.

"Italia," she murmured, stating the obvious before continuing to excavate the bag. Besides clothing, she procured several stakes, a set of rosary beads, an uncomfortably medieval looking cross-bow… "Not one for travelling light, was she?"

"Nonetheless, it seems she just flew in through the window, so either we're dealing with a far more complicated problem, or Mary Poppins is a werewolf and you just diced the bitch.”

She upturned the bag, giving it a final shake before tossing it aside and snatching up the passport. “Martina Bianchi.”

“Sister Martina Bianchi, I’ll wager,” I said, lifting a large, ugly wooden crucifix from the carnage. “Or close enough to it.”

“No bet here.” She carefully lifted one of the dead woman’s hands and a piece of her face with one of the bag’s shirts. “I need to run some tests.”

“You *need* to leave this house. If they know where you live, that’s your first priority. I’m sure under the circumstances, Patricia will—”

“No.”

The icy speed and finality of the reply stunned me. Patricia would have to be told soon enough. The targeting had been too precise. As for the choice of soldiers, first Luca, now a werewolf? The Scimitars may have drawn their ranks from devout members of supernatural family lines, determined to purge all evil from their self-loathing little hearts, but those Scimitars who suffered the misfortune of an actual transformation rarely lived long enough to second guess their choice. Unless they were being sent to Australia in the hope they’d die fighting for the holy cause… none of which explained how Sister Bianchi had invaded Isobel’s office in the first place.

“*Reylan!*”

“Sorry.”

“Dismembered werewolf ninja nun, remember? Where were you?”

“Just thinking about her, and how to deal with this. From the safety of elsewhere, would be a good start.”

“This is my home. I’m not leaving, and I’m not arguing this with you.”

"Isobel! We may not have the slightest idea why these people have chosen to target you, or me, but if they've sent two assassins already, human or otherwise, I'd bank on them sending more."

"And if they can send those assassins into a locked room with supernatural protections? Let's not fool ourselves into thinking there's some safe haven they can't reach. At least if they come here, I can defend myself."

I cast another glance at the door that had made such bloody short work of our assailant. True to her claim, Isobel could take care of herself, and I'd quite enough on my plate without hovering over my former protégés.

Protégé. Singular.

"Not that I don't appreciate it," she said, her tone now more conciliatory. "But who's looking after you?"

"What?"

"One of them also got into *your* house, and you don't have the protections I have."

"I'm sure between myself, Brett and… we'll be fine."

"And who?" she asked, not missing a beat. "Not the old woman you've got up living upstairs?"

"No! Look, it doesn't matter."

"Two people just appeared in the city and tried to kill us, one of them is still out there and has killed since, never mind what he's turned *into*, and you've brought a stranger into your home? It matters."

"He's just some human. Someone else Luca attacked, who managed to escape. Maybe he scared the kid somehow."

"And do you know his name? His profession? Where he lives? Most importantly, why haven't you wiped his memory?"

"He's a priest—"

"Not a great start under the circumstances."

"I'll take care of it."

"And his memory?"

I could have told her about Iain's unusually resilient memory. Perhaps some part of me had come here with the intention of doing so. But the earnest, decisive look in her eye gave me pause. I'd seen that look before, and it spelt nothing pleasant for Iain. Not that she was necessarily wrong, but I wasn't prepared to take such action, yet. "I said, I'll take care of it."

Her expression deflated before she turned her back. "If you say so."

"Isobel—"

"Find your Death Shade. I'll deal with this." She pointed to the werewolf's remains.

Nodding grimly, I turned to take my leave.

"I'm really sorry I started that."

"Started what?" I asked.

"Us, lying to each other."

I left without another word.

CHAPTER SIX

The cab rumbled along Oxford Street, passing closing restaurants as they spilled patrons out into the surrounding bars and clubs. Part of me wondered if Luca was among them, somewhere, looking for his next fix. After the fate of the unfortunate suited man, I'd no idea when or if he'd do it again. Nor where. Of course, knowing something of how he'd met the man might provide me a clue, unless Luca was just flopping around the city at random.

No, he'd picked the guy up. That at least narrowed the possibilities to a world I knew.

Luca had also survived at least a full day's light. So, either Death Shades were impervious to sunlight—an idea I didn't wish to contemplate—or he'd found a suitable lair already. A lair, I could track down.

As for the 'werewolf ninja nun' who by now probably rested in several bags in Isobel's basement, I'd no idea where to begin. Even if this was some new Scimitar play to get rid of their cursed offspring, offering them redemption for doing God's work in the forms of their devils, it didn't explain why they were coming after *us*.

My connection to Ross explained why Luca came after me. But I'd been the only link between Ross and Isobel. Why target her? Were they targeting her at all? Or was I being followed?

"Stop the cab," I said absently.

"Huh?" the driver grunted. "Bus lane, mate. Can't—"

"Anywhere here then." I took out my wallet with grudging exaggeration and threw a twenty down on the passenger seat. I could have sworn the driver deliberately sped away from the curb before I'd regained my footing.

I shuffled out of the way of two groups of clubbers getting an early start to the evening in their half-dozen strong packs. The gauche fairy lights that framed the door of Waves blinked on and off, blue, pink, green, orange, red, purple, white, accompanying the gentle thump of an old Bananarama hit, promising a line-up of retro favourites that hadn't much changed since 1998. I'd not set foot inside in almost ten years.

Did the Scimitar know that? Even if they'd honoured their truce with Sydney all these years, there was no telling who they'd kept eyes on. Me, Patricia, Isobel… most certainly Ross.

That had to be it. They'd been watching Ross. My unwitting friend, kept alive not just by Patricia's diplomacy, but by his own unwitting usefulness. Had his death announced the time to strike? In any case, this meant they'd had agents in the city for years. I cast my eye over the river of faces wandering up and down Oxford Street. Years? Not exactly a comforting thought. I winced as the shutters flew up with a loud bang on the entrance to Blaze. A burly looking bouncer fastened them in place before disappearing back inside the still dark entryway. It would be at least two hours before the place saw any real life. I didn't know why I'd prematurely stopped the cab. If the Scimitar had been tracking me through Ross, they already knew where I lived. They knew where I went. They knew who my friends were. They knew of Deborah, and Brett.

"Reylan!"

I looked up to see my faithful Mannequin waving to me from a cheap but popular Thai restaurant, squeezed in between two leather and bondage shops. Clearly, I was late to the party. Peter, Iain, and Brett had demolished four or five dishes between them and were now tossing back the last of a bottle of wine, with the exception of Iain, whose glass remained conspicuously full.

"I take it the food crisis is averted?" I accepted the seat Brett pulled out for me.

"We were planning to meet up anyway," he said, indicating Peter.

"*If* you don't need Brett elsewhere," the older Mannequin added with a hint of caution. Good. Better it came from a peer than from me.

"That's fine. Planning a big night?"

"I promised to help Deborah fix her door. Sorry, I should have told you. I just assumed——"

"You assumed correctly. Give Deborah my regards."

Brett looked decidedly sheepish. "To be honest, I really don't think she wants to see or hear from you right now. She was this close to hanging up on me."

"Who's Deborah?"

I turned to Iain, suddenly aware of how open we were being in front of a human. One thrust into our world through no fault of his own, yes. But still one I wanted to keep as far from it all as possible. "She's the night manager at a Crown Street café I'm quite fond of. The only one open after dark."

"Oh! Valia's? I've seen her. Auburn bob? I haven't gone in, but I've seen her through the window."

"Except right now that window is a wooden board we managed to fix up last night," Brett added, checking his phone. "Her boss was either too cheap or too bitchy to get someone over there today."

"I thought there were contractors for that sort of thing," I said. "Damn it, I'll pay for them."

"No need." A glint of pride seeped into Peter's smile. "I've lived a long life. Picked up some skills."

I let out a discrete cough before catching Brett's eye. "Can we talk, alone?"

He wiped away the last drops of curry with a paper napkin, dutifully following me toward the exit. I couldn't help but cast a look back at Peter and Iain, who appeared to have fallen silent as I led Brett away.

"Everything okay?" he asked me with unmistakeable hesitation.

"I don't know. Why don't you tell me exactly how much you've told Peter about what happened, not to mention how much Iain has picked up? Then I'll tell you if it's all 'okay.'"

"Woah! I said nothing. *Nothing* important."

"Mmmhmm. Which is it? Nothing, or nothing important? In fact, why don't you explain what you mean by 'nothing important' because if you've convinced Peter to help you replace Deborah's door, you most definitely did not tell him 'nothing.'"

"I didn't get into details. I just told him the truth, that I couldn't hang out because a friend needed some help installing a new door. He offered to help. He doesn't know anything about our crazy mate."

"I see. What about our *other* mate? You didn't think putting Iain in the same space with Peter would cause problems?"

"None yet. We chatted for a bit. He seems like a nice enough guy. Told him the basics about you and me, like you said. Told him Pete was in the same boat as me, just with another Blood Shade. Nothing he doesn't already understand."

"And did *he* say anything to Peter about this?"

"No. I told him not to. I thought Peter might tell Colin. Well, he'd have to, I guess."

"Yes, he would. Peter's not stupid, Brett. I know he's done a terrific job teaching you a lot of what you need to know, but you're still not thinking like a Mannequin. Having a human around who just happens to be 'hanging out' with you looks extremely suspicious. I assure you, Peter will mention whatever he's learned to Colin, and there will be questions."

"I'm sorry. Honestly, I didn't think it… Shit."

I shook my head as Peter and Iain resumed conversation. Relating all he could learn about the human to Colin was part of Peter's job and I couldn't blame him for it. But I could ensure both he and Colin were distracted while I worked out what to do with the human. "It's all right. I'll deal with Iain, and hopefully find our other little friend. As for Peter, tell him the Scimitars have broken the truce. He'll know what that means."

"Okay," Brett nodded as Peter and Iain joined us.

"We making a move?" Peter asked.

"I see no reason to keep Deborah waiting," I said. "Enjoy yourselves."

"See you in the morning."

The two of them disappeared into the night, leaving a somewhat bemused looking Iain at my side.

"Something on your mind?" I asked.

"No, no. It's just… such an odd relationship."

"Neither a servant, nor a friend," I explained. "I mean, the colloquial comparison is to a pet, but—"

"Ouch." The priest's smirk quickly disappeared as soon as we reached the street and he looked me in the eye. "I suppose I'm not just heading home tonight?"

"We need to find the boy who attacked you."

"Boy? Is that what you'd call it?"

"He's a lot of things." None of my compatriots needed to know about our hellish werewolf encounter. But whether it was tiredness, hunger, or just plain concern, something in my face betrayed me.

Iain's hand was on my shoulder. "You need a plan. Not to mention a stiff drink."

"I'm afraid that's not going to settle my nerves."

"No, but it'll help settle mine. You do realise drinking alone is a sin?"

The smile tugged at my lips.

"I saw that," the priest said, returning one of his own. "Come on. I know just the place."

* * *

The Kraken and Kitten—I paused to read the sign several times before following Iain inside—was not the kind of venue I'd come to conflate with Oxford Street. Set just one block away, in the ground floor of an aging, six storey apartment block, it hid behind an unassuming façade of wrought iron and ivy.

"Come on," Iain called, holding open the front door. "First one is on me."

"Which would you like me to point out first?" I asked, stepping inside. "That we're pushed for time, or that I don't drink?"

"If you had the slightest idea where to start looking, you'd be out there now, instead of checking in on your servant. You certainly wouldn't have agreed to a drink with me." He hung up his jacket, or rather, my jacket, on a hook behind a stool at one of the high tables. "Besides, I have an idea."

"Fine," I pulled out my own stool. "Do enthral me. Why are we here?"

"Jacket, off, now." He fell immediately silent as I narrowed my eyes at him. "Too familiar?"

"A touch."

"Sorry. I'm afraid youth outreach has its own language, and once you get used to it—"

"Yes, I can imagine." I gave the room a once over, my jacket still in place. Every furnishing and table, the wallpaper, every decoration, and even the servers' clothing had been chosen with a distinct sense of anachronism. There was a dash of old Hollywood, a healthy shake of Weimar Berlin, and the gentle, oddly sophisticated garishness of Paris' Golden Age. That was just what I recognised, having lived in each of those eras myself.

"A place for those who feel out of place," Iain waved to the bartender, "but aren't sure just where it is they're dreaming of. Can I get two Gin Blackbirds, Charlie?"

"For the last time, I don't—"

"You'll drink, and with any luck, leave with something far more valuable." Iain tossed his head at a tall, somewhat lanky young man lounging across a battered leather couch tucked into the corner. "A couple of fifties and you'll find young Paul over there very obliging. He gives the place a touch of Kleist Casino, if you know your Isherwood."

"Yes, yes, very fetching. For your information, some of us went to the *actual* Kleist Casino. For all I know, I fed on Isherwood."

He stared at me, the disbelief plain on his face. "I don't know if you're putting me on."

"And you never will."

"Well, I can't guarantee you any famous writers, but one hundred will get you half an hour with Paul. You can feed until your—"

"Just a minute," I said, lowering my voice as the dark purple drinks arrived. "Are you pimping that boy out?"

"Are you looking for a drink in the face?" He scowled, for the first time looking genuinely fearless. "I would do no such thing!"

For a moment, I stared at him, wide-eyed at his outburst. "You're certainly doing your best to enable it. And may I just say, Father, that you seem to have adjusted awfully well for a man who not twenty-four hours ago was attacked by a being beyond human? At least if your present boldness is any indication."

"Brett explained some things. As for the rest, it's as I told you. I've been reading whatever I could find about you for most of my adult life. The only reason I haven't gotten closer is—and please don't take this personally—I haven't wanted to."

"That's certainly a wiser decision than throwing a drink in my face. In the interest of your future well-being, I'd warn you against threatening those above you in the food chain. As for... 'Paul,' he's very attractive, but I don't see—"

"To spell it out plainly, I know most of these boys. I've earned their trust, which is not the easiest thing to do, as you can imagine. They do what they need to. I just keep an eye on them and offer a friendly ear when they're in trouble. Get them drug or sexual health counselling, which... Well, not to perpetuate stereotypes, but there's a need. Paul's a good kid, besides being quite knowledgeable and... well connected on the street."

"Ah," I said, suddenly feeling dense.

"Yes. 'Ah.' Do you trust me?"

I didn't appear to have much choice.

"Hey man, how's it going?" The voice came from over my shoulder.

Before I knew it, Paul was looming over our table, flashing a million-dollar smile that beamed above a smooth, gently muscular chest I could just make out under a half-unbuttoned shirt.

"Paul, always good to see you." Iain accepted a hug while deflecting the boy's kiss to his cheek with a knowing smile. "Paul, this is Rey."

I shot a look back at Iain. The boy had hardly wandered over by chance, but more than that, where had Iain picked up the nickname 'Rey?' Only Ross and Jorgas had ever called me that.

"How's your night?" asked Paul, putting out a hand and doing his best to compensate for the gruff, unmistakeably Australian edge in his voice with customary politeness.

"Next question?" I answered, admiring his firm grip as he took my hand. Clearly, I'd been sized up as potential trade already. The boy was keen to show off his strength, along with the perfectly even white teeth he now flashed me.

"Reckon I can make it better?"

Iain chuckled under his breath. "Slow night, Paul? Let the man finish his drink, at least."

"Can't promise I'll be around that long, can I?" The boy smiled at me again. "Come chat when you've loosened up."

I watched Paul re-settle himself on the couch, popping one more button on his shirt as he winked at me. "I thought you said he could help us."

"He will, in more ways than one, if you're patient. Now he's hooked you, he's not going anywhere."

"You've known him a while, then?"

"Paul's something of a fixture, pushing… I want to say thirty. I try not to ask how long they've been at it. Paul's lucky. Tried the junk, as a lot of them do, but soon tired of it. Then, shrewd enough to realise he'd found something he enjoyed that he was good at, he applied himself accordingly. I slip him some cash here and there to keep an eye on the others."

"What about the girls?"

Iain shook his head. "Not my world. They're mostly based around the Cross, and that means tiptoeing around pimps and gangs. No thank you. Unless you're talking about the high-end girls, and most of them—"

"Have the protection of an agency, of course."

"You speak from experience?"

I shrugged. "Only when I'm feeling particularly lazy, or when Brett needs a companion."

He nodded, taking a sip of his drink. "You really care about him, don't you?"

"I extended his life. His well-being and happiness are my responsibility," I picked up my own drink and sniffed at it, instantly recoiling at the pungent odour of gin, blackberry, and elderflower.

Iain smiled. "Don't force yourself if you're not feeling it. They're my one boozy weakness. Trust me, I can finish two."

I waved away his concerns, lifted the glass to my lips, and tried a sip, letting the clash of sweet and sour flavours wash over my tongue before swallowing it down. "It's um… different."

"Good different?"

A mild, uncomfortable heat rebounded in my throat, followed by a sourness that quickly rose to the back of my mouth.

"Will you excuse me?" I quickly rolled off my chair and ran for what I hoped were the toilets.

"Second door on the right," Iain called after me.

I burst through the doors, threw myself at the sink and spat out the vile purple brew. The long red stream it had aggravated followed immediately, Jackson Pollocking the sink with an alarming crimson pattern. Fortunately, a day's passing since my last meal had left little to bring up. I washed the stray drops from my chin, then set about trying to clean the rest of the—

"Holy fuck, mate! Are you all right?"

I looked up to see Paul's horrified gaze darting between me and the bloody basin.

"Yes, I… I'm fine, thanks. Just a bit sick."

"Man, you're pale as! I'm calling an ambulance."

"No, it's fine." I quickly washed the mess down the basin and shut off the water. "I just needed to throw up. Please, put the phone away, it's nothing."

"Throw up? That was blood!"

I grabbed his wrist as he began to dial, locking eye contact before he could question me. "Paul, I appreciate the concern, I do. But what you saw wasn't blood."

"It… it wasn't," he murmured in semi-conscious agreement.

"No. In fact, I'm not even feeling sick anymore." I edged closer as the hypnosis gently erased the last minute or so of his memory. "How are you feeling, Paul?"

He grinned, pushing his shoulders back to open his shirt wider as I slipped a hand inside and stroked the firm, cool flesh of his abdomen. "How do I feel to you?"

More ways than one, indeed. I smiled, tilting my head back to brush his lips with my own. I planted a series of gentle kisses across his cheek, slowly working my way down his neck and suckling at his throat, tasting just a hint of blood through his skin. It was rich, fragrant, and inviting. Iain had been right. The boy took care of himself. I took hold of his hips and eased him inside one of the cubicles, letting him slam the door behind us. With a graceful shrug, he tossed the shirt off his shoulders and leaned back against the wall, extending his full, sinewy torso for my appreciation. The smooth chest, the thin trail of hairs that disappeared beneath the lip of his trousers, the dark, soft hair of his underarms, and the scent of him.

"Fine," I whispered, raking my fangs over his shoulder as I kissed him there. "Absolutely fine."

*   *   *

"I guess an apology would be redundant?" Iain asked as I resumed my seat.

"He was perfectly lovely, thank you."

"I can tell. A certain cliché about cats and cream comes to mind. Do you think I'd recommend you rubbish?"

"How would you even know the difference? You don't strike me as the blood geek type."

"The what?"

"Blood geek," I repeated, just a little relieved that at least some of our slang had been kept from him. "A human so obsessed with Blood Shades, or vampires, as they no doubt call us, that they make a habit of tasting blood themselves."

"Oh. I take it they're not popular with the genuine article?"

"To be blunt, one human attacking another is not our problem. On the contrary. The more blood geeks there are, the less plausible the genuine article seems. It's hard to silence rumour, but you can send it on a long diversion from the truth."

"I can see how that'd work." He raised one corner of his mouth into a humourless smile. "You have a cold streak, don't you?"

"Don't you?"

"Me?"

"I imagine your line of work requires a certain emotional distance from the people you help?"

"A professional distance, yes. But if you're talking about the misconception that psychotherapists are more likely to themselves be psychopaths—"

"I wouldn't make that leap."

"Nonetheless, some do. Why wouldn't they? It's a catchy, repeatable line. I'm *not* a psychotherapist, just so you know.

But my line of work requires a firm hand, and so, yes, some emotional distance. Occasionally, that isn't enough."

"You do get attached, then?" In some way, I could tell. Something in the way he'd spoken about Paul…

He nodded. "At which point, I find them another counsellor, or the aforementioned psychotherapist."

"Assuming they're not a psychopath?"

"Right." Iain grinned as he lifted his drink.

"Did you always want to be a counsellor?" I slid the remainder of my own drink over to him.

"Long enough to bring the dream to fruition. I think if you have a gift and a desire to help young people… Well, you're not so inexperienced in this yourself."

"Come again?"

"Brett. And the boy who attacked me? Somehow, I sense your interest there is more than superficial. So, why? What does it do for you?"

I hesitated, relieved that Brett had told him nothing of Jorgas. Yet I remained hesitant to answer.

"A purpose?" he guessed. "A sense of symbiosis with the world, rather than just feeding on it? I imagine that would get tiring after… I'm sorry. I shouldn't be asking."

"It's fine," I answered reflexively. "I suppose I don't much think about it."

"Neither do I."

For a moment, we sat in comfortable silence, Iain sipping his drink while I watched. I'd no intention of playing tricks, or even making eye contact. I simply sat, regarding the man before me, almost forgetting the strange and deadly circumstances that had brought us together.

"Hey man, how's it going?" A familiar voice over my shoulder said for the second time that evening.

"Paul," said Iain, extending a hand and saving me an awkward encounter with the boy whose short-term memory

I'd erased not fifteen minutes earlier. "I was hoping we'd run into you. Have you met my friend, Rey?"

The boy flashed what was now an all too familiar devilish smile. "I think I'd remember if I'd been that lucky."

You think so, kid?

"He's with me tonight," cautioned Iain. "Be nice."

"I'm always nice."

"Actually, I'm hoping you can help us. Rey's looking for someone."

I opened Luca's passport and showed Paul the photograph.

"Hey, cute!"

"We're wondering if you might have seen him among the other 'cute' boys, along the Wall or somewhere?"

Paul screwed up his nose, seemingly offended. "You know I don't do that anymore."

"Of course." Iain took out his wallet and handed Paul a crisp fifty-dollar note. "But if this kid is, I'm sure someone you know must have seen him."

Paul pocketed the note with a smirk before taking out his mobile and photographing the passport page. He tapped a few commands into the phone before putting it away. "You'll know soon enough."

I wondered how many of Sydney's finest street hustlers had just received Luca's passport details. Still, identity theft was the least of Luca's problems right now. In fact, with an identity and family like Luca's, it might have been desirable.

I watched in silence as Iain and Paul continued chatting. Iain asked after several of the boys by name, smiling and laughing with an easy, familiar air as Paul related this or that absurd story. His face darkened as Paul relayed that another boy named Neil had attempted suicide, again. But seeing the seemingly unflappable priest listen with such nonchalance made it easier to understand how he'd come to take Blood Shades so wholly in his stride.

Paul pulled out his phone when it buzzed, opening a picture message from somebody named 'Ace.'

"This him?" Paul turned the picture around for our inspection. "Scar on his neck?"

"Yes! When was this taken? Where?"

"Just now." Paul tapped out a response. "Ace says to find him some new turf. Having too many new guys around scares the regulars."

"Thank you," I said, grabbing my jacket. "I don't think that'll be a problem much longer."

"For sure." Paul smirked, pushing his shoulders back to make a show of his athletic chest. "So are you in that much of a hurry, or—"

"Another time," I said, pecking him on the cheek. Hey, the past was 'another time.'

Iain put on his own jacket and downed the rest of his drink as Paul returned to the sofa, his cocky smile unshaken. "You see? Good company, valuable information, and fresh blood. Don't say I don't show a man a good time."

"Iain, you've helped tremendously, but you're not coming."

"And what if this kid's already moved on? How do plan on convincing Ace or any of the other boys to tell you what they know?"

"I assure you, this 'Ace' will be far less co-operative if he's…" I trailed off, realising I hadn't in fact shared with Iain just what Luca *could* do to those who crossed his path. "I just don't want to see you hurt again."

"And I don't want you running after a wild goose. You need me. Besides, this time, you'll be there to protect me, won't you?"

I tried and failed to suppress a smile as we headed for the door. Tonight's forecast? Fresh rent boy and toxic purple booze with a chance of grievous bodily harm. No-one could accuse my new acquaintance of boring me.

CHAPTER SEVEN

Throat scar or not, the lure of fresh meat on the block had proved too tempting for at least one of the Wall's drive-by clients. Luca was gone by the time Iain and I traversed the short walk to the stretch of Darlinghurst Road made famous by the boys who traded on their natural assets in the shadow of the old courthouse and gaol. It hadn't taken long to find Ace, the surly-looking, self-appointed ringleader of the strip's head-turning homos for hire. With his ashen hair and acne-scarred face, he'd hardly risen to the post on good looks. From the muscles that stretched under his too-small navy singlet, to a complete absence of body fat, and bulging biceps lined with prominent veins, Ace seemed the type to favour intimidation over allure.

He'd infused his thuggish appearance with such unexpected charm upon seeing Iain, that I'd understood the boy's business model immediately. My companion, of course, wasn't buying it. In truth, Ace hadn't taken much softening, instead settling for our promise to remove his newest competitor from the block once we found him. That competitor had sped off in a BMW belonging to one of Ace's regulars, instantly burning any bridges to the boys of the Wall.

We did however learn that the car's owner preferred to take Ace to one of the local saunas and conduct business there.

Iain took this too in his stride and came with me. I tried to imagine the priest stealing away from his official duties to roam the dark halls dressed in a towel. How much did Iain Grieg have to surprise me in one night?

"Assuming he is here—"

"He is," I said. "The car Ace described is parked a couple of blocks back."

"I saw it. How do you propose we get him away from his client and out the door?"

"Any way I have to." This included broken bones or even killing Luca if necessary. Prior to what I'd seen at Isobel's, I would have given the boy every possible reprieve. But we were dealing with a beast of legend, far beyond the experience of any of us. "I want you out at the first sign of danger. Do what you can to keep any bystanders out of our way if you want to be useful, but *not* at the expense of your own safety, understood?"

"Yes, sir." A hint of amusement lightened his voice.

I wasn't exactly obliged to keep Iain safe. In fact, had I shared the old school ruthlessness of certain Blood Shades, putting him in Luca's path would have been one way to deal with his resilient memory. I dismissed the notion immediately. We were doing this together. God help me.

"Entry for two, please," I said to the cashier.

"Lockers okay? Private rooms are full until half past one."

I stared back at the man like he'd hit me in the face with a frozen salmon.

"Two lockers will be fine, thanks," Iain said, quickly rescuing me.

I looked at him as the man momentarily left the counter. "Knowledgeable, aren't you?"

"I've talked at least a dozen addicts out of suicide, counselled more delinquent youth than I can remember, and been attacked by two vamp… Blood Shades. I like to think I've earned a break on the 'celibacy' thing."

"I wasn't judging." I smiled as the man returned with our keys.

Iain led me to an open room containing several rows of lockers. He stopped at the number that matched his key and took off his jacket.

"Wait a moment." I raised my hand as he went to undo the top buttons of his shirt. "We're not here to enjoy the facilities. We're here to get Luca out and then leave."

"Yes, and if you don't want to draw far too much attention to yourself, your towel's in the locker."

I reluctantly shucked off my jacket as Iain popped the last few buttons of his shirt to reveal a smooth, trim white torso and— "My god."

"I know. Not such a fan of the sun myself. Blame Irish-Polish skin."

"No, your back!"

He glanced over his shoulder before flashing me a shy smile. My eye had fallen on the elaborate carpet of black, blue, and yellow scales inked into Iain's back, forming the coiled shape of a Chinese dragon.

"My protector," he said, removing his shoes and socks.

I stripped off my shirt, hoping I wouldn't blind half the place with my pasty hue. "Are you sure you're a priest?"

He laughed, slipping off his trousers before wrapping the towel around his waist and letting his underwear follow. "I guess I always saw it as the natural route to counselling. My Dad didn't exactly push me into the secular wing of that profession."

I shucked off my shoes and pants, and let my underwear slide to the floor, trying to ignore the pungent smell of disinfectant, leather, sweat, soap, sex, and amyl nitrate that hung on the air. "It's not too late to change your mind about this. You don't owe me anything."

"Not a chance."

"Fine." I lowered my voice as a burly, bored-looking patron with a small, keg-shaped torso sauntered past, casting an eye over both of us. "You're not to put yourself in danger for any reason. If you find him, let me know and come straight back here. Or better still, go home and text me. You've already gone above and beyond."

"Text you? Where are you planning to put your phone? I promise I'll be careful. Trust me, I'm not going another round with this kid."

I tightened my towel with a slight smile, casting an eye into the darkness of the hallway leading to what I assumed was the cruising area. A slender young blonde man emerged, lazily threading his fingers through his hair before disappearing into the dark hallway.

Christ. These humans had no inkling of the danger that walked the halls with them.

"The fellow at the front said all the private rooms were full," I said. "I think we can assume the man who hired Luca would be using one."

"Very probable, if they could get one. Come on, rooms are this way."

"Woah, hold on there, Padre." I caught his arm. "You direct, I'll lead."

"Looking out for me?" He said with a smile.

"More than you know."

*   *   *

A search that seemed infinitely longer than its supposed fifteen minutes interrupted several combinations of two, three, or more gentlemen in various states of undress and a greater variety of sexual predicaments than I knew existed. It seemed that patrons who made use of the 'private rooms' were more than willing to take advantage of their flexibility, even if the supposed privacy was an optional after thought. Our efforts to find Luca and his 'client' had netted us just two angry snarls to fuck off, both of which were delivered through a door far enough ajar to confirm Luca was not inside. I supposed two such dismissals against five invitations to join in wasn't a bad average, though the memory of interrupting a man's rhythm mid-double-fisting would likely remain a source of regret for the rest of my extended life.

By this point, I was beyond worrying what the good father thought.

Luca was nowhere to be found. Had we made a mistake? Had Luca somehow talked his trade into renting a hotel room, or even inviting him back home? If so, we were screwed, and so was his client.

"Not the outcome you were hoping for." Iain returned his attention to me as a muscular young Asian man tossed him an inviting glance.

This didn't make sense. The car was parked nearby, and we had a knowledgeable lead on the sauna. Luca had to be here, somewhere. But there was no detecting his scent over the powerful aromas, both human and chemical, that mingled in the darkness. At least I wasn't smelling blood, yet.

"Have we missed them?"

"No." I supposed it was possible that Luca had simply taken his fill of sex—and money—from the human and let him be.

Sure. And Isobel's secluded lifestyle was no more than a cover for hot yoga and salsa classes being run out of her home. Not bloody likely. My heart skipped as a slight, athletic young man with dark hair and a profile not dissimilar to Luca's crossed our path. Not Luca. Absolutely not Luca. I needed to be careful, lest I injure some hapless human.

"Love your ink, man," the young stranger said as he rounded Iain.

"Thanks."

For all my supernatural gifts, I was feeling decidedly upstaged. But then, I couldn't argue. From his sharp, striking features to his just-athletic-enough body, to… god, even to his scent! No wonder Luca had found Iain irresistible. Even the priest's modest, unassuming demeanour commanded attention.

"Perhaps they're just taking their time? Or they went to the steam room to relax?"

Steam room? Again, my naivete was showing. I imagined something not unlike the Turkish baths I'd known in Berlin, where the focus had been on relaxation until… Well, humans will be humans.

"I don't suppose you can smell him?" Again, the priest's intuition impressed me.

"I've been trying, looking for anything that's not human. Whatever he's become, he's not one of us. I can't say exactly what it is, but there's a difference. I can't make it out on the air." Then again, maybe the combined scents of cleaning chemicals, horny, testosterone-soaked humans, and raw sexual exchange had made it nigh impossible to smell anything else.

"Thought yet of what you'll do when you do find him?"

Good question. With all my concern for Iain's life, had I spared a thought for what Luca could do to me? In a steam room, no less. My enhanced Blood Shade vision would give me an edge, but I had to assume Luca possessed the same gifts. That didn't bode well for any humans caught in the fray. It seemed unlikely that Luca would attack a human so publicly, but could I be sure? The present lack of screaming encouraged me, assuming he'd brought his prey here at all. Assuming he was still here and hadn't already… No. I'd smell a dead body and fresh blood well enough, chemicals or no chemicals. Too many 'ifs.'

"We could try the rooms again?" Iain suggested.

"I'm not sure that'll do much good."

"I've got an idea. Trust me?"

An idea? I was more or less certain Iain wouldn't find Luca within the rooms. If the boy was still here, there was only one place he'd be. "I'll check the steam room. If you do see him or anything suspicious—"

"I'll come and grab you. I know the brief. I just want to see if I can make our lives a bit easier." He disappeared up the darkened hall, attracting the stare of yet another admirer who tripped on the flimsy carpet before righting himself and pretending nothing had happened.

God speed, Father.

I tried not to gag as the scent of chlorinated steam filled my nostrils. The heat wasn't doing me any favours either. I'd adapted well enough to Australia's warm climate years ago, but concentrated heat wasn't something Blood Shades took to instinctively. Perhaps it would have the same effect on Luca, driving him out. Or perhaps I was looking for any excuse to leave.

I tried to ignore the residual scents of sex that hung on the steam. The damp, dimly lit room was largely empty, save for two dark shapes looming on opposite sides of a tiled barrier. Fresh steam rose from behind one of the figures, who turned briefly to face me before resuming his forward gaze. The other remained motionless. In the dark, it was impossible to make out just how tall or... No. Not Luca. They were both too solidly built. Even the leaner of the two struck a figure far too imposing for the young man as he got to his feet and stood, a clear inch or two taller than me. I could barely make out the white teeth of a smile through the steam, even with his face just inches from my own.

Warm fingers touched my left flank as he explored my damp flesh. Caressing the small of my back, he leaned closer, delicately inhaling the scent of my neck. Instinctively, I brought my hands up to his solid trunk. With at least twenty years on my apparent age, he nonetheless possessed a body clearly maintained by regular exercise, a punishing gym regimen, or both. Though I remained full from Paul's generous donation, this tall, dark, steam-shrouded stranger made for tempting seconds.

As the man's fingers descended further, teasing the cleft of my backside, I watched the other man, who'd glanced at me before, get up and leave, spilling white light into the dampness of the room as he let us be. Briefly illuminated, the man who'd failed to acknowledge my presence before remained still. It seemed my first impressions of the room had failed to detect my muscular admirer at all.

My would-be companion's hungry sigh set off a rumble in my stomach I couldn't dismiss. God, he smelled good! Rich and complex, the scent seemed almost familiar, but mixed with all the others in the room, I couldn't quite place it.

I gently clasped his wrist, breaking his hold on my backside. He immediately brought his other hand up to caress the back of my head, lips brushing over mine as he cupped the back of my neck. Nice try, sexy. But I would have to put this encounter on ice for another—

The man's hand refused to budge. I'd been careful not to use my full Blood Shade strength against him, lest I break something, but if this continued... I let his lips brush mine once more as he leaned close, bringing my ear close to his mouth.

"*Maledetto.*" He clapped a hand over my mouth, silencing my scream as the blade went into my flank, then shoved me away into the darkness. I landed hard, collapsing over the slick tile bench in a manner that would have broken several ribs had I been human. But I was not human, and this guy, along with his compatriot who now blocked my escape route, clearly knew it. My gaze darted between the two of them as I licked my fingers and tried to seal at least part of the wound now draining precious blood from my side. It refused to close.

If my natural Blood Shade defences weren't closing the wound, the weapon had to be laced with something, either chemical or mystical. The man's word for me revealed who my assailants were, even if their faces remained obscured. We were way past talking this out.

The younger one lunged at me, throwing a punch that missed my face by inches as I ducked and landed one of my own into his side. I followed it with a kick that was somewhat clumsier than I would have liked, but nonetheless threw off his balance on the wet floor. I could make out the blade of another knife in his hand as he flailed. The distraction gave sexy chops just enough time to launch another attack. His blade nicked the skin below my right pectoral as I tried to retreat. But there was nowhere to go. Ignoring the pain, I dropped to the floor, using the slickness of it to pivot my entire body, catching the man's leg with my own and bringing him down. I heard a sharp yelp followed by a piece of wood clattering to the floor and rolling away.

I didn't need Blood Shade senses to identify the lost weapon. If either of these two rendered me unconscious, there was plenty more they could do before they finally killed me, and if they were Scimitars, I wasn't prepared to discount the possibility of exquisite torture.

The younger man leaped upon me again with a vicious snarl, his knife missing my shoulder by inches. I grabbed hold of his arm before he could raise it for another strike, pulled his body close, and sank my fangs deep into his exposed throat. I clapped a hand over his mouth as he screamed, but pain soon gave way to ecstasy as his entire body went rigid, locking itself into my grasp. Even in furious combat, the beauty of this experience couldn't be denied. Fingers that seconds before had gone for my throat, now gripped my body with sensual hunger. The sudden swell of his erection pushed against me, beyond mere sexual arousal as our heartbeats synched and the flow of his blood became one with mine. Feeding into me, sustaining me, eagerly trading his life force for the sensation of my touch. I should have been more careful. Somewhere, in the recesses of my mind, I remembered Luca. Remembered the awful taste of his blood when I'd fed on him in order to defend myself. But no such taint affected this man's flavour. He was all human. Rich, fit, complex, unmistakeably European, and completely delicious.

My heart jumped as I saw his comrade rise to his feet, bearing down on us with the blade that had found its mark on me twice already. Barely thinking, I shielded myself with my companion, covering the man's mouth again to muffle his scream as the knife went deep into his back. His body jerked violently, the combined sensations of the arousing feed and violent penetration more than he could stand as he ejaculated, his scream fading into choked sighs. I licked the last drops of blood from his wound, feeling the man's heartbeat falter as he collapsed on top of me, eyes frozen as he took his last breaths.

I rolled the young thug's body off me, snatched up his knife and sprang to my feet. One down. Could I drink another? As the wounds in my torso refused to heal, I felt more than justified. I watched the man's dark shape with caution as he circled me in the steam. With full Blood Shade speed, I could have tackled him to the ground and ended this within seconds. But in such a tight space, without steady footing… Not to mention several dozen humans outside.

And now I had a dead body on my hands, not to mention a powerful, very much living one determined to make me pay for defending myself. I had to finish him off here, or at least render him unconscious. One body I could perhaps sneak out, with Iain's help. Two was pushing it. But first—

A damp white towel in the face was far from the attack I'd anticipated. I pulled it off me just in time to see the door to the room swing shut. I bolted after him, emerging from the room just in time to hear a crisply accented European voice.

"Excuse me, could I get a fresh towel?"

"Clean towels are at reception. You lose yours?"

"Yes. Sorry," the thug said, casting a glance at me over the clueless attendant's shoulder. The understanding that passed silently between us was clear. The Scimitar valued discretion as much as I did. No human could be allowed to find the body in the steam room. "I'm embarrassed to ask, but could you bring me one?" The man made a show of covering his nakedness.

The attendant conceded with a barely disguised harrumph. "Wait here."

With a smile that could have greased a thousand breakfast fry-ups, the bastard let him go.

I found myself studying the man, now that I could see his face. The sharp, dark lines and flowing black hair, greying at the tips. The pronounced Roman nose. He jolted me with recognition, just as Luca had. The same features, approaching a healthy fifty. A long scar ran from his left eye down his cheek.

"Go on," he said quietly in Italian. "The question's killing you."

"In that case, it's doing a better job than you. Are the Scimitar's finest all waging the Lord's war with towels these days, or was that just a distraction while you *ran away*?"

"A good soldier knows when the secondary objective is more trouble than it's worth."

Secondary objective? Rude. "I suppose you're not going to tell me who the primary is?"

"Why should I? Why don't you use some of that towering Blood Shade intellect? You already know the answer, among others."

True enough. The added muscle mass, the lines of twenty years, and a hefty battle scar couldn't hide the fact that I'd just met another of Ross's kin. One who'd been a key player in my friend's exile.

"Sal," I said, my voice barely a whisper. "My god."

"God has forsaken you and all your kind."

"Don't start with me! What are you doing here? What are *any* of you doing here? I thought Patricia made an agreement with you. With *you*, personally."

"She did, and the time has come to end it. The decision was not mine, Blood Shade. Besides, you are a fine one to talk of agreements."

"What are you talking about?"

"He was my brother, daemon."

"Ross was my friend."

"Yet you seduced him? Until he met a death that should have been yours."

Shit. How much did this guy know? *How* did he know?

"What's the matter? Upset you couldn't finish the job yourself?" I could see in the faint tightening of his muscles that he was holding back the urge to throw himself at me and do whatever damage his limited brute force could accomplish. But the man had one quality the other Scimitars I'd encountered, including Luca, lacked. Composure. At least he wasn't under the illusion that I'd actually *killed* Ross. "Don't try and tell me that's why the Scimitar is here."

"I'm not here for the Scimitar. I'm here for me."

"But you're not here for *me*. 'Secondary objective.' Your words."

He nodded.

"So, you're here for Luca."

Another silent nod. If the man was making me work for answers, I had to choose my words with care.

"I'm afraid his life has gotten… complicated."

The attendant returned with two fresh, fluffy towels before I could continue. Sal thanked him with another greasy smile, covering his modesty before the attendant offered the other towel to me. I waved him away, not taking my eyes off the Scimitar.

"I'll take one," came Iain's cheerful voice, distracting both of us. He accepted the towel from the attendant, holding the man's eye just a fraction longer than I would have thought necessary. That did it. My new friend was clearly a shameless flirt with anyone and everyone who crossed his path.

"Are you going to introduce me?" He threw the fresh towel over his shoulder as the attendant left us.

"No," I said quietly. "Iain…"

His cheerful demeanour darkened, picking up on my tone.

"And you are?" Sal asked, his assassin's smile now downright punchable.

"Iain," I repeated. "Get dressed and leave, *now*."

I started as a loud alarm began shrieking just above our heads, following by an automated voice.

Attention. The fire alarm system has been activated. Please move to the nearest exit and evacuate via the stairs in an orderly manner.

"I guess we should do as they say," said Iain.

"That's not going to be possible just now," I said, not taking my eyes off Sal. We weren't going anywhere.

"Okay. So, what about—"

"*Iain*," I repeated, bordering on irritated. "I'll see you at home."

This time, he left without argument. It was a calculated risk. If Luca was among the grumpy looking, semi-naked men being ushered out of the club without so much as the chance to collect their clothes, I was putting Iain, not to mention the rest of them, in grave danger. But if we hadn't found Luca by now, the risk seemed mild. Sal, on the other hand, was a very clear, present, and obvious danger.

Sal raised an eyebrow at me, tilting his head in the direction of the steam room.

I almost laughed. Had the gesture come from any other man, I might have been flattered. I took his cue, following him inside. I was ready for him to try anything. But the man wasn't that foolish. Instead, he resumed his seat, ignoring the still shape of his dead comrade on the floor. I folded my arms, leaning against the wall in one of the darker sections of the room.

"I can't tell you where Luca is," I said.

"That's evident. What do you mean by 'complicated?'"

I paused, unsure just how much to reveal. "Let's just say I don't think he's quite the young man you thought you knew."

"Meaning what?"

"Oh, no, no, no. My turn for questions, Sal—" I shut up as the door to the steam room swung open, and a hideous white light spread through the mist, just wide enough to illuminate the Scimitar's bloodied body.

"Did you blokes hear the fire alarm? Hey, what the—"

I closed the space between the attendant and myself in less than a second, scrunching the top of his shirt in my fist and locking his gaze to mine. "There's nobody here," I told him firmly. "Everyone's safely out of the club, and you should be too. Leave, and don't come back or let anyone else back in for at least half an hour. Do you understand?"

"Yes," the man stammered. "Yes, I... I'm going now."

I didn't particularly need to maintain eye contact with the man, but I held it anyway. Perhaps to make sure he complied. Perhaps to ensure he didn't catch another glimpse of the corpse. Whatever the reason, I held it a moment too long.

I doubled over in pain as a solid kick sent me sprawling on the damp floor. I reached out and yanked the dagger from the dead assassin's back, looking up just in time to see the steam room's door close. Unwilling to risk losing Salvatore in the crowd of men who by now had to be milling outside, I dived after him, only to be grabbed by solid arms and thrown hard into the window that overlooked the darkened halls of the club. Glass shattered around me. I barely felt the impact, landing in the bed of shards. I winced, trying to keep my breath steady as I got to my feet and saw the broken window a few feet above my head. Even if I did manage to climb back through without cutting myself to ribbons, Salvatore had bought himself enough time to disappear anywhere in this labyrinth of dark rooms, bathed in dim red light and the smell of sex. Even if I wasn't his primary goal, I couldn't just let him go. I listened for the bang of a locker, footsteps, heavy breathing… anything at all that might have betrayed the man's whereabouts.

The sound of heavy gasps some way up the corridor broke my concentration. Ordinary human hearing would have likely missed them, but I knew those sounds all too well. This was all I needed. Two stupid humans too horny to put it away until the danger had passed. Curious though, that a fire alarm should just happen to go off tonight. Just as Salvatore and I had found ourselves locked in stalemate.

Iain's handiwork?

That question would wait. I had at least two humans in the throes of passion to eject from the premises before I could direct my energy back toward kicking a certain holy crusader's arse.

I quickly found the sole remaining closed door and knocked. The 'happy couple' didn't miss a beat, continuing their steady rhythm of moans, gasps, and faint whimpers of *oh yeah, use me, harder, deeper, oh yeah, daddy*, and other human verbalisations that rarely failed to put me off my food.

I hammered on the door. "Break it up, boys!"

No answer. I did not have time for this. I sent the door swinging off its hinges with one swift kick. The fuckers could bill me.

Empty, save for the porn movie playing at top volume on a small television in one corner of the ceiling. How the hell had Salva—

My scream buried the sounds of the movie as the knife entered my side. I rounded on Salvatore and lunged at him. But I wasn't going far with a blade in my flank, and I was losing blood fast. I slammed the room's door shut just as Salvatore dived at me again. Managing to slide the bolt home. I quickly backed off as a tattoo of loud bangs hammered against the door. Then, all was still.

I reached around for the knife and prised it out, finally losing my battle not to scream as it came free. Even as blood poured from the wound, I felt a rush of relief, but what if the blade was laced with the same chemical? Fresh intake of blood or not, my healing abilities still lagged.

I turned off the blasted television and listened for any sound that might have given Salvatore away. Nothing. Not a single breath in the now silent corridor. I crept from the room, padding silently past the open doors and abandoned bunks.

The long sword came through my side without warning, sending a fresh wave of pain through my body. Again, the wound stubbornly refused to heal. Despite wielding such a weapon, Salvatore hadn't gone for my head. This wasn't about killing me. This was about punishing me for Ross. For setting

Ross free and encouraging his true nature. The bastard blamed me.

I wasn't about to give him another chance. I dove into a dark corridor coming up on my right and weaved my way through the labyrinth, ducking behind darkened wood panels, keeping beyond the range of dim red lights. Salvatore was still on my trail, but my Blood Shade senses offered me a keen advantage. Eventually, I'd have to escape. Any escape would do at this point. I dove toward the light just up on my left, only to find, not a room, but a series of none too sturdy looking wooden doors on either side of a large leather mat, suspended from the ceiling by thick chains. A tiny wooden stool sat on the floor at one end of the mat.

Oh.

Salvatore could not have been more than a few steps behind me. I snatched up the small stool and belted it across the man's face, raising it again only to have him artfully pivot in my direction, sword in hand. I dived under the sling as the sword glanced off the metal chains. He came at me again, trying to compensate for his moving target as the sword this time sliced into black leather. The chains jerked violently as a corner of the sling fell away, leaving one of the chains loose. I grabbed hold of it and pulled down with my full weight, staggering to regain my feet as it came loose from the ceiling. Not much of a weapon, but it would do.

Salvatore's self-satisfied smirk did little for my confidence as we circled one another. If I could only stun him long enough to—

Pain gripped me again as I evaded his first attack, then another. If I couldn't stop the bleeding, I'd need another round of fresh blood, and if it came from Salvatore, that would end my best chance of learning what was happening to Luca.

I let him lunge again, then attacked, wrapping the chain around his neck and pulling it hard toward me. The move caught him off balance, just long enough for me to whip around behind him and pull again, dragging the man off his feet. He refused to let go of the sword, even as I dragged us both toward one of the rooms and wrenched open the door. I could hear the man choking. If I could take just enough blood to restore myself without killing him, his fight would be over.

He choked as I drew the chains up, thrashing his sword around like a child in a tantrum. I could smell the richness of his blood as it pumped just below the surface of his skin, right up until the moment I bit him. That was how Salvatore Depuratore became the first man to punch me in the face mid-feed.

I jerked myself away and choked down the little blood I'd managed to get out of him. It was all the opportunity Salvatore needed. Blood still ebbing from his shoulder, he thrust at me with the damn sword once more. Chain still in hand, I narrowly escaped the tiny confines of the room, throwing the door shut behind me, hearing the sword break wood as it landed again. With few alternatives, I looped the chain through the door handle, then ran it through the handle of the neighbouring door, looping it there as well. It wouldn't hold for long, but all I needed was time to get away.

I scurried back through the darkened maze, the light of the locker area already in sight. Just a few more steps. My side was killing me.

With a great crash and the sound of metal sliding to the floor, I knew Salvatore was on my tail. Diving to my left, I limped back toward the steam room, where I'd at least a chance to lose him in the gloom.

Salvatore lunged for the steam room door before I could get near it. Instinctively, I reached behind me for the wooden handle and dove into the dry sauna instead, slamming the door shut behind me and holding it fast. I ducked as the small glass window at the top of the door shattered. Then came the now all too familiar sound of metal against wood as Salvatore hacked away at my feeble sanctuary.

Wood. Why did gay men insist on making everything wood?

I backed away, catching my attacker off balance as the door suddenly gave way. I caught his arm and nimbly flipped him into the wall. As he came at me again, I dove out of the way and swung myself up onto his back, trying to regain my hold on his throat. But the man had at least thirty pounds of raw muscle on me, and in my current state, my 'superior' Blood Shade strength meant little as he grabbed me by the hair and wrenched me off toward—

He slammed the side of my face into the burning coals. A sword couldn't kill me. Even a stake through the heart would inflict no more than a deathlike paralysis, but fire? I burned as readily as any human.

My sanctuary now a torture chamber, it took every ounce of strength I had to brace myself on the wooden guard-rail— no longer cursing the gay propensity for all things wood—and break free, slamming the back of my head into what I assumed was the man's nose. Ignoring the odour of lightly charred Blood Shade flesh, I caught Salvatore's free hand and bit into it until it was good and bleeding. Ignoring the tempting scent, I threw open the door and hauled myself free. But I'd lost a lot of blood. My movements were sluggish and I didn't hear Salvatore approach until he'd nicked my arm again with his sword.

I startled, whirling round and retreating up the corridor, not taking my eyes off the Scimitar. I needed a weapon. Anything! I yelped as my foot hit something metal and I fell, my head striking something on the way down.

Salvatore grabbed hold of the weight rack and sent it toppling onto me before I could get away. I lay pinned in agony, sure he'd broken several ribs. Nonetheless I tried to push the rack full of thirty and forty-pound weights from my chest. But there was no budging it. Not while I was bleeding, hungry, and disoriented from the blow to my head and the gaping wound in my side.

I heard the Scimitar's heavy footsteps and lifted my head. Standing in the doorway, he looked not unlike a pornographic parody of some ancient gladiator, blood streaked across his face and chest, bathed in red light, which shone off the long, thick blade of the sword he'd returned with.

Of all the ways I'd envisioned or even skirted my death—trapped and left to burn in sunlight, ripped limb from limb by a crazed werewolf, consumed by some flesh-eating hell beast from another reality—being decapitated by a naked Catholic zealot while pinned under a bench press in a Sydney sex club hadn't been the most probable. Yet its likelihood increased with each step the man took toward me… then plummeted as Sal's eyes rolled back within his head. His muscular form collapsed in a heap beside me, sword clattering harmlessly against the bench press frame.

Iain stood wide eyed and panting as he clutched the small free weight he'd landed with such precision on the back of my enemy's skull.

"I told you to get out!" I hoped that somewhere within my abrasive tone lay wisps of gratitude.

"You're welcome." He lifted one of the weights off the rack, followed by another. Some four or five weights later, I managed to prise myself free, not taking my eyes off Sal's now motionless body.

"What are you going to do with him?"

"Them."

"What?"

"There's another one dead in the steam room."

"And this one?"

Pulling my lips back in a silent snarl, I could resist it no longer. I dove upon Sal, snatching him up and burying my teeth in his throat. I barely heard Iain's protest as the blood delivered on the promise of the bastard's fit body. The man stirred with the first pangs of semi-consciousness, trying with futility to push me away. But part of him didn't want to. Like his brutish lieutenant before him, Sal surrendered to my embrace as I wrapped my body around his, draining him in long, steady gulps.

"Reylan, *stop!*"

Even as a slightly off flavour crept into Sal's blood, even as his heart began to slow, I continued feeding. Just a few more sips and—

A spray of blood erupted from the man's throat as the metal struck the back of my head. I pushed my meal away and rounded on Iain, but the man was ready for me, pushing me hard against the wall and holding the cross bar against my throat.

"Listen! *Listen to me!*"

Fury bristled through me, longing to be freed. Longing to pounce on this presumptuous human who'd dared interrupt my feeding. Who now dared to hold *me* against my will and tell me to—

"He's down. You've won. You've fed. Now for god's sake…"

This didn't make any sense. High on fresh blood, particularly Salvatore's, I should have been able to push myself free and toss Iain aside like a rag doll. Yet as I gazed into those dark, earnest eyes, eyes that in that moment glistened with genuine fear, I couldn't bring myself to raise a hand against him. The resistance drained from my body as my muscles relaxed. I glanced down at Sal, who lay on the floor, bleeding profusely from the neck.

I'd lost all control. Panicked in my underfed, injured state, I'd allowed the monster that survived upon the life's blood of humanity to feast on my prey without conscience. The thought of accidentally killing Sal didn't bother me. What bothered me, was how close Iain had come to joining him.

Apparently satisfied I'd regained a hold of myself, Iain withdrew the iron bar from my throat. I returned to Sal's side and gently licked closed his wound before lowering him to the floor to recover. He wouldn't give us any more trouble. I'd drained him too near death for that, which worried me. Somewhere in my darkest of hearts, I knew how close Iain had come to being next.

"You're a damn fool." I wiped the last of the blood from my lips. "Interrupting a frenzied Blood Shade mid feed. And for what? To spare the life of some brutish zealot who'd happily kill us both?"

"And just how many brutish zealots do you have to kill before you're no better than they are?"

"We're nothing alike at all!" I snapped. "When we kill Scimitars, it's in self-defence."

"Is that what just happened between us? Self-defence?"

I silenced him with a look before picking up Sal's sword. Confident the discussion was over, I inspected the functional, almost spartan hilt. The weapon was light, despite its obvious strength, which, on consideration, shouldn't have surprised me. An organisation of professional killers needed practical weapons, particularly against an enemy to whom guns posed little or no threat.

"What's a 'Scimitar,' exactly?"

"Let's just say not all the Lord's servants share your open mindedness when it comes to people like us. Descended from supernatural family lines, they fancy themselves holy warriors, charged by God to hunt and destroy supernatural beings."

"Despite being born that way themselves?"

I shook my head, lowering the sword. "It's not that simple. The state of being a Blood Shade, werewolf, Cloak Walker… Or one of any number of other permutations might be hereditary, but it's not consistent. The gene can lay dormant for several generations of human before taking over. Even when it does, it typically won't do so until the individual reaches their early twenties, by which point they've already reached adulthood as a human. Maybe even settled into adult human life."

"That must be quite a shock."

"It was," I admitted. "But for the poor devils born to the families of the Scimitar, it's a death sentence. Their acolytes are expected to serve the cause faithfully their entire lives, and if they do suffer the misfortune of a change—"

"Honour killings." Iain did nothing to hide his shudder. "Barbaric."

"The one remaining road, in their eyes, to salvation. And only if the subject surrenders willingly."

"But they only hunt supernaturals?"

"Don't think for a moment that your humanity would have saved you. If they see you at my side—and if they're watching me, you can assume they have—then in their eyes, you've chosen the wrong side. Find us a fire exit, will you?" My strength replenished by his blood, I dragged Salvatore along the short hall leading to the lockers. Checking the number against the key on his wristband, and dropping his prone form where I could keep an eye on it, I took out a worn-looking black t-shirt, plus leather jacket and pants, both of which offered fruitlessly empty pockets. His backpack, however… wallet, passport in the name of Salvatore Depuratore, born Naples, Italy, 1977 and a rolled-up knapsack that unfurled to reveal a half dozen small but vicious looking hand blades and two wooden stakes, together with a small pistol, already loaded for good measure. No doubt my unconscious foe was handy with each and every one of them.

"There's one leading onto some stairs around this corner and down the hall," Iain's voice called. "Where are you?"

"Locker area," I answered, taking the gun from its lining.

Iain's eyes widened as he caught sight of Sal's armoury.

"Here," I said, handing him the gun.

"Reylan, what the hell? I don't—"

"Wait here while I get the other one. I very much doubt he'll give you any trouble. But if he does—"

"Just answer me one thing. How do you know him?"

"I beg your pardon?"

"His face. Did you think I wouldn't notice? Same nose. Same jawline."

I fished out Sal's passport and held it up where Iain could see it. "Same last name. He's here for the same reason we are, or at least he claimed to be. It seems I was just an opportune distraction."

"Opportune?"

"Can we discuss this *after* we've disposed of these men?"

"Disposed? You're really going to kill him?"

This gave me pause. I owed Sal nothing. Not even his life. But after Luca, the woman at Isobel's house, and now Salvatore and his thuggish sidekick… Even putting their 'agreement' with Patricia aside, this concentrated barrage seemed odd for the Scimitars. Killing Sal could destroy a valuable opportunity, though perhaps the answer lay in his own words, 'I'm not here for the Scimitar.' In any case, Salvatore had answers. I intended to find them, and judging by the off flavour that had crept through his blood, I needed to find them soon.

"I'm not going to kill him," I said. "Though he might wish I had."

CHAPTER EIGHT

"Bloody hell." The familiar voice of Kelvin emanated from the doorway. "I swear, I'm gonna buy a hearse and start running a shuttle service."

I shifted Salvatore's limp weight in my arms. "Will you help us get them out of sight, please?"

Relief spread across Brett's face as Kelvin took part of the dead Scimitar's weight. Salvatore, I could manage on my own, but even the smaller thug's body, densely packed as it was with lean muscle, was a challenge for my human servant.

We'd hastily wrapped the men in sheets from the sauna, leaving Iain with strict instructions to go to my home and wait for our return. Perhaps I should have ordered him back to his own house, but the man's unusually resilient memory still troubled me. I wasn't prepared to let him vanish into the night just yet.

"Where's Patricia?" I gently kicked the door shut behind me as we moved the bodies into the sitting room.

"Hold your horses," the Cloak Walker said. "She'll come see you when... Is that who I think it is?"

Confident he was still dead to the world, I tilted Salvatore's face toward the light. "I think Patricia will want to see us now."

"Is he—"

"Alive? Yes, though he might need some time. Possibly a blood transfusion, if you can spare any." I assumed Sophia's newfound knowledge would offer some way of discerning the man's blood type to ensure compatibility. If not… oh well.

"Blood? What did you—"

"What I had to do. I availed myself of the situation." I omitted the part about Iain coming perilously close to being dessert.

"All right, next question. They're both naked. Do I even want to know?"

"I was wondering that too," said Brett. "That and a bunch of other stuff, like who they are, how the hell they found you, why this guy looks just like—"

"Will the both of you stop it?" I finally snapped. "Besides fighting off two professional assassins, I've been just a bit preoccupied this evening."

In fairness, I'd not explained a damn thing to Brett when I'd collected him from Valia's. Nor to Deborah, and certainly not to Peter who'd still been hanging about. After the merry old time I'd had introducing Brett to the world of BDSM clubs, was he ready for gay saunas? The Scimitars, it seemed, had no such hang-ups. To them, it was just another hunting ground.

"I'll explain everything when Patricia arrives."

"Then there's no need to wait." The former nun's gaze fell upon Salvatore's face. "Ball room. Now."

*　*　*

"So, he is related to that kid who attacked you?" Brett asked, after I'd done my best to summarise how events had led me to fighting Scimitars in a sauna. I'd altered the facts ever so slightly to omit Iain's presence.

105

"Quite closely, I'll bet," Patricia said. "I'll have Sophia analyse a blood sample."

"But you already know who he is?"

"Of course. I presume that's your reason for bringing them here?" The former nun directed her question to me, rather than answering Brett.

"It seemed prudent. The fact that the Scimitars are in Sydney at all violates an agreement made personally between the two of you."

"Yet he claimed he wasn't here for the Scimitar, correct?"

"So he said."

She regarded the man strapped firmly underneath a sheet to a table in the Arcadia Trust's ball room come medical bay. "And you believe he was at the sauna looking for Luca?"

"Just as I was, yes."

A flicker of annoyance crossed Patricia's face as she took off her glasses and cleaned them. "Overlooking the fact that you managed to lose Luca within hours of taking him into your custody—"

"Sister, as I made pointedly clear to you—"

"I'm aware of the circumstances, thank you. They hardly lessen your problem. Still, you said he wasn't at the sauna."

"Correct. I couldn't find him and nor did these two."

"Meaning he's still out there somewhere, potentially killing again."

"If he does, we'll know soon enough," said Kelvin.

"He won't," I said before anyone could humour that less than comforting thought. I turned to look at Salvatore's almost comatose form. "Not if we have some help in finding him."

"No fucking way!" the Cloak Walker snarled. "Just who do you think you're—"

"Leave us," Patricia said in the general direction of Kelvin's voice.

"But this is—"

Kelvin." She turned toward Brett, raising that same bloody single eyebrow I knew too well. "Now."

"Reylan?"

"Wait for me at home," I told him. There'd be time for explanations later. Frankly, I was more interested in seeing what Patricia and I could come up with without the constant interjections of her invisible guard dog.

Only when both men had left us alone did I hear what Patricia really thought.

"Have you completely lost your mind? Bad enough you lose track of the boy. Now you expect *this* man to help us?"

"He's critically injured and his right-hand bully boy is dead. Between you and I, we've all the reason in the world to kill him, yet we haven't. What if he's telling the truth? What if he is here alone, without Scimitar backing or protection?"

"But the other—"

"Easy enough to bring one thug along for the ride. Now he's alone, and we're the only ones keeping him alive. Whether he likes it or not, I'd say that leaves him precious few options."

"You'd say?" Patricia parroted back with uncharacteristic sarcasm. Call it childishness, but I couldn't deny my mild satisfaction at putting her on the back foot. "This man hates every one of your kind, and from what you've told me, he blames you for Ross's 'corruption.' Probably even his death. He'll die before he lifts a finger to help us."

"In which case, we lose what?"

The irritation in her face gave way to something quite different. Respect. I knew Patricia to be a cold woman when it came to safeguarding her charges. I was learning when to fight her and when to give way, and my willingness to work with Salvatore—with his cooperation or otherwise—did not extend to alienating her.

"You're both punching above your weight." There was no mistaking that voice. Wakey wakey, arsehole.

"Is that so?" I approached the table where he remained strapped down. "Then perhaps you'd care to enlighten us? What are we dealing with, Salvatore? Who is Luca to you? What's happened—"

"Well, listen to you. All the questions. No answers. Poor, lost little daemon, talking tough without a clue."

"I think I'm starting to piece it together."

"Then you don't need my help." The man's sneer spread into a grin as he looked at Patricia. "Good to see you again, Sister."

"I suggest you be nice to Reylan. Right now, he's the only thing standing between you and enforcement of our agreement."

I wasn't sure how to take that. As of this moment, I'd stayed Patricia's hand against two Scimitars. That, in principle, was two too many.

A low, clucking laughter burst from the man strapped to the table. "Agreement? Yes. What of our 'agreement?'"

"Don't worry," said Patricia. "I'd no illusions that you had any intention of keeping it."

Salvatore gasped, his face barely containing an obvious burst of pain.

"What's wrong with him now?" I asked.

"I don't know. I'll call Sophia."

"Don't bother," the man choked out, ignoring the fact that Patricia was already on her way out. "I'm sorry to dent your precious daemon ego, but my death won't be your handiwork."

"That depends on how forthcoming you are with me."

He laughed again, a sound not unlike a large rat trying to gnaw through a skirting board. "The man who doesn't age is getting impatient. Your existence is a never-ending maze of contradictions."

Immortal or not, I wasn't prepared to push the boundaries of it by enduring this idiot's sophistry.

"I will never understand why God would grant such a gift to—"

"And Satan was the most beautiful of all angels," I pointed out. "Do you really want to spend your last earthly hours crying foul at the god whose mercy you'll be begging so soon?"

"Hours? Planning to finish the job quickly after all, Blood Shade?"

"I haven't decided yet."

He smiled, this time sparing me the contemptuous laughter. "You can smell it, can't you?"

My mouth flattened into a steely grimace. "I could taste it."

"Stomach cancer. Too far advanced to stop at this point. And if you're even thinking about using some of that precious Blood Shade—"

"Believe me, that offer is not on the table."

"Just as well. You already damned one of our family in Ross. I won't let you—"

"Better make that two."

All the cockiness drained from his face. "What are you talking about?"

"He found me, Salvatore. I don't know what he was doing here, or why, or how we weren't warned. But Luca found me, and I assure you, in that exchange, I was not the one 'punching above my weight.'"

The man's face twisted with renewed contempt. "You should have killed him! He would not have hesitated to do the same."

"Yes, he made that perfectly clear. Unlike some, I have grave reservations about killing children, or sending them into battles where they are grossly outmatched."

"Now listen, Blood Shade—"

"No, you listen to me. We can continue this pissing contest until that tumour works its way through your innards and eats whatever black heart beats in your chest. Right now, I have bigger concerns, such as who Luca may kill next."

"Next?" He seemed genuinely taken aback.

"Posing as a hustler, he's killed at least one of his clients."

For the first time during our conversation, Salvatore had no answer. He wouldn't even look at me. He just stared at the ceiling, breathing as steadily as his obvious discomfort would allow.

"You knew he would change, didn't you?"

"Impossible!" he said, snapping out of his silence. "If that were so, I would have killed him myself."

"I don't think you were given that chance. I don't think Luca's here with your consent at all." Met only with silence, I pressed him further. "You said you weren't here on the Scimitar's behalf. What's going on, Salvatore?"

Patricia returned with Sophia and Giorgios at her side.

"By the time you realise what's been done, you'll be too late," the man said, waiting until the three were in earshot of his hoarse croaking. "For what it's worth, you're right. My permission was not sought for what has been done to him, nor did I send…" He trailed off, offering Patricia another less than sincere smile. "What does it matter? Your fates are sealed as sure as mine."

Sophia looked over the incapacitated Scimitar, ignoring the difficulty of being barely tall enough to see over him. "I'll be the judge of that."

"Let me save you some time, little daemon. Stomach cancer. Beyond treatment, not that I suppose you're offering any."

"You suppose correctly," said Patricia.

I frowned. "Just as you're not offering me any answers, Salvatore."

"I owe you nothing." The man wheezed another cough before his eyes closed.

Sophia took hold of his limp hand. "He's telling the truth. Best let him rest."

"We're not done, Sophia."

"If you plan to get anything more out of this man at all, I assure you, you are, at least for now. He wasn't joking about it being in its final stages. He needs rest."

"We'll have him under constant observation," Patricia added. "Don't worry. Come back tomorrow. We'll get his cooperation one way or another."

They say you can smell Cloak Walkers, even if you can't see them, since their invisibility makes it impossible for them to properly clean themselves. This uncharitable myth notwithstanding, I didn't need to smell Kelvin to know he'd entered the room. One way or another, indeed.

"Let's hope for his sake he's feeling more cooperative tomorrow." I left Sophia and Kelvin to examine their prisoner.

A troubled expression crept through Patricia's face as she turned to me one last time. "What do you suppose that meant? His permission?"

We'd made such a hash of the whole business. The best thing may have been to kill Salvatore and focus our time and energies on Luca. But I couldn't. In some strange way, I owed it to the boy. "Salvatore might not be in the running for Father of the Year, but I very much doubt he condones what's been done to his son."

Patricia nodded without a flicker of surprise. Of course, she was no fool. She'd worked out the connection just as I had. "Whatever that is. We still have no idea what he's become. But he needs your blood to survive, doesn't he?"

"Honestly? Without knowing what he's turned into, I can't know. Right now, he seems more interested in the blood of others."

Patricia's expression hardened again as she toyed with her collar. "Resolve this. Do what you have to do." Before I could answer, she turned and stalked toward her office.

It wasn't until my shoulders relaxed that I realised how tense the entire visit had been, and only then did I hear a small boy's voice behind me.

"There's something you should see."

I turned to see Giorgios, the younger and smaller of the two Prematures. I'd rarely seen him apart from his sister. Without waiting for my answer, he turned and led me to the Trust's library. I swallowed as the smell of archaic dust and old books filled my nostrils. As on my previous visits, the room was so dimly lit, I could barely see more than a few feet in front of me. Yet the volumes on these shelves—millions of pages on supernatural lore from every nation, from times long forgotten, empires long dead—what I wouldn't have given for a few hours—

The light of a computerised tablet near blinded me as it broke the gloom, looking decidedly anachronistic as it bathed Giorgios's face in its blue glow. The boy beckoned me closer until I was looking over his shoulder at the pad. A grainy black and white video unmistakeably showed us the sauna. Was it legal to have cameras inside the place? In any case, there was no disbelieving what I now saw.

"Why do you have this?"

A familiar, slim shouldered figure in a towel came into view. Luca. The figure in the image came to an abrupt stop in the hallway. While the video was too grainy to make out any sort of facial expression, there was no mistaking him. Nor was there any mistaking… No. Impossible! He would have told me. Surely, he would have told me if… I clenched my fists as I watched Iain approach the perfectly still Luca, whisper something in his ear, then walk out of shot as if nothing had happened.

"How did you get this?"

The boy didn't answer, nor did he have to. I'd already been played.

CHAPTER NINE

I closed my front door quietly behind me, making sure Dorotha's upstairs apartment door was safely closed. I didn't think the Scimitars would go after a defenceless old woman, much less a fellow 'good Catholic,' but at this point, I couldn't discount it.

"Iain?"

The only response came with the faint skittering of paws. Demetrius spilled into the hall, rubbing himself against my ankles. That accounted for one member of my household, at least. I set the cat down silently on the stairs leading to Dorotha's door before rounding the partition into my living room.

There, on the dimly lit couch sat Iain, silently shushing me with a bony white finger against his lips. In his lap slept Luca, as human and unthreatening as I'd ever seen him.

I froze, unable to speak, unable to move, unable to do a bloody thing as I fought the temptation to… Hell, I think I wanted to laugh. Asleep! Right there on my couch! The man he'd 'attacked' stroking his hair.

Iain just smiled at me again, carefully easing himself out from under Luca and replacing his knees with a cushion from the end of the couch. "I suppose you want an explanation?"

"Assuming you have one I'm going to believe." Of all the possible scenarios that had gone through my head—a trap, Iain playing dumb, an empty house—the sight of Luca sleeping peacefully in the man's lap had blindsided me almost as much as the boy's attack.

"I can't promise that," he answered, leading me into the kitchen. "I made him some tea. Can you drink tea?"

I tossed my jacket over the kitchen counter. Had the entire evening been one big charade? A little bribe for the local rent boys to back up his story and… Fuck! May someone stake and burn me if I ever indulged my inner Good Samaritan again!

"Tea, I can digest, yes," I answered calmly. Iain was shielding his hand, and if I wanted to undo the Scimitars, I'd need to do the same. "Though why you'd offer it to a creature that almost killed you eludes me, as does why you'd bring him inside in the first place."

He frowned as he filled the kettle. "About that—"

"He could have killed you. To be perfectly blunt, I'm surprised he didn't." I should have been so lucky.

"He was waiting for you, Reylan. As in literally waiting on the doorstep when I got back. I didn't know what to do. I tried not to let him see me at first, but he recognised me."

"Recognised you? As a former victim?"

"He's been following us. He wants help, but he's terrified you're going to kill him. When I tried to leave, he practically begged me to come back. Maybe he finds me less threatening?"

"You are less threatening."

"Thanks. Anyway, I didn't know what to do. He seemed in control of whatever he is. I barely recognised him at first, but he knew where we'd been. He remembered me offering him help right before he attacked me."

I wanted to hand the bastard an Oscar. "You risked your life, mine, and my tenant's in bringing him here alone."

"And you being here would have made that much difference?" He plonked the kettle down on the burner before his expression calmed. "I'm sorry, that was out of line."

I wasn't so easily distracted by his performative outburst. "In any case, we need to secure him. If he loses control of whatever's inside him again, I can't promise protection to you or anyone else in his path."

He gave me a reticent nod. "And how do we accomplish that?"

Easing him aside, I opened the third of the kitchen drawers he'd been blocking and retrieved a ball of genuine silver twine. I'd first procured it at a small occult shop in Bratislava, more as a novelty than anything else. Now, I was about to test its strength against a creature I barely had a word for.

"You're kidding."

"This thread is pure silver, designed to restrain a captured werewolf in human form. If the wolf changes shape or expands, the silver cuts right through its flesh and bone. I'm not assuming Luca's transformations work exactly the same way, but if it's strong enough to bind a wolf, I'd say it's the best chance we've got." I flinched despite myself as Iain grabbed my arm, though if he noticed, he didn't show it.

"You told me werewolves didn't exist," he said. "I asked you that exact question and you lied to my face."

Damn. I'd fucked up there. Not that his ignorance had been any less of a pretence.

I gently unhooked his fingers from my arm. "Remember just how much danger you're in, knowing *we* exist. You'll forgive me if I don't go throwing more exotic and terrible creatures on the bonfire that is your impeccable memory."

For the briefest moment, I wondered if I'd made a second, graver mistake. Had I just given the game away? I was in no shape to fight two Scimitars at once, and the sooner I had the twine around Luca's hands and feet, the better I'd feel about confronting Iain.

"You're right," he conceded at last. "I don't want to know. In fact, when you work out what *he* is, I don't want to know that either. Then I think you should wipe my memory, and if you can't do it, find a Blood Shade who can. I'm done. I'm out. Clearly, this is all way beyond my pay grade, and it's not as if any of you want me involved anyhow."

Wise words, far too late.

"You're sure?"

"If what you say is true then it's only a matter of time before I'm somebody's loose end. I don't see any way that can end well, do you? Besides, we don't even know if you can do it."

His logic, however manufactured, was infallible. The very idea of a Scimitar immune to Blood Shade hypnosis… Whoever he was, he'd been quite a coup for their ranks.

I rounded the corner into the living room and stopped. There was Luca, sitting up, looking straight at me. No trace of gloating marred his expression. His eyes were wide, his dark fringe hanging over his forehead in sharp barbs held together by dried sweat, lips ever so slightly parted, longing me to speak so he didn't have to. This wasn't a man after my blood. He needed my help. But I could hardly rely on him in this state to help me against Iain. The charade would have to continue a little longer.

"Luca," I said quietly, raising my hands slowly so he could see the silver thread.

"What did you do to me?" He practically breathed the accusation. "Why do I feel so sick?"

How I wished I had answers for him. What had I done? I wasn't about to blame my taking him as a Mannequin for the creature he'd turned into. That, by any measurable law of nature, did not happen.

"You were injured," I tried to explain. "I fed you a little of my blood—"

"*Perversione!*" he spat out, rising to his feet.

"Sit down." I threw the force of the loyalty I'd imposed on him behind my voice. Whether it had the desired effect, or whether his quick compliance was thanks to his weakened state, I couldn't say. Standing had caused him obvious pain. Only once he'd calmed did I continue. "In truth, I don't know what you are. But I do know that it'll put you and anyone near you in great danger, if you don't accept our help."

He crossed his arms over his stomach, looking away in a vain attempt to hide his shame.

"We both know you've been raised and trained to kill, Luca."

"To kill daemons!"

"To kill people like me! Blood shades, werewolves, Shapers. Men and women who are *different*. Who have gifts deemed 'unholy' by your miserable ideology. Oh, but this is something else, isn't it?"

"Another daemon vampire! Descended of Satan. Prince of liars!"

Nice to know I had pedigree.

"That same blood that flows through you, Luca. Just like it flowed through Ross."

His head spun to face me, eyes widening at the name.

"Ah, yes. You know Ross, don't you? Or you did, by reputation at least. Don't tell me the resemblance is some accident. What was he to you, Luca Depuratore?"

"*Enough!*"

"He never mentioned you. Not once. Did he even know about you? A shame. You would have liked him. You might well dismiss him as a traitor, but I assure you, he's the only reason you're still alive."

"He… he…" If there was more to that sentence, Luca wasn't getting it out.

"Reylan," Iain said, gently touching my arm. "What are you doing? What's the point of this?"

I silently bit my lip, not taking my eyes off Luca. Maybe I'd pushed far enough. Perhaps even risked him transforming and attacking us. But I had to know, just as the boy had to know that he'd been lied to his entire life. Only then, could we help him.

We? Damn it, *I*. Iain could go to hell!

"My uncle," Luca finally admitted, his voice little more than a whisper. "My father is Salvatore Depuratore. The man you call Ross is my father's brother."

"But you never met him?" Iain asked.

"Of course he didn't," I said, not taking my eyes off the boy. "The Scimitar would never allow that. Instead, they fed you a diet of endless lies about your 'evil' uncle who surrendered to the daemon. Until at last, they were ready to send you after him. To succeed where Salvatore had failed so many years ago. Except, your uncle was already dead."

Luca snarled again. "He died because of—"

"Because of what? Because of me? Is there some logic behind that accusation, Luca? Or are we Blood Shades just the cause of every ill in the Scimitar's world?"

Not a word.

"Very well, here's some logic for you to think over. Ross died saving my life, and the lives of others like me, not because he was asked to, but because that's the sort of man he was. That's the man your army of blessed 'holy warriors' tried to murder. And when he did die, it wasn't by the hand of some other 'daemon.' Oh no. He was killed by a man, Luca. A *human* man with a gun, and not just any sort of gun. A weapon *your* holy brothers and sisters developed to help them kill men like Ross more efficiently. Well, *if* we ever choose to let you return home, Luca, you can tell them it works beautifully. That it burns a man alive from the inside out. I can't begin to imagine the pain—"

"Enough!" the boy bellowed, choking on the end of the word.

"How many more innocent people have you helped end in the name of this crusade?"

"Maledetto!"

"Oh, we're back to this again? How many, Luca?"

"Maledetto!"

"How many people have you killed?"

He didn't answer at first, his breath heaving as he tried to stare me down. But I would not be moved. Let him look. Let him see his sins plainly reflected in my eyes. Let them burn into his soul. It wasn't my place to punish him. But he would punish himself, sure enough. I could feel Iain's eyes on us both, his silence as potent as our own.

"Four," Luca said at last.

"And do you remember their faces? Do you remember their names? Were you even told their names?"

Again, only silence.

"How old are you, Luca?" I wanted to hear him say it. I wanted Iain to hear him say it.

He struggled to shape the word, as if his English had failed him, which I knew wasn't the case. "Seventeen."

"Seventeen," I said quietly. "God must be proud of you, with four kills to your name. Tell me, does that include the man you eviscerated after he paid you to suck his dick, or are you trying to purge that from memory? Because from what I've seen, Luca, you've got one hell of a weapon inside you. I wonder how long your illustrious holy comrades will tolerate it before they decide you need 'saving?'"

A small choke was my only warning before he pitched forward and began sobbing quietly into my shoulder. I had him. Broken, exhausted, but not destroyed. Ross had been different. Ross had come willingly, eager to escape his family's evil. Luca… Yet, I'd given Jorgas that same second chance. He'd grabbed hold of it and thrived, before leaving me.

Iain had stood there silently throughout our exchange, barely breathing, his tension palpable when Luca's temper flared. The bastard was good. Had he even convinced himself? Or had the Scimitar altered his memory? The conspiracy theories were endless, and I knew better than to humour them, lest I send myself mad.

"Do you want my help?" I asked once the boy had composed himself enough to look me in the eye, tears drying on the shelves of his high cheekbones. I wasn't about to force him. All his life, he'd been forced into this action or that. No more. He had to want to be free.

"They'll kill me," he said quietly.

"Accept my help and you'll have my protection. That's the deal. I don't know quite what you are yet, or how you can control it. But we're going to find out. You do as I tell you and I promise, you will get through this."

"What… what if—"

"The world is full of 'what ifs,' Luca. Possibilities. Uncertainty. Risk. Consequence. *Choice.* And that is frightening. Don't think I don't understand. What if you run away from the Scimitar and they send your own flesh and blood after you? That's the choice your uncle made, one that brought him pain and fear. But he survived it. He thrived."

The boy swallowed, but said nothing.

"Are you hungry?"

He shook his head. "Tired."

"Yes, I suspect so." I smiled at him. "You can have Brett's b—"

Luca's lips were on mine before I could finish, the sour taste of whatever he'd done for food, or perhaps just the lack of it, still raw on his breath.

I took hold of his arms and prised him off me. "That's not why you're here."

"Why not?" he shot back. "You don't want me? You wanted me in the club."

"That was different. That was…" I trailed off. There was no point explaining Blood Shade asexuality and the intricacies of hunting and feeding to an exhausted boy locked in a battle with his own daemons, both spiritual and physical. "We have a lot to discuss. But you need sleep. You can have Brett's bed tonight."

With a little help, he got to his feet, eyes darting from me to Iain and back again. "Why do you help me?"

Why indeed?

"Sleep first. Answers to your questions after, I promise."

He seemed satisfied with that, allowing me to lead him to Brett's room. Then I pulled out the ball of silver twine.

"What is this? You tie me up?"

"It's just a precaution." I raised my hands, letting him see the twine. "Strong fibres coated in genuine silver. It has… certain properties that might help restrain the creature living inside you."

He took hold of the loose end of twine, firmly pulling on it to test its strength, his scepticism plain. Apparently satisfied, he stripped off his clothes and let me snip off two pieces long enough to bind his wrists and ankles together. I'd omitted the part about the twine's ability to sever a shifting creature's hands and feet with brutal efficiency. I didn't think Luca was in any such danger. I saw no reason to worry him.

I helped the boy get into bed, pulling the duvet over him. "We're going to get you through this. That's a promise."

He reached out with his bound hands and squeezed my wrist. "*Maledetto*." The curse sounded almost sweet.

I brushed a lock of hair off his forehead. "Welcome to the *maledettos*."

The boy fell asleep so quickly, I couldn't even be sure he'd heard.

*   *   *

"You were very quiet," I said, finding Iain waiting for me on the couch.

He offered me a weak smile. "Feeling a bit out of my league."

I almost snorted. "One of the things I learned very quickly about this existence is that the 'league' is constantly changing. There's no getting used to it."

"Do you really think he'll be okay?"

"Without knowing for certain what he is, I honestly don't know."

Iain's discomfort, or at least his show of it, was all too easy to read. The man was a consummate actor. A consummate liar.

"Can I see that?" he asked, nodding at the ball of twine in my hand.

I watched him puzzle over it. "I can't explain how it stays so strong. Scissors will cut clean through it, but there's no breaking it apart with your bare hands. Not even with my strength."

"Interesting," he said, passing it back. "Do you have a lot of this stuff?"

"Stuff?"

"I'm hesitant to use the word 'magick.'"

I didn't answer him right away. With Luca secured, I had to handle this carefully. Iain couldn't simply ignore the fact that Luca had just turned his back on the Scimitar. If anything, it gave him more reason than ever to try and neutralise me, after which he could take, and perhaps even kill Luca without my interference. Yet I also couldn't risk the boy waking up, knowing what I was about to do. There was only one place we could go.

"Let me show you."

*   *   *

Besides being something of a rarity in Darlinghurst townhouses, my basement is not a space I'm inclined to share with strangers. Dry and secure, it's where I keep my collection from years of travels. Tapestries dating back centuries before my birth, artefacts, knick knacks, and even antiquated weapons. All secure within four dry, sound-deadening walls.

Iain let out a low whistle, eyes widening as he took it all in. "Impressive."

"A century and a half gives one ample opportunity to collect."

"No kidding!" He looked at me, silently imploring permission before lifting an 18th century Venetian stage dagger from its shelf and holding it up to the light. The fact that he'd gone straight for the weapons did not escape my notice.

I took the dagger from him and replaced it on the shelf.

"Who's your friend" he asked, nodding at the skull in the corner of the room.

"That's Trotsky."

"No!"

"Check the hole at the top where the ice pick went in."

His eyes narrowed as he lifted the skull and peered closely at the hole. "Wow. Except of course, Trotsky was killed with an ice axe that would have decimated his skull, not left a neat little hole like this one."

124

I smiled, still enjoying my little joke. "Impressive. Though you're no fun at all."

"If it makes you feel better, I had to think about it."

"There's something to be said for indulging people's willingness to believe nonsense, for better or worse."

He smirked, replacing the skull where he found it. "Please. You're talking to a Catholic priest."

"Really not at one with conventional Papal wisdom, are you, Father?"

"Okay, first of all, please don't ever call me 'Father.' You're almost five times my age and it's weird. Secondly, I've never seen religious doctrine as a having any value unto itself. You've only got to look at our young friend upstairs. He has no sense of morality because he's never needed one. He's been fed a narrative his entire life that purports to be all he needs and replaces all rational thought. It's allowed these... What did you call them?"

"Scimitars."

"These Scimitars have been able to control him through it, as they control all their soldiers, I assume. Now, the lie is failing him, so what do they do? Destroy him, or give him a new narrative that leads him to destroy himself?"

The man had an interesting point. But what was Iain's role in such a narrative? He'd found Luca at the baths, only to let him go. If Salvatore was working against the Scimitar's goals, whose side was Iain on? Had I misjudged his game completely?

Iain glanced back at the skull. "They do always seem so happy, don't they? The dead. Always smiling."

"I suppose they do. That would explain the Scimitar's willingness to pick fights they can't hope to win. Believe me, Iain, should any of their brave soldiers cross my path, they *will* be destroyed."

The priest's confused stare lasted barely a second before I pounced. He cried out, only for his scream to fall muffled beneath my grip. His carotid artery raced less than an inch from my face as his heart leapt with raw panic.

I couldn't let Luca see this. It had to be done here, in private. And how Iain's scent now intoxicated me! The smell of precisely the kind of young man I favoured as a companion, enriched by fear more typical of the thugs I'd occasionally seized off the street. I savoured it, along with the sound of his screams, muffled by my unyielding grip.

"Come now. Surely you and your Scimitar comrades aren't afraid to die in a holy cause?"

His muffled screams became louder as he tried to wrench my arm away.

"Sorry, what was that?" I inhaled his scent, tightening my grip.

He was shaking, actually shaking in my arms. This was odd. I knew mercifully little of the Scimitar's training methods and conditioning, but I did know their soldiers to be unwaveringly faithful, supposedly blessed by God to act as his army. They certainly did not fear death at the hands of a 'daemon.'

But he had to be Scimitar! Why else would Luca respond to his orders? And yet, one seed of doubt... Damn it!

"I hope you're listening closely, because I'm willing to play the fool for only so long. When I take my hand away, one of two things will happen. Either you will tell me who the fuck you are and what you're really doing here, or you're going to scream, in which case, I'm going to take a large chunk out of your neck and gorge myself on your blood until I can drink no more. Then I'll feed whatever's left of your pathetic, twitching corpse to Luca. Do you understand? And do *not* lie to me, because I can smell it on you."

"All right!" he barked as soon as I released him, backing into the wall. Such a relief that he was willing to talk. I hadn't at all fancied the prospect of getting blood out of those tapestries. "I'm not quite who you think I am."

I snarled, bearing down on him. "You waste my time with the obvious."

"I'm not a Scimitar!" He cowered as I stopped inches from his throat. "I know who they are, of course. I know… a little of your history with them, and I know who the boy is. I *don't* know what he's becoming—"

"That's all very interesting." I grabbed hold of his throat and squeezed again. "But it's not an answer to my question. *Who are you?* We can start with your name."

"Iain Grieg," he choked out, "is my real name."

"Oh, yes?"

"Yes! The one I use now, anyway. The Scimitar… they're the reason I revealed myself to you."

Changed names? Uncanny knowledge of the night's affairs? *Revealed* himself?

"You're a Shaper."

He nodded, tapping the back of the hand around his throat. He gasped as I quickly released him. "Among other things," he got out between wheezes.

"Then why should Luca obey you? Answer me, or I'll feed you to him, I swear!"

"If you can rein in that most vengeance-happy of monstrosities flowing through your veins, I can explain! We both know that if I'd introduced myself to you as a Shaper from the get go, you wouldn't have trusted me."

"I've no reason to trust you now."

"Yes, you do! Damn it, Blood Shade, we're on the same side! You New Worlders may think yourselves separate and protected from supernatural politics, but I can assure you, when the Scimitar comes after us, they come after *you*. A silent contract protects us all. Can you at least put your bone-headed superiority complex aside long enough to recognise that?"

"Us?" I asked, now circling him. "You're not just any Shaper, then? You're on official House of Magick business."

He nodded. "I am truly sorry for the deception, but—"

"Did Luca really attack you? Did you even see him the night I found you?"

The man swallowed, clearly considering his answer before wisely settling on what I already knew to be the truth. "I hid as he passed me. The wounds were by my own hand."

"Odd, isn't it, that he just happened to rush by you in his panicked state?" I began to put the circumstances leading up to our meeting together in my head. "Odd that he'd just happen to lead me to your exact hiding spot while rushing to escape. Tell me that was a coincidence, Iain."

He stared at me, breath heaving.

"Tell me that was a coincidence, and I will kill you where you stand right now."

"It's called a lure," he spat out quickly. "A spell based upon the ancient Sirens, only where they sang, we… send a kind of psychic beacon"

"Psychic?"

Christ. I'd opened my home, and trusted my life to a manipulator of the mind. To a fucking Warlock.

"I know perfectly well how Shapers of my quarter are regarded. But I have only acted in your best interests, Reylan, I swear."

"I saw you in footage from the sauna's cameras. You whispered something in Luca's ear. He left immediately, and the next thing I know, he's sitting on my couch. How?"

"A mind as conflicted and troubled as his is easily compelled. I sent him here."

"Oh, thanks for that!"

"And now, he's secured in your guest room, frightened out of his mind, yes, but safe, as are others who might have crossed his path. I'm also pretty handy at improvising a weapon or two at the gym, in case you'd forgotten. Since I'm sure my word means nothing to you right now, look at my actions."

Could he be telling the truth? His very identity as a Warlock explained his secrecy, much as it alarmed me.

"There are still two questions bothering the hell out of me, *Iain*. What brought you here? And how long have you been watching me?"

"Ego-crushing as I'm sure this will be, I didn't come to Sydney for you. There's a small organisation with which I believe you're acquainted. Supernatural in nature, but led by a mundane. A former nun, I believe."

Ding, ding, ding. I was ready to solve the puzzle.

"I take it by your expression that I needn't elaborate?"

"And when I became involved with their business?"

"You became my business. That includes your friends, and your battles. I've been wanting to congratulate you on your handling of the Patron incursion. That saved us all a lot of trouble. The mundane population too, I expect."

"While you stood idly by and watched? Damn it, man! Good people died that night!"

"Your protégé? I know. You weren't the only one to lose good people."

"Elspeth and Matthias worked for Patricia."

"No, they cooperated with Patricia. They worked for me."

I believed him. The trace of bitterness in his tone suggested the loss had been hard felt.

"I don't hold your scepticism against you. Perhaps there's little I can do to ease your mind." He crossed the room, slowly, making no attempt to hide his reach for the book. "I trust you've found our little gift useful?"

The book of Temporal Echoes, with living history written and imbued within each page, allowing the user to relive it frame by frame in their mind's eye. I'd already taken two trips through the nasty thing's collection. One to a colony of Blood Shades and werewolves in ancient Bulgaria that had ended in disaster, the other to a day in Jorgas's life. A day that should not, by any sense of logic, have been found within the book's pages of death.

"No, I did not. What was it? Some feeble attempt to warn me away from Jorgas?"

"I suppose I shouldn't be surprised. I did try to tell the powers that be that your personal life was none of our concern, but old prejudices die hard. It was felt that the book might deter your relationship with the Flesh Master. It turns out all we needed to do to end things was leave you be." His face fell as he caught the full brunt of my glare. "I'm sorry, that was callous."

Callous or not, he was right. Whatever affection I'd shared with Jorgas had served us for as long as it had and was now best forgotten.

"Why make yourself known now?"

"The Scimitar is a threat to us all. We've nothing to gain by leaving Sydney to fend for itself."

"But the Prematures, Sophia and Giorgios, they hold all of Elspeth and Matthias's memories."

"Actually, and not by accident, I assure you, they hold only Elspeth and Matthias's magickal knowledge. Any details of me, the House, or our operations have been concealed. You understand, I just can't give Patricia Bakker that kind of information. As for what happens now, we're both in a quandary."

"A quandary?"

"Now that I'm discovered, my instructions are to return to Europe, and leave you to fend for yourself."

I nodded, opening the door. "Safe travels, Shaper. And take your bloody book with you."

He crossed to where I held the door open and gently swung it shut. "The quandary is, you need me, and… to be honest, I don't want to leave."

"What on earth are you talking about?"

"I've met dozens of Blood Shades, Reylan. I've watched them, studied them. I've even had one feed on me. I didn't make that up. Her inability to remove my memory of the incident made me realise for the first time what I was and what I could do. But I've never met one like you. I can see why Bakker likes you. Why the wolf liked you."

"Iain, I appreciate all you've done for me here, but…"

"Are you saying you feel nothing for me?"

"Right now? Nothing good."

This of course wasn't entirely true. I'd desired him ever since laying eyes on him at the sauna. Perhaps even before then. But that was impossible. Sexual attraction meant nothing to us, and attachment to a man over whom I held no psychic power, who might well have held such power over me… No. A veritable ocean of reasons made this a terrible idea.

"I can change that," he whispered, so close now I could almost taste his breath, enriched by the scent of his blood. "Unless my abilities frighten you?"

I took hold of his upper arms, yet even as this act stopped him, it weakened my resolve. His body, flesh, blood, and bone, so easily broken in my grasp. Like any other companion, except perhaps for the richness of his blood. Could his magickal abilities have enhanced it in some way? In that moment I didn't care. I was too tempted to just pull him into the sharp, beautiful kiss that would sate my hunger and drive his desire beyond understanding. Or perhaps he understood me perfectly as his lips brushed mine, right before his tongue speared into my mouth. His fingers slipped between the buttons of my shirt, and against better sense, I let them stay, kissing him deeper. Was I being manipulated? Seduced by unnatural means?

I couldn't have cared less.

I delicately punctured his tongue in a dead spot I'd once found, perfect for sampling the blood of a companion. Oh, how sweet it would have been to surrender to temptation and take him right then and there. The richness of his blood, tempered by the subtle textures of a man who took good care of his body and mind. And yet there was something else. A faint, almost effervescent quality as the blood hit my tongue. I pulled him closer, perhaps against better judgement. Again, I simply did not care. I closed my eyes, a great shudder going through me as he heaved against my body, pushing deeper, oblivious to the fact that I'd tasted him. But the taste had been enough. Curiosity sated, I now wanted to simply enjoy him as human. Both of us could pretend to be human, just for an instant, couldn't we?

I could swear his lips had grown warmer. His touch firmer, and strangely familiar. His scent had taken on a harder, roughened quality that belied the mild appearance of a fresh-faced priest. Of course, his Shaper nature belied it as well, but this was something else. Something entrancing and wonderful.

He had both our shirts open before I'd realised he was working their buttons. The heat of his body brought its own temptations as our hearts beat against one another, his scent almost overwhelming me. I desired his body, not his blood. This was insane. I wanted sex! Good old fashioned, sweaty, very human sex with this man. More than wanting it, I needed it, like I'd known his body and made it part of my own already. A great smile crossed my face as our kiss finally broke and I opened my eyes.

My mouth fell open as he stepped away from me.

"Jorgas," I whispered.

The familiar, muscular frame of the young werewolf was unmistakeable. The tattoos I'd so enjoyed lavishing with attention during our tristes, the tiger wrapped over his shoulder, stalking the faux silver nipple ring he wore, while colourful red, orange and blue flames covered his opposite shoulder. And that hard, yet strangely beautiful face… I'd never seen it so inscrutable.

"Jorgas."

He didn't respond, eyes fixed on me as mine were on him. The room seemed so much darker now, to the point I could barely make out detail at all. There was only Jorgas, who seemed almost to radiate his own light as he stood before me, dressed only in tattered jeans. He slipped his arms around the small of my back, pulling me close, mouth teasing my neck as our slow dance continued. He tilted his head to where his lips grazed my ear, and I inhaled deep of his scent. Fit, muscular, and vaguely musky in that way typical of men in their early twenties. I wanted his blood now. I wanted all of him, any way I could have him, including the way he now kissed my ear.

"I told you to kill me," he whispered.

I should have stopped dancing. Instead, I ran my fingers through that familiar, lovely mess of dark brown hair. He rested his head on my shoulder again, inhaling deeply, savouring my scent as much as I did his. I watched him bring a hand up between us. But where a human hand ought to have been grew a gigantic wolf's paw, with deadly sharp talons on its end. I watched as he dragged it across his naked throat. Blood spurted over his chest and mine. His body jerked and convulsed twice, three times. I caught him as he collapsed, his body convulsing again as he tried to grab my arms, pulling us closer. The scent of the blood near overwhelmed me as stray drops splashed my face. Jorgas opened his mouth in a failed attempt to speak, my effort to hush him rewarded only by a few stray drops of blood on my tongue. Oh, to taste that again!

133

To have its sweetness and heat, the taste of his anger, confusion, and arrogance teasing me once more after he'd abandoned me.

And he had abandoned me.

He cried out weakly as I latched my mouth onto the wound, letting the blood flow to sate my hunger once more, as rich, dark, and untamed as I remembered. The steady thrum of his pulse synched with mine, which grew stronger and louder as his began to quiet. It wasn't long before it slowed.

"Reylan," he gasped, fingers digging into my back. But his strength had waned, his heartbeat barely more than a murmur as more of the delicious blood bubbled over my tongue.

I didn't stop. I couldn't. I refused. He wasn't leaving me this time. I made sure of it. He was dead before he'd even released his grip. His life, his last gift to me.

"You should hide the body."

I didn't recognise the male, unmistakeably European voice, but it felt familiar. I tried to turn around and face the speaker, but my body refused. All I could do was stare into Jorgas's lifeless eyes. The life that had surrendered itself to my hunger. The speaker's tone had betrayed no surprise or outrage at the young werewolf's death. "I think we should, yes."

"We?" the voice laughed. "It's not my problem! Oh, don't look distraught. It's in your nature, and did he, or did he not wish for you to kill him?"

This didn't make sense. Yes, in a moment of shame and weakness, Jorgas had begged me to end his life. But that had been months ago, when he'd known me only as some mark he'd tried to mug in the street. I'd instead wound up witness to an unbidden transformation, and the carnage wrought by his wolf state. But that was ancient history! His mastery over his changes had grown in leaps and bounds since—

"I asked you a question," the speaker said.

I turned to see… Patricia?

Impossible! The voice had not been hers. I looked back at the man in my arms… only he wasn't Jorgas anymore. Instead, the dead eyes of a man he'd mortally wounded stared back at me. A man I'd been forced to kill before his own injuries dragged out the job. Rory.

"Tell me, Reylan," Patricia continued. But still, it was not her voice. "How many people have died to protect your secrets?"

Had I been human, I might have comforted myself with the knowledge that what I was seeing wasn't real. Yet in that moment, I knew with absolute certainty that my thoughts were as real as any action in the physical world. Would they also have physical consequences?

Consequences. I'd known there would be consequences for Rory's death, mercy killing or not. But Patricia knew about Rory already. She'd mentioned him to me distinctly, knowing full well the choice I'd made.

I squared my shoulders, tightening my grip around the corpse as I fixed the mocking figure with a stare. "You're not Patricia Bakker."

The thing tilted its head, seemingly befuddled by this accusation. "And that's not Jorgas, is it?"

I looked down at the body again, only to drop it in disgust. Rory's once muscular body was emaciated, his healthy skin parched white, all blood and colour drained from his face. How was any of it possible?

"Reylan," came a soft spoken, extremely familiar voice behind me.

In Patricia's place stood Isobel. She said nothing more. She simply approached Rory's dead body with that same curious glint in her eye that I recognised oh so well. Tilting her head not unlike some bemused bird, she kneeled beside Rory and gently blew upon his forehead.

I watched, mesmerised as piece by piece, faint traces of movement returned to Rory's body. His breathing resumed a steady rhythm in his chest before he choked out the first signs of life. Isobel remained perfectly still, kneeling beside him even as I approached her. I could have called her name, though she appeared to be in some sort of trance.

Both Isobel and Rory turned and snarled at me with such rage, I instantly jumped back, crying out in panic as I stumbled and fell hard on my backside.

*   *   *

"What? Hey, calm down! Reylan, it's me! It's just me!"

I stared at Iain in disbelief from my completely undignified position on the floor, my legs tangled in bed clothes. "Iain? What the hell are you doing in bed with me?"

"Okay," he said. "Not the most flattering pillow talk, but I'll bite. Yes, I went to bed with you. You invited me, remember?"

"I most certainly did not!"

"Yes, you did. I said 'Maybe we should take this upstairs?' to which you said 'I think we should, yes.' Sounds like an invitation to me. As for what we've *done* in your bed, nothing ungentlemanly, I promise you. You seemed a bit out of sorts, and I wasn't about to just take advantage."

Sure enough, the man was dressed in a white t-shirt I recognised as one of Brett's and loose-fitting underwear. For that matter, so was I, and there was certainly no evidence beside the bed to suggest anything more had transpired than he'd claimed.

"But I remember us kissing!"

"We kissed, yes, which was…" he trailed off, face lighting up in a sheepish smile. "When we came up here, I wanted to do so much more. It's just that you seemed… I don't know. If I didn't know better, I'd say you were stoned."

I slowly got to my feet, untangling them from the sheet I'd managed to carry with me in my sudden somnambular exodus.

"Are you all right?"

I nodded. Had the sun even set? A dream…

He smiled at me again. "You're almost more beautiful when you're asleep. So still."

"I'll add that to my Grindr profile." I'd been still all right. Blood Shades didn't dream! We barely even drew breath. There's good reason legends of our existence are so closely tied to tales and superstitions of death. Yet obviously, I'd not only dreamed, but made my way upstairs and into bed with Iain beside me. "What time is it?"

Iain reached for his phone on my nightstand. "Just after six. The sun's just set, if that's what you're asking."

So, I *had* slept through the day. I snatched up my pants from the floor and pulled them on. "Brett?"

"In here," he called from the living room. Sure enough, there he was, laid out on the couch with a comforter over his long, pale body. "What's up?"

"Up?" I realised how absurd my agitation must have looked. How could Brett possibly understand how disconcerting my experience had been? "When did you get home?"

"I don't know. Four in the morning? Five, maybe? Then, I see you're not here, and my door's locked. Then you and your friend come upstairs and you're acting all weird, like I can't get two words out of you. What the hell's going on, man?"

"Maybe I can explain?" Iain looked at me with sympathy that bordered on annoying. "It's as I told you, Reylan. You agreed we should come upstairs, and then you just seemed off. Like you couldn't focus on me, or Brett, or on anything else at all. What else could we do but put you to bed?" He stripped off the t-shirt and passed it back to Brett. "Thanks."

"No worries. Hey, sweet ink!"

Iain laughed, glancing over his shoulder at the colourful dragon. "Thanks."

"Mine washed out. Something to do with Reylan's blood."

"Well, not many people get to see this one. A bit controversial in my line of work."

"Is that work as a priest, or a Shaper?" I asked.

The two of them stared at me. Well, to hell with their stares! I'd still no recollection of getting from my basement to my bed. None at all! I'd had a nightmare, which ought to have been impossible, and the only connection between the two was a Shaper I'd…. Dear gods, why had I kissed the man? A warlock, no less! I'd gleaned precious little about them from my previous conversations with Shapers, but even Iain had admitted he knew damn well how Shapers of his quarter were regarded. And now, to piece together the time I'd lost, I had only his good word.

Yet had anything he'd told me about the incident been untrue?

"You're a Shaper?" Brett asked. "You didn't tell me that."

"We're not normally that eager to share," Iain admitted. "But I suppose, if Reylan knows, you should too. There's a growing sentiment within the House of Magick that Australia and New Zealand have been neglected for far too long. Now, lo and behold, you're under attack by Scimitars—"

"Not that it seemed to bother the House of Magick when a Patron slipped in and took up residence under our city," I pointed out.

"I can't rationalise every decision the House makes. For that matter, it's better the less you know. Surely that makes sense to you?"

"Do you know what else makes sense to me, Iain? You leaving. Right now."

"I'm sorry?"

"You say you're here with no intent to do harm? Fine. I'll choose to believe you based on your actions. But we didn't ask for your help, nor the House of Magick's. If you want to fight the Scimitar in whatever way you see fit, that's entirely your prerogative. But as far as my home and my life are concerned, I'm asking you to go."

"You don't trust me." His eyes took on that infuriating hurt puppy dog quality that seemed to melt humans so reliably. No such luck here.

"I don't know who you are to trust! A priest? A Scimitar? A Shaper? At what point do we get the full story?"

"If I withhold information, it's only to keep you safe."

"Indeed! So, think then how safe we'll be with you gone. Go back to 'observing' if you must. It's what you were sent here to do. But if you or anyone from the House of Magick interferes with me or mine again—"

A loud knock interrupted us. Bloody impeccable timing.

"Get dressed. I want you gone in five minutes."

The Shaper squared his shoulders, but said nothing, retreating to the bedroom. Nice to know I was going to get some cooperation.

"Good evening, Mister Raymond. I hope I am not disturbing you?"

I summoned a kindly smile for Dorotha, only to realise it was genuine. The very sight of the human woman drew me back to a life before nights with the Arcadia Trust, Scimitars, or Shapers were commonplace. But the feeling of warm familiarity vanished once I saw the worry on her face. Her pallid, almost chalky complexion, and the great folds under her eyes.

So much for getting rid of her before Iain returned.

"Dorotha, please come in."

She followed me hesitantly into the living room, her movements furtive and timid, even before she spotted Brett standing in his underwear.

"Oh, good heaven! I so sorry Mister Raymond! I did not know you were having one of your special parties!"

"You're interrupting nothing," I said, gently steering her toward the couch, away from my Mannequin's mostly naked form.

"I ah… I should take a shower anyway." Brett disappeared in the direction of the bathroom.

"Sit down." I took Dorotha's hand in my own. "Whatever is the matter? Can I get you some tea?"

She waved away my concern, though how aware she was of my presence was hard to say. "Mister Raymond, forgive me. I… I do not know what happened. I sleep so poorly last night, then try to sleep this afternoon, just for an hour, perhaps. But… Oh, but it does not matter. Here, I have mail for you."

"Thank you," I said, putting the envelopes aside without looking at them. "What happened when you tried to sleep?"

She offered me a faintly maternal smile. "The kind of silliness that overexcites an old woman, Mister Raymond. Bad dreams. Is nothing, I promise you."

Bad dreams? Was there any point in asking for details? Iain. There could be no other explanation. If it happened again, after the man was gone, then I'd worry about it.

"Perhaps something to help you sleep?" Speak of the devil. Iain emerged from the bedroom dressed in the same clothes he'd arrived in. "Surely, Reylan, either you or your… friend have something?"

I bristled at Iain, catching him with a glare before he managed to out Brett as my Mannequin. Though we'd said nothing specific, I was sure Dorotha had dismissed him as a lingering 'gentleman caller,' a misconception I was happy to humour if it kept her out of our hair.

"Please." She waved him away before offering her hand with an apologetic smile. "It is nothing, but thank you—"

Before Iain could introduce himself, or indeed, before any of us could react, my elderly tenant leapt back with a loud shriek.

"Dorotha!"

She didn't answer me. Rather, the strangest sounds gargled from deep within her throat. Words of some sort perhaps, but nothing in any language I knew. It wasn't Polish either. Over and over she muttered them, like an incantation, backing away from us all the while as they grew louder and louder.

"What did you do?" I demanded of Iain, trying to calm her without success. "Answer me! What did you—"

"Daemon," she continued, arms now flailing. "*Daemon!*"

That word I knew. Was she talking about me? I tried to take hold of her, only to receive the sharp raking of nails down my face.

"Dorotha, stop!"

More words, some recognisably Polish now, interspersed with the occasional *'daemon'* as she thrashed some more. It took me a moment, once I could finally focus, to see Iain had grasped hold of both her wrists, finally holding her still.

"Pray with me, Sister!" The flat line of his face confirmed that no, this was not some tasteless joke. Having assumed the role of priest and comfort giver, it seemed Father Iain Grieg was perfectly able to slip into it at will. He now held both my tenant's hands in his, keeping a soothing, even tone even as she wailed. "*Pray with me!*"

I jumped as he barked the words then went right back to the incantation, words I recognised no more than I had Dorotha's ramblings. They weren't Latin, or if they were, they were of a form so old I'd no way of... Wait, they weren't...

Yes, they were speaking in unison now! Over and over and over, a little quieter each time as Dorotha's quaking slowed.

"Iain," I said, not wanting to break whatever spell I assumed he'd used to calm her. "Iain!"

He fixed on me with eyes as black as onyx, their whites utterly consumed.

I froze. Had the man just turned his magicks on me? What the hell was I seeing? What had he and Dorotha been saying? "Brett!" I called, hoping I wasn't calling my Mannequin into danger.

The black drained from Iain's eyes before my Mannequin could reach us, leaving them the same handsome, dark brown I'd first seen in the alley. There could be no denying what I'd just witnessed, but they were definitely the eyes of a man and nothing more.

"Everything all right?" Brett asked.

I'd no honest answer for him. No idea.

"Everything will be fine," Iain said, slowly bringing Dorotha to her feet.

I watched as the woman's agitation eased. Watched her hands stop shaking as she slowly released her vicelike grip on Iain's sleeves.

"She just took a turn," Iain put a hand on Dorotha's shoulder. "A very frightening one, but nothing we can't—"

"I saw…" she began. "I know not the word for it!"

"Are you all right?" I put a gentle arm around her shoulders.

Taking a few more seconds to compose herself, the woman nodded. "Yes, Mister Raymond. It was almost like my dream, but… Forgive me. I not—"

"Father Iain Grieg," the Shaper pre-empted, taking her hand once more. "You gave us quite a fright, sister."

"Oh! Father? Mister Raymond, you did not—"

"Iain, this is Dorotha, my upstairs tenant," I said with a hint of possessiveness. "Brett, will you entertain Dorotha for a moment? I need a word with Father Grieg in private. Now."

As Brett sat Dorotha down, I closed my bedroom door behind Iain and myself—hardly a room I wanted to share with him, but one that afforded us privacy, except from Demetrius. The cat watched us in silence, ginger tail flicking back and forward with wary regularity.

"Do you really need to ask?" Iain muttered.

"I just want to hear it from you. What the hell just happened in there, and what did you do to my tenant?"

"Will you calm down? I don't know what happened to her. If you're asking for a magickal explanation, there are literally hundreds of possible spells and random combinations of psychic energy that can cause that sort of fit. I'm sorry I can't give you a better… diagnosis, but I'm not some sort of psychic EMT. What I can do and did do, is reach into her mind with a mild spell to calm her down. Nothing more."

"You cast a spell on her without so much as—"

"What would you have had me do?"

Even as my fingers twitched, and I fought the urge to launch myself at his throat, I had no answer. He was right. I wasn't angry at what he'd done. I was angry because I didn't understand it.

"Iain, look me in the eye and promise me you weren't the cause of what just happened to Dorotha." I waited, searching his face for the deception. The lie he was conjuring to excuse his actions, but none came.

"I can't," he replied at last. "I wish I could. But she's clairvoyant, at least in part. It's… unlikely that what she experienced was a reaction to my own psychic energies, but it's not impossible. I did what I could, which was to ground her mind, focusing her on her present location and time."

"By continuing your masquerade as a priest? Don't tell me what happened in there was an exorcism!"

He rolled his eyes. "I hope you, of all people, have learned enough to know daemonic possession is a myth. She's a woman of faith. To such a person, suggestion is a powerful tool. Nonetheless, what I did in there won't be enough."

"What the hell does that mean?"

"I overheard pieces of your conversation. Nightmares, and now this? I can't promise you these aren't symptoms of a more serious problem. I need more time with her to know."

"You can't be serious?"

He raised his hands. "Up to you. I'm not going to kidnap the poor dear, if that's what worries you. I'm just warning you, she may have been exposed to something very dangerous, and if she's clairvoyant… I don't want to fill your head with scenarios before I have something concrete to tell you. But if you care about this woman at all, I strongly suggest you not ignore this, and frankly? I'm the best expert you've got."

I resisted an audible sigh to no avail.

"I know what you're thinking. Again, if you doubt my words, look at my actions. I represent the House of Magick's interests. I make no secret of that. That doesn't mean… Hell, it has *never* meant working against you. Let me help Dorotha, if I can. If after that you never want to see me again? Fine."

It made enough sense. If this was an apology for his deception, what did I stand to lose in letting him make it? God knew I had enough enemies knocking at my door.

"I think you should do what you must for Dorotha, and that I should do what I must for Luca. Then… I don't know. If these Scimitar attacks continue—"

"Then you might need me again. So be it."

I swore, if he was lying...

"Everything okay?" Brett asked as we rejoined them. "What's the plan?"

"That depends. How are you feeling, sister?" asked Iain before I could answer. Though he had his back to me, I could tell by the sudden flush in Dorotha's cheeks that he'd turned his boyish charms on her. "I was about to go to Saint Barnabas to pray. Perhaps you'd like to join me?"

Oh, he was good.

"Oh, Father, I… I would not impose so—"

"Sister, God does not expect us to face our fears alone."

The woman hesitated at first, regarding Iain's hand as though merely touching the handsome 'priest' would corrupt her soul to decadence. Perhaps it would, but if it brought her some comfort, who was I to stand in their way? Still, if he harmed her in any way…

"Thank you, Father. I think I would like that. Mister Raymond, I so sorry to have worried you."

"You're never a bother, Dorotha. I hope you'll come back later, when you're feeling better." Though it hadn't included him, the invitation was as much for Iain's benefit as hers. If the Shaper wanted me to judge him by his actions, that's what I would do. I would see Dorotha again, safe and sound with all her faculties intact.

Mumbling the usual pleasantries and sending them on their way, I began to second guess myself. This, I supposed was only natural, but I had to come back to the facts. Iain had certainly concealed the truth, but with reason. Warlocks were near universally mistrusted, even by other Shapers. Yet save for that one great omission, he'd raised no hand against us.

Brett turned to me as soon as they'd gone. "What the hell was that about?"

I shook my head, unable to give him an honest answer. "Something well beyond me."

"And you just let her go with that priest?"

"That priest specialises in mind magicks. He was very disturbed by what just happened here, and frankly, so was I."

"No shit. I thought you didn't trust Shapers."

"What makes you think I trust him?"

Brett's brow furrowed in that charmingly obvious way it did when he knew he wasn't about to like what I had to say.

"If Luca's not already awake, he will be soon. While I attend to him, I need you to tail Iain. Keep your distance and don't interfere unless he takes Dorotha somewhere you can't follow. Let me know immediately if they seem to be taking too long, or if anything else feels wrong to you. Just make sure she gets to Saint Barnabas and back in one piece."

"Christ, if that's all you wanted, I could have taken her to pray!"

I shook my head. "Iain mentioned one very important truth. Suggestion is powerful. Better she believes she has the guidance and friendship of a priest. Unless you see some sign he's actually working against us, I'd rather not start a fight."

"And what if he realises he's being tailed?"

"Don't worry about that. He already knows."

CHAPTER TEN

I didn't relish the prospect of bringing Luca to meet his father, but the boy had been denied the truth his whole life. I wasn't prepared to indulge that lie anymore. He deserved to know all the man had put him through. The cold reality of what the Scimitar stood for. I doubted Salvatore could further damage the boy in his current state.

"Should I get the morgue ready?" grumbled Kelvin as the heavy door swung open.

"Not this time." I ignored Luca's perplexed stare. He'd figure out the disembodied voice soon enough. "I trust Patricia is in?"

"Yeah, pretty boy, Patricia is *in*. She's a bit busy right now. Is this importa…" Had he only now recognised Luca? "Step inside, slowly. The kid first."

"He's calmed down since our last briefing. You have my word."

"Yeah? That's real fuckin' reassuring. If he tries any bullshit, I'm taking him out, and it'll be your fault, understood?"

If Kelvin kept up this sparkling display of personality, he'd be welcome to try.

"Please," I said, stepping inside after Luca, "inform Patricia we're here."

A few seconds passed before I heard the Cloak Walker stomp away.

"And a pot of tea, please, Kelvin."

"Fuck off."

Even Luca smirked a little. "And he is… what?"

"A Cloak Walker," I replied. "A man who—"

"You think I'm an idiot? I mean, what does he do?"

"Have you ever heard of an organisation called the Arcadia Trust?"

His eyes widened, his shoulders tightening as his breath quickened.

"Yes, I thought so."

"Reylan."

I turned to see Patricia approaching us from her office, dressed in one of her crisp, cream linen suits. Her attention wasn't focused on me, but rather on my young companion.

"Do you know where you are?" she asked him.

"He told me."

"Then you know perfectly well it's in your best interests to cooperate."

"Patricia, if I may? We've reached an understanding—"

"While I'm pleased the boy has earned your trust, Reylan, you'll forgive me if that doesn't infer mine. I have lives other than my own to consider."

"As do I."

Brett. Dorotha. Luca. Possibly… no, Iain could damn well take care of himself.

"You know what is happening to me?" Luca asked, quietly.

"I'm afraid not," she said, seeming disarmed by the boy's sudden vulnerability. "But we're doing our best to find out. You need to understand, this isn't going to be easy. You're going to have to answer some hard questions. Probably ask some as well."

"Ask?" He frowned. "Ask what? Who?"

So much for easing him into it.

"Luca," I said. "We have—"

"Last night, your father and another man attacked Reylan at a club in the city." Patricia's tone, all business once more.

"My… No, you are lying!"

"In a moment, you'll see that I'm not. The other man was killed and I'm afraid your father isn't in great shape either."

"Not entirely our doing," I cut in, just in time to stop a barrage of accusations from the young man. "He's not a well man, Luca."

The boy swallowed, not looking either of us in the eye. "I know this. Everyone knows it. Cancer. Still, he fights."

"Luca," I'd no wish to let Patricia break the bad news. "He won't be fighting any more. He knows it and I think so do you."

"He should not be here! He—"

"He came looking for you. I just got in the way."

Again, barely a reaction as he considered my words. What I wouldn't have given for Iain's powers in that moment.

"You want me to see him?"

"He's not going anywhere. To be honest, I don't know how long he's got."

"Patricia," I cautioned.

"Just what, Reylan, will be served by more lies? Every minute we spend here is a minute Salvatore loses. One we lose if we expect to get any answers."

"Take me to him," said Luca. "I want to see."

Patricia led us both to the ball room and eased open the door, spilling faint light into the room before raising the dimmers. No attempt had been made in my absence to make Salvatore more comfortable. The man remained strapped to the same table, a sheet thrown over his body, his chest rising and falling with steady breath.

"Is that the fallen lady of Christ I smell?" he called. "Or the sodomite daemon? Both, perhaps?"

"Papa?"

That sealed it. No way in *hell* were we leaving the two of them alone.

"What are you doing here?" the boy continued in Italian.

Salvatore tilted his head, flashing me a wan smile. "Since I assume our daemon friend will be translating for the good sister either now or later, you can save us all time by speaking English."

"Use any bloody language you want," said Patricia. "Just answer his question."

"Why are you making him ask questions to which you already know the answer? Tell me, Sister, did you tell him anything before you brought him in here? Or was it just 'Oh, he's your father. He'll talk to you. Go forth and interrogate?'"

"What is he talking about?" Luca asked. "You know why he is here?"

"He came here to find you, Luca. What I'm not clear on, Salvatore, is why."

"And there, daemon, lies an excellent question. Why would a man facing death fly halfway across the world to retrieve a wayward child?" The man in question took a deep breath before continuing. "You made your choice, boy. You knew that choice would have consequences."

"The others made the same choice!" the boy shot back.

"They aren't family."

"Gentlemen, please." I didn't at all like where this was going. "What choice is he talking about, Luca?"

Silence.

"This is about what's happening to you, isn't it? What you're becoming, which, Salvatore, is—"

"Spare me the details, Blood Shade. I know. He's becoming an abomination, like you. You need tell me nothing else."

It was my turn to remain silent. Like me? Not exactly. But what Salvatore didn't know wouldn't hurt him—or us.

"You know damn well the curse that infects our blood," the man continued. "The Scimitar of Light? Do you even remember what that means, boy? The one path left to us, to die with a pure soul, and you would spit in the eye of God himself?"

"Papa, we can't eliminate them as humans! How many have to die before you see that? The only way we have a chance is—"

"Blasphemy? Wicked sorcery? Taunting the horrors in their own hell and emerging as the very daemons we've sworn to fight?"

'In their own hell?' I didn't like any part of that question at all, nor the tone with which Salvatore had said it, but Luca answered with renewed determination before I could ask.

"Papa, it would cure you. You'd never have to fear death again. We could spend eternity doing God's…"

The look on Salvatore's face could have rent the very flesh from Luca's. "If my arms were not tied, I would beat you with such fierceness, we'd soon see how 'immortal' your daemon has made you."

"Papa, please!"

"I'm going to die, boy. But I will die with a clean soul. He will reward me, as I sit at His right hand."

"And what of your brother, Salvatore?" I asked. "Oh yes, Luca knows all about that too. Will you also sit at Ross's side? Or is his sacrifice meaningless?"

"My brother had his chance to repent, Blood Shade." His sudden switch to the non-derogatory term did not escape me. "He chose the offerings of Satan. So be it. It's too late for him, but not for you, Luca."

"Enough," Patricia said. "What did you mean, 'taunting the horrors in their own hell?'"

"Repent," the man continued, ignoring her. "and by your own hand, if you must, end it. There is no hope for the Scimitar. They've chosen their path. This… perversion of all we are. But you and I, Luca, can still be saved, together. Repent your sins, and take your life with a pure—"

"Answer the question, Salvatore!"

"Luca, are you even hearing this?" I asked. "Is this what the Scimitar stands for? Your own father, telling you to kill yourself? Slitting your throat?"

Patricia shot me a look but said nothing, having reached the same conclusion about Luca's scar.

"No," the boy finally got out. "No, we didn't… This isn't—"

"Would you be separated from Him forever?" Salvatore said through a sneer. "Condemned like the daemons you've slain? I raised you to be better. To *know* we were better."

"Damn it, Salvatore! Is that all you can say to your son?"

"Oh, Blood Shade. We both know he's no son of mine."

"If you're going to burden that old cliché…" I trailed off, seeing Luca's face.

Oh.

"That's not possible," said Patricia. "Blood Shades are asexual, even impotent!"

"Don't play the fool, Sister. My brother wasn't born an abomination."

"Yes, it's possible," I said. "It's extremely rare, but not at all unheard of for Blood Shades to give birth or father children before their change."

Still, I'd never, to my knowledge, met one. Trust Ross to beat those particular odds.

"No," Luca murmured. "No, it is not possible!"

"Haven't you been listening, boy? Not one of your mother's finer moments, rest her soul. But at least her soul does rest. That coward, on the other hand—"

"Shut up! No more of your lying!"

"*Lying?* Oh, poor baby, Luca. I'm the only one left to tell you any truth! Who else are you going to believe? Our comrades, who now sell their souls to Satan? The devils that surround us? A dead pervert who refused to even claim you as his own?"

"That's not—"

"*I* raised you as my own, Luca! Snatched you from the jaws of the beast and washed you clean and pure, and now this? You disgust me. You disgust God. Unless you act now. Do it, boy. Repent of these wrongs and find His mercy."

"Luca, put the knife down." It shouldn't have surprised me that the Scimitar had taught its agents all manner of tricks for concealing weapons, but for fuck's sake...

"Luca," Patricia whispered. "Please, you don't need to be part of this anymore."

"Even now, they're lying to you, boy. You know that, don't you? I raised you to be a better man than your wretched father!"

I jumped as Luca plunged the knife down into Salvatore's chest in one swift movement.

Salvatore choked on a scream before the boy ripped the knife away and brought it down again, stabbing the man over and over. He got four or five in before an unseen force knocked him to the ground and sent the bloody knife skittering across the floor. As Patricia flew to Salvatore's side, I dove for the knife. One of my kitchen knives. Note to self.

"Reylan, help me!"

I turned toward the voice, only to see Luca struggling under Kelvin's weight, and unmistakeably starting to change. The colour was draining from his face, his already dark brown eyes becoming shiny black pits as his mouth curled into a fierce, hissing snarl. I pounced upon his shoulders, pinning him to the floor, but I could still feel the strength of his awful alter-ego bursting through, threatening to break our hold and wreak havoc at any moment.

"Reylan," Patricia called. "A little help?"

"Bit busy!" I locked my eyes with Luca's. "Listen to me! It's all right. Nobody's going to hurt you! *Luca!*"

"*Maledetto!*"

"Reylan, I can't hold this kid much—"

Luca threw him off with a fierce snarl. Out of options, I used all my strength to plunge the knife into the boy's shoulder, pinning him to the wooden floor. He screamed like some raucous beast from the pit, but it soon faded into something comfortingly human as the darkness drained from his eyes, and the colour returned to his face.

"Jesus! What the hell is he?"

I remembered Patricia's plea. "Get Sophia. Quickly!"

"It doesn't matter," the nun said as she approached us. "Salvatore's dead."

I heard Kelvin leave the room as I stroked Luca's hair and tried to keep him calm. Hopefully, his 'enhanced' physiology would do most of the healing work, just as our own did. It was only a kitchen knife, after all, not that that distinction had spared Salvatore. In a perverse way, the man had died exactly the way he'd hoped. Fighting an abomination.

"What happened?" Sophia rushed to my side, zipping open a small bag to reveal gauze, antiseptic, a small pair of scissors, and other decidedly human healing implements. Of course. She carried Elspeth's healing knowledge, but none of her expertise.

"We had to stop something before it started," I said. "He should be all right now."

"What do you mean, 'stop something?'"

"I'm sorry, this is going to hurt." I ignored Luca's scream as I pulled the knife from his shoulder, immediately pressing my lips to the wound and sealing it shut with a long, deep lick. I spat the sour, toxic blood out behind me, coughing up as much of it as I could manage. That reminder, I did not need.

"Any more blood on this floor, and we'll summon Pinhead," Kelvin muttered.

"Be quiet," Patricia said, giving Luca and I a look that bordered on imperious. "Stand him up."

"Give him a minute. The wound is still healing. I can't work miracles."

Patricia squatted to her haunches, her annoyance giving way to curiosity as she looked into the boy's eyes. "What are we going to do with you?"

Fair question. I didn't know where to start, and judging by Luca's silence, neither did he. He eased himself up, resting his head against my chest. I put an arm around his uninjured shoulder and gave it a gentle squeeze. If he was Ross's son, that made him family. That, I would not abandon.

"I'm sorry," I whispered. "It was the only way. I'm sorry."

"Is he stable?" Patricia asked.

"How are you feeling?" I asked him, making sure Patricia didn't miss my look of disdain.

He only curled tighter into my arms, gripping me as if for dear life.

"Here." Sophia handed me a square pillow half her own size.

I nodded thanks and eased Luca off me, helping him lay down. "You'll be all right. Nobody's going to hurt you."

"Reylan?" Patricia asked. "A word, in private?"

I glowered in what I guessed was Kelvin's direction.

"You want me to get him a blanket, too, pretty boy? Go on. We'll keep an eye on him."

"I'll be right back," I whispered, easing myself up and allowing Patricia to lead the way.

*   *   *

"Our lives grow ever more complicated."

"Noticed, had you?"

"You knew perfectly well the risk in bringing him here."

"That risk jumped considerably when you failed to check him for weapons!"

"Don't worry, Sister. I won't be underestimating his paranoia again, though I don't think his outburst is entirely our fault."

It was the only sensible explanation. With nothing to lose, of course Salvatore had wished his nephew dead. Why not provoke Luca into trying to kill us? Either would have secured the boy's place in the Scimitar's twisted vision of paradise. If Salvatore was to be the first victim of the boy's rage, then so be it.

"In any case, so much for finding out what Salvatore meant by… 'taunting daemons in their own hell' or whatever it was he said."

"I wouldn't worry. Whatever he meant, it sounded to me like he wanted no part of it. I think we'll find Luca a far better source of information, when he's ready."

"Let us hope that's not too late," Patricia muttered. "He's staying with you for now, isn't he?"

I shook my head. Knowing Luca's true parentage, I felt more obligated than ever. Yet could I continue risking Brett's life, after what we'd just seen?

"Reylan," the nun continued, her voice now quiet, even compassionate. "You're not honour bound to rescue every stray that comes to your door."

"I know that." But did I believe it? I'd felt obliged to take care of Luca when I'd thought him Ross's nephew. I now felt doubly so. I'd brought a werewolf through my door, and trusted him to control his impulses. But extenuating circumstances aside, Luca was another species entirely.

"What do you know about Death Shades?" I asked.

Patricia frowned. "Then you *do* know what he's turning into?"

"Just a theory from someone more knowledgeable than I."

The sister's expression darkened, ever so slightly. "I trust Isobel is well?"

"I trust you've not reconsidered your position?"

She dismissed my question with a faint flicker of annoyance. "Death Shades?"

"So they're called. They're rare. So rare, it's unclear whether they evolve naturally, like us, or emerge as some sort of mutation, or by accident. One story claims them to be a Blood Shade and werewolf's joint offspring, but I gather that's a myth to deter the two species from mating."

"An accident?" she asked. "Do you think something happened when you tried to claim Luca as a Mannequin? Or when Sophia—"

"Between our attempts to heal him, his natural body chemistry, the fact that he's too young to know for certain if he was destined to turn into a Blood Shade on his own, and whatever the hell Salvatore was talking about… I don't bloody know! You see this face?" I said, pointing to my most dumbfounded expression. "Isobel is giving me this face right now, and she's the Library of Alexandria on these matters, compared to my third-grade science essay. I simply don't know enough about this beast to give you a credible explanation. More importantly, I can't tell you if it will eventually take him over completely, or how long he's got. If I could guarantee the boy's safety, I would. But I don't have the resources, nor any idea what to prepare for if this gets worse."

"You're suggesting we do? You saw what happened when Sophia tried to heal him."

"You're still better equipped than I to contain him. The wine cellar? Not an ideal solution I grant you, but until we know what he's facing... Okay, what's that look?"

She raised a single eyebrow in that arch manner I'd come to despise.

"Sister?" I asked. "What haven't you told me?"

*   *   *

The main house of the Arcadia Trust backed onto a small, well-maintained courtyard with a large, heavy wooden trapdoor in its centre. Beneath, was a wine cellar the size of a small bedroom. I'd had the dubious privilege of climbing inside only once, but I knew it to be one of the safest spaces to hold a powerful and dangerous supernatural being with little self-control. Not quite the description I'd have given its present occupant.

"Ross left us quite a legacy," said Patricia.

"Pleeeeeeasse!" The girl below was chained to a heavy supporting pillar. "Let me go. I need to find him. Need to see him. He'll tell you. He'll know."

Suzette. The girl who'd mistaken Brett and I for a couple the night we'd first met at the Black Soul. The girl Ross had rushed to hospital after her mishap with Sklav, or so he'd said.

The girl Ross had made his fucking Mannequin before his untimely death.

"She turned up here looking for him. Don't ask me how she found the place. It didn't take us long to realise something was very, very wrong."

The moonlight caught the girl's face, illuminating her wild, desperate eyes, surrounded by dark circles. An irregular twitch had seized her shoulders, neck and mouth, and it was evident she'd been crying for hours, hungry for Ross's blood, which nobody else could provide.

"What are you going to do?" I knew in my darkest of hearts that that question had only one answer.

Patricia shook her head. "We can't let her starve. But we also can't—"

"You might have to."

"She's not a wounded animal, Reylan."

"Patricia, that is *precisely* what she is. An animal you can't take care of, or even feed. And if you let her go, that hunger will take over to the point she tears—"

"I know perfectly well the consequences of starving a Mannequin, thank you."

A shrill scream erupted from the cellar, followed by the smashing of bottles against concrete walls. The rich aroma of fine wines emerged.

"Not her first tantrum. Will you please talk to her?"

"And say what? 'Sorry, your condition's terminal. Hold still while we kill you quickly?'"

"Reylan, she doesn't even know what she is. Please?"

Ugh. Fine. If I couldn't ease the girl's physical pain or hunger, perhaps I could at least help her make sense of it all.

"Suzette?"

Another bottle broke against the wall. "I need it! Where is he? You don't know what this is like! Just a drop of it, that's all. On my tongue, at the back of my throat—"

"*Suzette!*" This time, I released just a little Blood Shade fury into my voice to let her know who was in charge. "That's enough! I know you're frightened and hungry, but you must listen to me. Do you understand?"

I heard only the opening of the house's back door, which closed after Luca.

"Suzette, do you understand?"

"Yes," came a tiny voice from the bottom of the cellar.

"Good. Now listen carefully. The man you're looking for, Ross, isn't here. He isn't coming back, either."

Another scream erupted from the cellar.

"*Enough!*" I silenced her again. "You know I'm telling you the truth. I'm sorry. I very much wish it wasn't. But I'm afraid Ross isn't coming back to any of us."

"No! No, you're lying! It's not true."

"I have… a friend, very much like you. Someone whose life I saved, just as Ross saved yours. That comes at a cost, Suzette. The hunger you're feeling right now? There's no sating it. No substitute will do, only the Blood Shade whose life force extended yours."

"Blood Shade? What's that? I don't understand."

"But you do understand I'm telling you the truth, don't you? You know he's gone. You felt it the moment it happened. You've been trying to make sense of it ever since. Trying to work out what it is your body so desperately needs, with only a faint knowledge of the man who did this to you. The one who left you behind."

"No. No! He wouldn't leave me. He—"

"He did what was necessary to save your life, Suzette. Then he did what was necessary to save someone else's life at the cost of his own."

"Please! I need it!"

"I'm truly sorry for what's happened to you, but there's nothing we can do."

Several more anguished sobs, and then. "You're… you're like him. Can't you help me? Please? I just need a few drops. I can't even sleep. It fucking hurts, arsehole!"

"Suzette," I said, ignoring her outburst. "If that were an option, I would, but drinking my blood would only make the pain ten times worse."

"Oh god!" she sobbed, her voice sliding up into a high-pitched whine. "Why is this happening to me? I don't understand. It hurts!"

"What is happening to her?" The question came from the last source I'd expected. Luca.

"She needs blood," I explained. "Your father's blood. Without it, she'll die."

It took the boy a moment to comprehend what I'd said, but once he did, the sudden clarity in his eyes seemed almost triumphant.

"She is a sycophant?" he asked. "Like your friend?"

"I suppose so. The word is Mannequin, but yes. She needs her Blood Shade master's blood to survive."

"But she cannot drink yours?"

Kelvin offered his own helpful explanation before I could answer. "If a Mannequin drinks from more than one vampire, they go crazy. She'd probably start killing a whole bunch of people. We're *not* going through that shit again."

"Indeed not," Patricia said. "Why do you ask?"

"Patricia," I said. "It pains me to say this again, but the best thing we can do for her—"

"I was addressing Luca. Why do you ask such a thing?"

"I carry the blood of my father."

I couldn't believe what I was hearing. "That's insane. That's positively insane. I hate to remind you, Luca, but you're turning into a completely different species, one we barely understand as it is."

"The alternative is to murder her," said Patricia.

"Yes, damn it! To spare her a slow and painful death, yes."

"What? Oh my god! I can hear you! I can fucking hear you, you bastard!"

"Shut up and let 'em think!" Kelvin answered.

"Luca, this is madness. We have no reason to believe your blood will ease her suffering in the slightest."

"We've no reason to believe it won't," Patricia said.

"What of the risks to Luca? Have you stopped to consider those?"

"It doesn't matter," the boy interrupted. "I want to do this."

"Luca," I said, almost pleading. "You've just gotten your life back."

He looked at the desperate, but mercifully silent girl in the cellar. "Then it doesn't matter if she ends it."

I could have argued, but even my best objection had seemed trite. The boy had no family and no real future, at least, not until we worked out what it meant to be a Death Shade and how... *if* he could control it. A future? From the moment he'd plunged the knife into Salvatore, he'd certainly severed ties to the past.

"Fine," I said. "If it's what you want."

Patricia nodded approvingly. "No point in taking foolish risks. Kelvin, go to the kitchen and fetch a plastic bottle or bowl of some kind. Something that won't break easily. It'll be safer if Luca bleeds into that, then she can drink—"

"I appreciate your caution, but I'm afraid it doesn't work that way," I said. "The feeding has to be vein to mouth, or we can forget the whole idea."

"What are you doing?" the girl called out again. "What are you guys talking about?"

I ignored her, instead taking Luca by the shoulders. "I'm going down there with you."

He nodded before descending to the cellar's floor. I nimbly dropped myself in after him, giving the boy and his 'patient' just enough space to size each other up.

Suzette was in worse shape than I'd thought. Tears had streamed down her face, but so had blood, down her arms and across her cheeks in an attempt to taste at least some of what fate had denied her. It was with slack-jawed wonder that she now stared at Luca, who took one careful step toward her, then fell still.

"It's all right," he said. "I want to help you."

Suzette threw me a panicked look.

Luca held up both empty hands. "I'm here to help. I promise."

"You… you look like him. I don't know how I remember, but your face, your voice, even your smell… How can you look so much like him?"

I watched Luca step closer as he slowly gained her confidence, despite having been little more than a deranged monster himself just moments ago. It was as if now, knowing his lineage, the boy had channelled his father's talent for calming storms before they arose.

"Will you try with me?" he asked.

"Yes."

He ran a thumb down his wrist before giving me an apologetic look. "Can you help me, please?"

Of course. The boy had no mastery over his fangs. Keeping an eye on Suzette, I extended two delicate incisors and pierced the wrist he'd held out for me. He winced before the inherent pleasure of the bite won out, leaving him with that unmistakeable, blissed-out grin on his face.

The girl didn't miss a beat, rushing forward and falling flat to the floor as she yanked hard on her chain.

"Slow down," I said. "You'll hurt yourself."

One cautious foot at a time, Luca advanced until he was close enough for her to latch onto his wrist. He shuddered as the sudden force of Suzette's hunger grabbed hold. I could hear his pulse quickening, even as hers slowed.

"Not too much," I cautioned him. "Just take the edge off, don't let her—"

The boy's face contorted into an ugly grimace as Suzette gripped his arm tighter and continued to drink.

"All right, that's enough. Suzette?"

The girl didn't acknowledge me, but instead kept drinking, gripping Luca's arm tighter and tighter.

"Let go," Luca got out.

"Reylan, what's going on?" called Patricia from above.

"Suzette, enough!" I dove forward, grabbing Luca with one hand and Suzette with the other. "Let him go!"

With no alternative, I grabbed a fistful of her hair and wrenched her off Luca's arm, allowing her screech to fill the chamber. I toppled with Luca into the darkness before scrambling to my feet, fearing this could trigger the boy's monstrous state. But there came no such change.

"Are you all right?" I asked.

"Yes," he said, his breath slowing.

"Can you lick it closed?"

"Lick it?"

"Like this."

Seeing me imitate the gesture on my own arm, Luca tentatively licked closed the wounds. Satisfied he was none the worse for wear, I turned my attention to the crumpled heap in the darkness.

"Suzette?"

The girl's head rose, all distress now swept away by the blissed-out ecstasy of a much-needed feed. Would Luca's blood poison her as it had poisoned me? Judging by her expression, it didn't seem likely.

"Much better. So, so much better."

"Reylan? What's happening down there?"

"It's all right." At least, I hoped so. "I'll be up in a bit. Luca?"

"I'll come soon," Luca said, still catching his breath. "Don't worry, I won't get close."

Satisfied neither he nor Suzette were in any more immediate danger, I scaled the ladder to meet a mildly perplexed Patricia above.

"What happened down there?"

"Just the voraciousness of a first feeding. Luca's blood did the trick, but I don't think she's had blood since Ross first claimed her. Hopefully that'll help slow her mental degradation."

"Slow it? You don't sound optimistic."

"I'm not. All we've done is buy her time. Even if Luca can offer a long-term solution, the boy barely knows what he is, much less how to manage it. Add the responsibility of a Mannequin, and it doesn't bode well for either of them. We need to free her from the addiction."

"How do we do that?"

"I've not the slightest idea. Her condition is both physical and psychological. There's certainly no mundane way to undo it."

"Then we get Sophia to look into some not so 'mundane' options," said Kelvin.

"That could take weeks. Sophia's not even a proper Shaper."

"You've a better suggestion?" Patricia asked. "I'm not bringing Isobel into this, so don't even ask."

I clenched my fists. Isobel would have been precisely the person to ask, not that even her expertise offered any guarantees. "Keep Luca secured. I'll be back before the night's out."

There was an alternative. And gods, how I hated grovelling.

CHAPTER ELEVEN

Though not quite a cathedral, Saint Barnabas was the sort of church built more as a monument to its congregation's riches than their supposed god. No expense had been spared, from the painstakingly maintained marble steps to the gargantuan front doors, to the intricate stained-glass windows that during the day—I assumed—set the upper echelons of the main chapel ablaze with coloured light. A scattering of gargoyles sat atop the roof, at least upon those nights the little beasts had chosen to stay put. I wagered few small dogs or cats lived in the former workers' cottages that surrounded Saint Barnabas.

I passed under the humble, badly weathered wooden cross that hung above the vast doors as some odd testament to Christ's humility. One had to credit these modern-day Pharisees with a nice try.

The church remained open at all hours, though given Surry Hills's proximity to Oxford Street's nightly conclave of debauchery and sin, few took advantage after dark. Iain and Dorotha had been an exception. The latter approached me with a warm, matronly smile as I stepped over the threshold.

"Mister Raymond?" Her voice positively glowed in comparison to the fear that had gripped her in my living room. "What are you doing here?"

Good question 'Hi, Dorotha. I'm here to ask the Shaper I just kicked out of my house if he'd mind helping me cure a girl of a potentially deadly blood addiction.' Unable to think of a way my evening could get more awkward, I kept things simple. "I came to make sure you were all right."

"Everything is fine now, thank you. Your Father Grieg is a good man." She shot a clandestine look back at the altar before poking me in the ribs.

Please, no.

"And so handsome! I hope very much you will keep this one, Mister Raymond."

Sigh.

Her expression abruptly darkened, as if some terrible realisation had crossed her mind.

"What is it?"

"Are you feeling all right? You are not…" She pointed to the large crucifix above the main altar.

"Not what?"

"You can be in church? Is all right for you?"

"I think God's disdain for homosexuals has been somewhat exaggerated."

"No, no, not that. The other thing."

I could only summon a blank stare.

"You! Mister Ross! Miss Isobel! Nosferatu! I know this!" She clucked a final sigh and busied her way out. "You think I stupid old woman."

People of all self-aware species abuse the term 'speechless.' In that moment, it happened to be true. Not. One. Word.

I peered into the darkness of the chapel, trying to find Iain in the dim candlelight, calling his name a couple of times. I eased open the two confessionals. Worth a shot, I thought. I jumped as the front doors banged shut, and a new face entered the chapel. A woman I recognised as Jennifer Myers.

Jorgas's mother.

We'd never met, and I'd no reason to think she'd recognise me, particularly in her agitated state. The sight of the empty church seemed to calm her, as though she were afraid of being seen. She quietly made her way up the aisle and took a seat in one of the pews, staring at the crucifix that overhung the altar. She'd not even bothered to bless herself.

This was fortuitous. I should probably have left the grieving widow alone. I had, after all, witnessed her husband's death and done little to prevent it. But I had too many questions to let an opportunity like this escape me. If she knew Jorgas's whereabouts, and she was here, in a public place, seeking... solitude? The very fact she'd brought her grief here suggested her needs were not so simple. A charitable Blood Shade could at least lend a sympathetic ear.

A faint tilt of her head was the only sign she'd heard my approach.

"You choose an unusual hour to be close to God... my child."

Meh. I was already going to hell.

She frowned at me before lowering her face in apology. "Forgive me, Father. I thought you were someone else."

"Who might that be?" I asked, relieved her opening greeting hadn't led to an impromptu confession.

She shook her head, almost smiling. "I don't know why I'm surprised. Ever since Father O'Baer went away... I don't remember if we've met. I'm sorry."

"Father... Roger O'Hara," I said, quickly extending my hand.

I know what you're thinking, and you can keep it to yourself.

"Father O'Hara? I think you're a new one."

"I'll not be staying long," I said, resisting the urge to affect an Irish accent. "I'm here in an administrative capacity, just until Father O'Baer returns."

"And you felt you had to come talk to me?"

I wasn't sure how to answer that. Eager as I was, I wasn't about to grill her for information right away. "If you'll permit me. You seem troubled."

She looked me over with suspicion. "You don't know, do you?"

"If you're referring to your husband's death, yes, I do."

"Great. That's just great. I don't even know your name, but you know all about 'the widow Myers.' I should sell bloody t-shirts… I'm sorry, Father."

"I've heard far worse, child, even in here." I didn't want to push her, and I certainly didn't want to scare her away, but I had to know what she knew. Anything at all. "You have a son as well, don't you?"

"I hope so." She gave a quick snort of indignance, but it quickly gave way to a sob, then another as she pulled a tissue from her purse. "I really hope so."

"I'm sorry, I didn't mean to—"

She waved me away. "It's my own bloody fault. When William disappeared, I tried to find Billy. He wouldn't even answer his phone. Then, when they found William's body, I got so caught up in the funeral and worrying about things people were saying… I just thought that with his dad gone, Billy would come home. Where else is he going to go?"

"I'm sorry for all you've been through. For your loss—"

"I'm not sorry for that selfish bastard!" she snapped, putting the tissue away and wiping a stray tear with her hand. "Just, that now he's gone, I thought Billy would… I don't want to lose my son."

"They didn't get along?" I knew this already, of course, but I had to keep her talking.

"Not at all! Used to go at it like two wild dogs."

That part, I believed. I wondered whose side of the family carried the werewolf genes.

"It was Billy's choice to leave. There was no stopping him. I mean, he's a grown man. I just wish I knew where he was. What he's doing. He *says* he's all right, but—"

"Says?" I asked, briefly slipping from character. "So, you have talked to him?"

"For all the good it did. He hardly said anything. Not where he was staying, or what he was… Only that I'd woken him up. It was three in the afternoon! He reckoned he hadn't been sleeping. Nightmares, if you can believe that! Practically bit my head off for waking him up."

Nightmares? I knew Jorgas. He wasn't the type to complain about nightmares. Yet, he'd brought it up in a conversation with his mother? Even she'd thought it strange, assuming she was telling me the truth, and she'd no reason not to.

"How old is he?"

She tilted a faint smile in my direction. "Not much younger than you, I'd say, Father. He's twenty-three in March."

"Good genes." I excused my youthfulness with an embarrassed smile. It was easy to forget at times. "Forgive me, I'm sure you've heard this. He may just need some time. Let him work out what he's going through in his own way. Perhaps encourage him to come here, if you talk to him again."

"I told you, he—"

"He answered the phone," I pointed out. "He's not shutting you out, Jennifer."

She offered up a weak smile. "I should go."

I could have stopped her, even hypnotised her to get more, but what good would it have done? What knowledge was I hoping the woman possessed that she'd not already volunteered? Jorgas was her son, for god's sake, and for all the bitterness between him and his father, he'd never once spoken poorly of his mother. I watched the woman leave, confident that I knew all she did. As information, it was next to useless, but it made me feel better.

"You know, impersonating a priest is a crime in some jurisdictions, unless you're a stripper."

I near leapt out of my skin as Iain emerged from beside the main altar, an insufferable smirk on his handsome face. "How long have you been listening?"

"Just long enough to figure out who you were discussing, and that it was none of my business."

I couldn't resist rolling my eyes. "I suppose if you wanted to invade my privacy, I'd have no way to stop you."

"That's a bit low! Especially after I talked your old dear back to her senses."

"My old dear?"

"If I was the type to go rummaging inside other people's thoughts, you'd be no fun. You don't exactly keep your cards close to your chest." His smile softened into something a little less punchable. "You shouldn't feel guilt over caring, you know. It's not a bad quality."

"Who I care for, how much, and who I trust with that information—"

"Ah yes, trust. Should I be insulted or flattered you had me followed?"

I resisted an acerbic remark, silently cursing for what must have been the dozenth time that I needed his help. "Surely you expected nothing different?"

"Suit yourself. Hope we didn't bore Brett too much. Two people in prayer? Not exactly a show that wins Tonys. Speak of the devil."

I turned to see Brett standing at the end of the pew behind us.

"Hi," he murmured.

"Brett, I just need to talk to Iain. We won't be a minute."

"Won't we?" the Shaper asked. "Now I'm curious."

I sighed. "I need your help."

"*Again?*" he asked, eyes wide with smart-arse mockery.

"All right," I growled. "I deserve that. And you can tell me to fu… to get lost if you want. There's this girl—"

"Wow. You are full of surprises, but I don't do that sort of magick."

"It's not that! She's a Mannequin."

"I see. How many do you have?"

"She's not mine! The thing is, her Blood Shade died soon after making her. We've got her stabilised with substitute blood, but I don't think it's going to be enough."

"And you think I can break a Blood Shade thrall?"

"A deceased Blood Shade. Can you?"

"Well, I suppose I do know a thing or two that you don't."

"Such as?"

"Such as, that's not the real Brett. *Get down!*"

I hit the floor between the pews just in time as fire seared the air above me. Glancing upward, I saw another ball of flame heading straight for the Shaper's head.

"Iain!" I called out too late, as the flames wrapped around his face and shoulders… then passed right through them, disappearing against a large wooden column.

The priest smiled as his attacker dove upon him, only to vanish, letting 'Brett' slam face first into the singed column.

Reylan!

I heard Iain's voice, but there'd been no sound. No echo off the church's walls. The whole exchange had been telepathic. I'd been talking to an illusion.

I'm in the sacristy. Get over here as fast as—

The Brett-thing's head whipped around to reveal a ghastly mockery of my boy's handsome face. Where his mouth should have been, a gaping maw packed with dozens of needle shaped teeth now roared at me. His eyes burned with the kind of hot red fury I'd seen only in Blood Shades releasing the monstrosity they harboured inside them. But the face of a Blood Shade releasing such power remained otherwise unchanged. That meant—

The thing raised its hands, fingers curled around licks of blue flame.

I didn't wait for it to gain the advantage. With all my might I wrenched the loosest wooden beam from the pew and hurled it at the creature. It batted the beam away with a loud hiss. Taking a long step toward the shadow to its right, it vanished.

"What was that?" I no longer knew which way to turn.

Don't talk! Just get in here before it comes back.

It had been so long since I'd been in church, I had to think just what a sacristy was. But I quickly leaped up the stairs, around the altar, and disappeared into the small room, locking the door behind me.

"Is that what I think it is?" I asked.

"Ever fought a live daemon before?"

"No. I don't think I've even seen one. How did you—"

"Something was wrong. I felt it in the energy of the place. So, when Dorotha left, I ducked in here, just to be... Move!"

"What?"

The Shaper threw open the door and tossed me through before I realised what was happening. A second later, the door to the sacristy and much of the little room burst into blue flame. Only a charred frame remained in its wake.

I looked down the aisle to see not one, but two slender, human shapes, almost pitch black in the darkened nave. They were daemons, all right. Creatures of neither flesh nor shadow, instead flitting from one to the other as it suited their purposes. Their ability to mimic any being they touched, or channel the heat of their bodies into wildly destructive bursts of targeted flame, had not been exaggerated either.

There's the other one. I sensed her soon after you arrived.

"Great," I muttered. "Now that we're woefully outgunned, let's get out of here before they kill us."

"And do what? Leave them?"

I heard the distinct click of hooves as the demons slinked closer, long black tails flicking behind them. "Who are you?" I demanded. "What do you want?"

The only answer was another powerful bolt of flame, which seared the window sill above our heads. At least somebody was a lousy shot.

There's something not right here. They're unsure of themselves.

"Is that normal for daemons?"

Your guess is as good as mine, but I'd say no.

The female demon began to tumble toward us, falling and flipping hand over foot with an eerie grade, shadow blending into solid flesh as she came nearer and nearer the altar currently serving as our only shield. She landed with a sharp hiss, her angular features forming a nasty smile that hid a curtain of brutal teeth. The darkness lifted from around her eyes, their burning hot irises fading into a seductive brown. When she finally opened her mouth, it was as natural and unthreatening as any human woman, and just a little alluring. She shifted her weight from side to side, like a snake sizing up its prey. In over one and a half centuries, I'd never seen a daemon in person. Not one I'd recognised, anyway. The bastards kept to themselves, eschewing both houses in favour of their own solitary, narcissistic existence, taking the forms of humans unfortunate enough to cross their path.

Christ. Brett! What had happened to Brett?

"What do you want?" I asked. "Where's my Mannequin?"

The woman's smile mutated into something that quite frankly, left me preferring her daemon form. "The filth met the fate that awaits all servants of the beast. The fate that awaits all pervers—"

The thing let out a loud screech as Iain broke an effigy of the Madonna over her skull with a loud crack.

I looked up just in time to see a hungry ball of blue flame coming at us with frightening speed. Grabbing Iain's arm, I pulled us both to the floor. The woman raised her battered head, only to catch the full brunt of the unholy inferno. It set her hair ablaze, quickly followed by much of her clothing, parts of the altar, and a good portion of the furnishings behind us. Not that it seemed to bother her as she rose again, towering over the altar, letting ruined scraps of her clothing fall from her body in glowing, ashen fragments. The flames themselves quickly diminished, absorbed into her body, which had dropped all pretence of its human mask. What remained was one hundred percent daemon. And she was pissed.

Iain and I scrambled to our feet in time to see the male daemon join his counterpart, who hissed some foul curse at him, presumably about the wayward flames. Though daemonic vocal chords mutated her words, I recognised enough Italian to realise we were dealing with more bloody Scimitars. Daemons this time, to whose primary weapon— fire—my 'immortal' form was all too vulnerable. Still, we had them beaten on speed and accuracy, judging by the sluggishness and wayward targeting of their attacks.

I can also read their thoughts.

"Iain!"

Shut up! They're afraid. They're deathly afraid.

"Of us?"

The daemons stalked around to opposing sides of the altar, sizing us up, trying to intimidate us.

We're not going to beat them hand to hand. When I tell you, run!

"I'm not leaving—"

Go!

I could already feel the female ramping up another ball of blue hot death. I'd a hunch she'd be more accurate than her male lieutenant. I leapt over the altar and ran, feeling the heat of another fireball explode all too close behind me. I'd no objection to Saint Barnabas being reduced to a pile of rubble, provided we weren't inside when it happened. If only I could draw one of them away. Draw their fire so Iain could—

BE STILL.

I stumbled, knees buckling under me as the voice's sheer force echoed through my skull. It was Iain's, unlike I'd ever heard it before. Quiet, yet unquestionable, it left me physically shaken by its power, enough that it took every scrap of nerve and persistence I had to crawl behind one of the pillars next to the confessionals. Only then did I risk a look back at the altar, where Iain stood with arms outstretched, pointed squarely at each of the two daemons. The beasts seemed paralysed in his thrall. His gaze darted between them as he muttered some incantation. Even my Blood Shade hearing struggled to make it out. It was in no modern language, though it contained a good portion of Latin. A few words even sounded like Hebrew.

The female daemon hissed, and Iain's muttering grew louder, his glare fixed on her with pure malevolence. Snarls from the male daemon joined in with the cacophony, sending chills through me.

"Reylan!"

I looked behind me to see Brett's harrowed face peering out from the confessional. The rest of him soon followed, and I rushed to wrap him in a hug as sweet relief drowned my fear.

"She said you were dead." I kissed his cheeks, still not letting go of him.

"What's that guy doing with my face? At least it was my face."

"I'll explain later. You need to go, *now!*"

"What about Iain?"

I looked back at the altar. The two daemon bodies were alight with flame and it was clear by their cold expressions this had been no accident. They were summoning whatever magick they could to dispatch this pesky wizard who'd dared challenge them. But Iain's defences held firm. "I'll deal with that. I need you to contact Isobel. Tell her we need to meet urgently. Tonight! I'll text you the address."

A series of unsettling cracks above us joined the foul symphony.

"But—"

"Brett, go!" I barked, just as several stained-glass windows broke, showering shards of coloured glass over the pews.

My Mannequin knew better than to question me again. He bolted for the front door as I pulled out my phone and tapped out the address as fast as my supernatural abilities would allow, adding Isobel's phone number as an afterthought, so my servant could confirm she was in fact, home. At my age, it was easy to forget the benefits of technology.

Another window cracked above us as the flames danced higher and higher above the daemons. Whether it was their doing or Iain's, they were tearing the place apart, and Iain along with it.

Even as the man continued chanting, I could see the exertion on his face. The sweat pooling across his reddened brow, his face inflamed further by the heat of the daemons' primary weapon, which they'd charged to frightening intensity. If Iain lost control and they let loose now, there'd be nothing left of the Shaper who'd again saved my life.

Iain's chants grew louder and louder as he struggled to keep the two daemons at bay, more like angry curses now than incantations.

I ignored the din as I drew closer, feeling the heat off the daemons as they raised their clawed hands and extended them toward the Shaper. I flinched, narrowly ducking another long piece of broken glass that embedded itself in one of the front pews. It was better than nothing. I pulled the shard free and bounded up to the female daemon. The male shrieked some kind of warning, but I drove the glass home into her throat before she could stop me. I jumped away just in time to see the male turn his rage upon me, catching the now helpless female in a raging ball of flame that set her entire body into convulsions. She quickly lost control of her own inferno, which burst from her fingers and engulfed her comrade.

Iain's chanting grew louder still, all his attention fixed squarely on the two creatures as they continued to pour fire upon one another. As the flames around their bodies leapt higher, I heard the daemons roar, drowning out the sound of more falling glass.

Reylan, when I tell you, grab me and drop us both to the floor.

"What?" I took a moment to realise Iain had again reached out telepathically.

Now! Now, damn it!

I threw myself into him with full preternatural speed, knocking us both to the floor just as the two daemons exploded in a ball of blue flame and singed innards. I heard several more explosions as hot energy cracked and bounced off walls, pillars and pews. A stray bolt swooped uncomfortably close to my head as I covered the human, who'd curled into a tight ball beneath me, clinging to my hand as the deadly light show played out above us. Only once the fireworks had stopped did he let go. We peered over the altar at the burned-out husks of the two daemons, now splayed across the steps.

"What the hell did you do?" I asked.

He winced as he sat up, trying to get comfortable. "I just put the fear of God into them. They'd already changed into beings they considered damned and fallen. It wasn't hard for me to work on that guilt and turn them on each other."

"It looked like hard work to me." I brushed a strand of sweat-soaked black hair off his forehead. "You almost… Hell, you're still burning up!"

He began loosening the buttons of his shirt, letting the damp cloth fall away from his body. Faint, dark streaks crossed his flanks, making him look not unlike some bizarre, furless tiger.

"What the hell?"

"Residuals. They'll pass," he assured me, taking hold of my arm. "They're arcane, not poisonous. The daemons can't do anything with them now they're dead."

"I'm getting you water."

He obliged me with directions to a small kitchen off the ruined sacristy, gratefully sipping the water when I returned.

"So, do you enjoy having men shove you into the floor?"

He smiled. "I couldn't stop the manipulation. If either of them got hold of their senses, even for the second it took me to duck, they might have turned the fire right back on me."

I shook my head, collapsing next to him, grateful for a moment of rest. "Knowledgeable one, aren't you?"

"Protecting House interests," he answered, draining the rest of the water. "I need to know at least a little about different species I could encounter. Don't be intimidated. I've been at it since my teens. Once the House sees you, they arrange for your skills to be developed as quickly as possible."

"So, you're basically in service to them?" I felt almost foolish for asking, but I knew little to nothing about the House of Magick, and if they'd sent this man to collect information on us, I intended to collect a little of my own.

"Not indentured servitude, if that's what you're implying. I had a choice. I chose this. Shapers left on their own, hoping to find a mentor are walking recipes for disaster. Usually their powers just never find their full potential, but if by some fluke they do, it becomes a problem the House then has to deal with." Nothing he described sounded all that different from the House of Blood's own approach. Blood Shades left to find their own way in the world, lost to their hungers, without guidance? Messy. "Most every Shaper is both student and mentor during their lifetime. And nobody wants their blossoming abilities cut down for lack of guidance."

Was the mischievous glint in his eye just to wind me up? Could I say the same for the hand that had taken mine? His touch was so delicate, I'd barely felt it until now.

"Sorry," he whispered, withdrawing.

I gently caught his fingertips in mine. "I think I'm the one who should apologise, for throwing you out."

Iain's breath warmed my neck as he leaned closer. His lips were as warm and sweet as I remembered. The gentle quiver of his timidity—this man who knew I was a Blood Shade and didn't deny his fear—excited my hunger more than I wanted to admit. I knew his blood to be exquisite already, partly owing to the magick that flowed through him. Yet there was something else. Something I wasn't accustomed to as my hand slipped inside his open shirt and cupped his flesh. His chest pushed against mine as his kiss explored deeper, his touch lifting the lip of my shirt. It was as if the rest of the burned, broken church faded away. All I could smell, all I could taste, was this beautiful human. The feeling wasn't sexual, per se. I knew that was impossible. But something about the man evoked raw sensual pleasure as tongues, sweat, and smoky grime mingled between our bodies, and our shirts slipped to the floor.

"You shouldn't be doing this, should you?" I resisted the urge to pierce his lips they brushed mine.

"Shouldn't, can't, mustn't… You don't know how badly I've wanted you."

I hushed him quiet, tilting his head back and suckling gently at his neck, tasting the rich blood through the sweat I licked from his skin.

He tilted his head, catching my lips against his again. When we finally broke our hold, he smiled. "I want you promise me something."

"Yes?"

"That you won't bite me."

I couldn't deny this gave me pause. Though I was incapable of true sexual arousal, the bite, for me, *was* the arousal, and would surely inspire his own. "I suppose I can refrain. But—"

It was his turn to hush me, bringing a hand up to my cheek. "Trust me."

Just an hour earlier, trusting him would have seemed absurd. Now, as our lips reconnected and he lowered our bodies to the floor, I didn't just feel able. I felt compelled. The whiff of singed daemon passing my nose just made me smile. The things' corpses still smouldered, embers aglow in their clothing.

"Ever made love by burning daemon light?" I asked.

"Shhh," he purred. "Ever made love as a human?"

It was as if a high-pitched whine… No. A long, beautiful, sustained high note filled the back of my mind. An odd, sharp tingling crackled through my body. I closed my eyes as it dissipated. When I opened them, it was like looking at Iain anew. The man's face, his hair, and his body hadn't changed. But the natural smell of him aroused me with renewed vigour. I knew it was not simply the pull of his blood. The scent of his body, his strong jawline and piercing dark eyes, the edges of the dragon tattoo that peeked over his shoulder and around his flank, the thin trail of hair that led down his stomach, disappearing into trousers that bulged with a strong erection now pressed again my own.

I was hard. This was impossible. I could feign an erection with a concerted effort, and feeding on Jorgas's werewolf blood had never failed to raise one. But this time, I'd willed nothing, nor taken a sip of the human's blood. This human I no longer felt possessed to bite. Yet I had to have him. To pull every part of him deep inside me.

"What did you do?" I barely recognised my own feeble voice.

His only response was to free his belt, casting it aside before undoing the top button of his trousers, swooping down for another, much deeper kiss. Almost reflexively I grasped his back. He winced with a nervous laugh as I gripped his flesh.

"Careful. You still have Blood Shade strength."

Easing my grip a little, I let him explore, welcoming his tongue as it lavished my jaw, cheeks, neck, and shoulders with slow, powerful kisses. He suckled at my chest, his tongue stretching out under my arm before gently descending to circumnavigate my nipple.

"You taste… different," he murmured between kisses.

"Is that a problem?"

He didn't answer. Judge me by my actions, he'd said, and judging by the way he now followed the curve of my abs to the joyous depravity now promised by the bulge in my pants, I concluded that no, there was no problem at all.

He opened my trousers with the skill of a man who'd done so every night of his life, pausing as if to admire his prize, before lowering himself to nip the flesh of my inner thighs.

I gave the closest thing to a 'giggle' of which I was capable.

"Feel good?" he asked, not breaking the rhythm of his teasing.

"How… Ah!" I gasped, a great smile crossing my face. "How are you doing that?"

He grinned. "If I told you that, I really would have to kill you."

If I had a response, it escaped me as his tongue slid along the base of my shaft, announcing the rapidly approaching warmth of his mouth as he dove upon it. I'd simulated the action so many times, seen and indeed imitated the pleasure it gave the men I took to my bed. But the genuine, unrehearsed experience was…

Iain's tongue cut a rapid dance over parts of my manhood I'd never explored. He shushed me, somehow making it seem part of his repertoire, the tips of his fingers skimming my chest until they finally brushed my throat. He was caressing my chin and lips before I even noticed him leaning in to kiss me once more, his weight pushed with loving gentleness into mine. I let myself flatten into the floor, enjoying the sensation of his sex nudging my own, his tongue and strong hands exploring my preternaturally smooth skin, untouched by the sun in over a century. Feeling his hands wrap around my wrists, I grinned at him, bringing my weight up and flipping both of us over, returning his kiss.

He smiled as I withdrew.

"What?"

"Do you always have to be in control like that?"

"I don't know what you mean."

A sly glint crossed his eye. "Then lie down on the altar."

I gave his wrists another gentle squeeze, kissing the end of his nose. "Why would I do that?"

"I could make you. You'd never know. Or are you going to abuse the fact that I won't?"

I was nothing if not willing to humour him, standing up and leaning against the empty, draped altar. The smell of the burning daemons crossed my keen senses once more, only to be forgotten as Iain rolled lazily on his side, dark hair stuck to his forehead, his long, sinewy body streaked with ash, grime, and the shadowy residue of his spellcasting efforts. His smile, calculated to mock my own, was irresistible.

"What now?" I asked.

"I told you to lie down."

I eased my weight up on the altar and leaned back, swinging myself around lengthways so it would take my full height. Only my legs hung over its end. I turned my head to face the Shaper again. He hadn't moved, remaining perfectly still as we shared a lingering look.

"You are… ridiculously beautiful."

I thought of joking that he'd stolen the words from my mind, but thought better of it. The fact remained that I had never desired a human the way I now desired Iain Grieg.

"Close your eyes," he whispered.

I grinned. "You're really asking me to trust you."

"Yes, I am. Now, shut 'em!"

Yes sir! I rolled onto my back and did as I was told. I felt my trousers and briefs being slid from my hips, down the length of my legs to the floor. The breeze that passed over them was quickly replaced by Iain's warm breath as he kissed the inside of my thighs, gently licking his way up to… The man's tongue was beyond skilled.

We didn't have time for this. I needed to talk to… Who, again? Certainly nobody who'd make me feel like this. I shuddered as Iain's mouth enveloped my cock in one smooth movement. As he withdrew, his hands and arms slid smoothly along the sides of my body, his fingers spread wide until they teased the hair of my underarms. He kissed below my navel, cheekily flicking the tip of my cock one more time with his tongue.

I flinched so hard I almost leapt off the altar.

"Easy," Iain whispered. "Sensitive, are we?"

"Just… new at this." I tried to relax, a task made more difficult by the damp pressure of Iain's cock nudging my opening.

"Are you also new at this?" he asked, somehow managing to plant several kisses across my chest as he kept nudging.

"No, just—" A faint gasp escaped me as a particularly forceful nudge pushed hard against my breach, then retreated.

"It's been a while," the man guessed. "I can help you with that."

It was as if a wave poured from my brain down through my body, relaxing every muscle from the top of my forehead to the end of my toes. I barely felt Iain slide inside me until… I had no words for the sensation. I'd allowed so many men to go through the motion, redirecting my blood flow to engorge my cock and lessen the discomfort, playing the role of eager, mid-twenties bottom boy with conviction. Now, as Iain rocked back and forth with steady rhythm, letting the sensation peak each time he pushed forward, electrifying every fibre of my being as he pushed deeper and held for several seconds before withdrawing again, kissing my legs, shoulders, chest, lips, face, and anywhere else he could reach… Oh yes, I was new at this. But I was learning fast!

I arched my back as Iain gripped my shoulders and pushed harder, faster, his face filled with fierce exertion, lips peeling apart like a hungry animal about to dive on its prey.

"Lay back," said Iain.

"Huh? Oh!" As I did what I was told, the angle of his sex shifted. Whatever part of me he hit now, was a part neglected longer than my manhood had ever been. Probably my whole life.

It was Iain's turn to shudder as he covered my body with his, not breaking stride as he kissed me, moaning softly into my mouth. "So close. So… Oh!"

What he was doing now, I neither knew nor cared. The sensation of the man inside me, on top of me, all surrounding me, thrilled me in ways I'd never felt. The absolute trust and safety as I surrendered my body, the taste of his lips, the pleasure that washed off every inch of his being as he gorged himself on me—instead of the other way around—defied any description. So many men had yielded to me over the years. Accepted their place as mine. To give myself to one so completely, even just in body, was a new and wonderful experience.

Within seconds, I would drain him. Just not in the way I normally did.

He took my lips in another deep kiss, but I wasn't missing the grand finale, not even for such sweetness. I took a fistful of his hair and pulled him free, letting his final, bellowing cry escape into the darkened church as his seed erupted inside me. It took every ounce of self-control not to launch myself at his throat and draw deep as my nature desired. What rapture it would have been, to let the hot, thick pleasure of the man's blood coat my mouth and throat right as he emptied his lust into me. Yet I couldn't break my promise. Not to a man who'd shared with me such glorious pleasures.

After what felt like eons, Iain collapsed over me, exhausted, both our bodies soaked with sweat. A great smile replaced his rapture as he curled up under my arm and kissed the space beneath it.

"That was…" I got out at last. "My god!"

"If He can't hear you in here, He's not going to."

I smiled, stroking Iain's hair and kissing his forehead. "Somehow I don't think this is the place to come looking for Him."

"You're probably right. It didn't take me long to realise that when I arrived."

"Which was when, exactly? And why Saint Barnabas?"

He punctuated his silence with more kisses.

"Iain?"

"Can we enjoy what just happened, for a moment? Two dead daemons not withstanding?"

Fair point. In truth, I didn't want to move. "What did you do to me?"

He kissed my nipple, slid his hand across my chest and closed the space between our bodies. "That's just the start of what I could do, any time you want to let me into that extraordinary mind of yours."

I lingered on the thought with another kiss. Could I let Iain exert that kind of power over my mind, especially after he'd so expertly manipulated my body? Perhaps…

A faint buzzing came from the floor beyond our feet. My phone. I'd clean forgotten.

I eased myself off the altar and fished it from my pocket as Iain surveyed the daemonic carnage. Dim light illuminated the dark outlines of the dragon that covered his back.

"Reylan? *Reylan!* Jesus, are you there?"

"I… I'm here," I stammered, finally averting my eyes. "Brett?"

"Yeah, me! What the hell, man? I thought you wanted me to find Isobel, asap."

"Yes, yes of course. Wait, you're with her already?"

"No, I'm in a cab on my way to Colin's."

"Colin's? Why?"

Victoria House was no quick detour from Surry Hills. The imperious former heritage home now owned and occupied by the city's oldest Blood Shade occupied a stretch of land and gardens atop the cliffs of Watson's Bay. Prohibitively expensive real estate, far from the hum and thrum of Sydney's unwashed commoners. Not that I was bitter.

"Isobel's there! You should be too, as soon as you can get there. She turned up something you need to see."

"We'll be there as quick as we can."

"We?"

I'd shut off the call before I could reply, looking up to see Iain's still naked form silhouetted against the dim light. I found myself torn between responsibility to Isobel, and carnal desire for round two.

"We?" he echoed Brett's question, having I guessed heard both sides of the conversation in the silent church.

"You said it yourself. This concerns us all."

He pushed his shoulders back, stretching his arms behind him in a display that accentuated the shape of his torso. "And what are we going to do about these two?"

Bodies. I hated dealing with bodies, and we really didn't have time. I skimmed through the numbers on my phone and reluctantly hit dial. "Kelvin?" I didn't wait for the sarcastic reply. "I need a favour."

CHAPTER TWELVE

Not wishing to ponder the many expletives flung in my direction on Kelvin's arrival, nor just how large a favour I now owed him, I watched the increasingly grandiose houses of the eastern suburbs fly by the window of our cab. Iain, meanwhile, was watching me.

"Something the matter?" I asked.

"On the contrary. I didn't realise the Arcadia Trust held you in such high esteem."

"I think that's more about mutual best interest than fondness."

"Perhaps. But our friend's colourful language not withstanding, it can't be so bad, having those resources at your beck and call."

Beck and call? Had he missed the pleading, grovelling, and self-abasement that had finally brought Kelvin to my aid? I tipped the cab driver generously for his haste and discretion and sent him on his way, looking up at the looming walls of Victoria House as though it were a home for the criminally insane, rather than those insane enough to visit. Was I paranoid? No more than being rendered unconscious by the plants in the back garden was wont to make a man.

"So," Iain said. "The home of the infamous Colin."

I shook off the last of my reservations. "You expected lightning bolts?"

Ding dong.

Nice to hear Colin's bell still doing its best to undermine the house's inherent menace.

"Reylan, please come—" Peter went abruptly silent as his gaze fell upon Iain.

"Where's Isobel?" I asked, ignoring his surprise. "I understand it's urgent."

He led the way to a dimly lit study where the party had assembled. Brett, Isobel, Colin, and Colin's other Mannequins, the couple, Bryce and Tommy, and Genevieve.

All eyes were fixed on Iain.

"If it's easier, I can go." His confidence impressed me for a man being stared down by two powerful Blood Shades and five Mannequins.

"No, you can stay," I said, hoping I knew what I was doing. "I think what we need to discuss concerns everyone in this room."

"And how is that, Reylan?" Colin purred, his 400-year-old Haitian accent and 7-foot frame reminding us just whose house we were in.

"This is Iain, an envoy from the House of Magick."

Genevieve and Bryce's eyes flared. The latter clenched his fists, corded arms bulging in his t-shirt as his boyfriend shifted uncomfortably. Colin merely glowered as Peter, who sat closest to him, tensed. Isobel, for her part, remained implacable.

"The wolf was one thing, Reylan." Colin made no attempt to hide his annoyance. "His acceptance was not an open invitation for you to bring witch filth into this house."

"This 'witch filth' is the only reason I'm able to make this meeting at all. Assuming we're here to discuss the Scimitars,

I'd think the insight of the only Shaper with knowledge of their plan to be invaluable. Wouldn't you?"

The silence was thicker than the scent of Colin's blood, lingering on each of his Mannequins. Were they expecting trouble?

"If you vouch for him," Colin said at last, "then it will be a stake on your word."

It would have to do. I trusted Isobel, Colin, and Colin's people not to touch Iain. Could the Shaper offer me the same guarantee? He'd let Colin's slur wash over him with surprising grace.

"Why are we here?" I asked Isobel. "What did you find that you couldn't share with Patricia?"

"Testing my patience today, Reylan," Colin said.

"Patricia has been assisting in this matter from the outset. I thought we'd agreed to share our—"

"Reylan," Isobel's voice bore just a trace of hurt. "We both know Patricia won't want to hear anything I have to say."

"She will if it tells her what the Scimitars are up to."

"Isobel, is it?" If Iain had been at all nervous entering the den of such a powerful Blood Shade, he didn't show it now, looking Isobel directly in the eye. "I know I'm not exactly welcome here, but Reylan's right. For months, the House of Magick has been tracking Scimitar activity that seemed out of character. We've seen a substantial drop in the number of attacks in Europe over the last six months. Cities in North America have reported similar figures. We needed to know if the Scimitars were simply weakening, which, as I'm sure you now know, was not the case. Finally, my investigation brought me here."

"Lucky us," muttered Bryce.

"I propose an exchange of information. Perhaps we can help each other?"

"What about the other Shapers?" Brett asked. "Can't they help us out? We don't know how many more Scimitars are coming."

Iain's composure flickered just long enough to glower at Brett. "Assuming there *are* other Shapers in Sydney, which I can neither confirm nor deny in this room, they're not mine to command. I'm offering you—"

"Information," Colin said. "Very well, Shaper. Tell us what you know."

"I think," Iain said, turning to Isobel, "this is your show, my dear. I'll fill in the gaps."

"Reylan," Isobel answered, not taking her eyes off the man. "Tell your new friend that if he calls me 'my dear' one more time, he'll have trouble filling in anything ever again."

Iain grinned, whispering in my ear. "I like her. You were her mentor?"

"Gentlemen," Colin cautioned. "Proceed please, Isobel."

I could swear Iain's fingers brushed the back of my hand. Maybe I'd imagined it. Maybe it was just another of the Shaper's mental tricks. He seemed a cocky bastard, all of a sudden.

"I compared the remains of a werewolf who attacked Reylan and I in my sanctuary to residue found on Luca's clothing. Both feature energy residuals from a Wound."

This time, I grabbed Iain's arm, fixing him with a glare. Even Colin raised an eyebrow.

"Ah, sorry," said Brett. "Wound? Explain, please."

"An opening in our reality that if stable enough, allows creatures from other realities, including the realm of the Patrons, to enter our world. Creatures like Sklav."

Taunting the devils in their own hell. Bingo.

Genevieve's eyes went wide. "You're fucking kidding."

"So, wait." Brett said, getting to his feet. "You mean there could be another one of those things, like Sklav, in *our* world?"

"I did not say that. I'd say it's unlikely."

"But not impossible?" asked Peter.

"Let her speak." Colin's command silenced every Mannequin in the room, including my own.

"The residuals on the werewolf's remains match those found on Luca's belongings. Entities from the Patron's realm, such as Sklav, bear a distinctly different energy signature, native to the Wounds into their world. The wolf and Luca don't have it, ergo, they haven't been there."

"Just a minute," I said. "I thought a Wound in our reality *did* open into the Patron's realm."

Isobel shook her head. "It's more complicated than that. Think of the two Wounds as doorways connected by a corridor. A separate, micro reality, where each living being that enters both exists, yet doesn't exist at the same time."

"Like a… Schrödinger's hallway?" Brett asked.

She smiled at him, impressed. "For a Patron to leave their world and enter ours, or vice versa, both Wounds have to open in close enough succession that the individual can pass through. Depending on the individual, that passing has… physical consequences."

My throat tightened. This just got better and better. "What consequences?"

"Understand," Isobel said with unmistakeable hesitation, "the Houses know very little about how the Wounds open in this realm, much less any other, so it's difficult to determine any sort of rule or pattern. Since we can't safely enter these other realities, we know almost as little about them, except that they have a profound effect on mortal physiology. That's *any* mortal physiology, meaning Blood Shades, Mannequins, Flesh Masters, Cloak Walkers, beings who've been changed by direct contact with the Patrons—"

"Changed?" Colin asked. "You're talking about the Mutilated?"

"The creatures we call the Mutilated have already been abducted and pulled inside the Patrons' realm. Many of them come back mad, which, to be blunt, doesn't much help our research. What's more, the recollections of those lucky enough to remain coherent have always been so inconsistent, they're considered unreliable. All we know for certain is that they come back physically altered, presumably against their will."

"But these Scimitars aren't emerging as Mutilated," I said. "The one at your house was a werewolf. We just dispatched two daemons. Luca is… well, he's not the best example."

"Because they're not passing through the Patrons' realm at all. They're using the hallway as a conduit to move from one spot in our realm to another, and they're being awfully precise about it."

"No customs or immigration records," said Brett.

"No risk of being spotted by the usual informants," added Peter.

"Or being magickally detected or scryed," Isobel finished. "At least, not until it's too late."

"Speaking of magick," Colin said, practically purring. "You're awfully quiet, Shaper."

"It's a sound theory." Iain took a moment to confirm he had everyone's attention. Something shifted in his face, to the point I no longer saw my friend. Now, the man spoke for the House of Magick, and for all his handsomeness, he looked every bit the pompous ass that implied. "But you know it's incomplete. For instance, what would you say are the chances of two Wounds appearing right where the Scimitar need them?"

Brett shrugged. "Gotta be one in a million?"

"Exactly." Iain walked over to one of Colin's bookshelves, withdrew a thick volume and pretended to inspect its cover. "Unless of course you create the Wounds yourself."

"Oh, fuck off!" snarled Bryce.

"They're…" Brett began. "They can't be that crazy!"

"Did you forget you're dealing with people convinced their cause guarantees them eternity in paradise, who therefore have no fear of dying? The practice of creating a Wound is strictly forbidden by the House, of course. Not that the Scimitars give a damn."

"So, you possess this knowledge?" Isobel asked.

Iain scowled. "What part of 'strictly forbidden' did you miss? Those within the House who do know aren't sharing it about." Catching the expression on my face, he relented. "The point is, it's knowledge the Scimitars now have, and they're using it to conjure Wounds precisely where they want them. Entry and exit."

"And now, instead of killing those within their ranks unfortunate enough to go through a change, they send them through the Wounds to attack their enemies," I finished for him, having reached my own heinous conclusions. "Shock troops, bound for a glorious death."

"That's what we thought too, at first. But you're forgetting one very important detail."

"Which is?"

"The fact that they emerge changed, their dormant genes awakened."

"But that doesn't…" Isobel trailed off. "No! Changes are genetically pre-determined. They can't be induced!"

"The Scimitars come, almost without exception from supernatural family lines. Those families *all* carry the genes of one 'supernatural' species or another. Now they're being subjected to forces capable of radically altering physiology on levels we still don't understand."

"Altering?" I asked. "But only the Patrons' realm does that."

"Perhaps. But what happens if you're a human who already carries the genetic traits of other species? Let's say you get too close to this realm. Perhaps you even open a small Wound into it, too small for the Patrons to detect. Say that lets you expose yourself to just enough of their power to trigger a transformation, right before you emerge at any point on the globe you chose."

"With a massive genetic upgrade. That's... insane!"

"The things humans will do for blind faith. Don't let one or two diplomatic victories blind you to the fact that the Scimitars want us all dead."

"So, they're willing to become everything they've vowed to hunt and destroy, to make themselves better killers."

Iain smiled humourlessly. "When God no longer blesses your cause, make your appeal to the other guy."

"Could they be after a specific target?" Isobel asked. "Something they consider worth the risk?"

"The Trust?" Colin asked.

"Possibly," I said. "Patricia more or less forced them into a truce last time they were here. They might see this new 'technique' as a way to get her off the board once and for all."

"Or the Trust is a practice run for a larger assault. On one of the Houses, perhaps."

"Either way, they're bloody particular about their targets. I don't know where Luca materialised, but that werewolf managed to emerge *inside* Isobel's house, and those daemons knew exactly where to find Iain and I, at Saint Barnabas."

"What about Salvatore?" Brett asked. "Isn't he Ross's brother?"

"Was," I corrected him. "He's dead, and in any case, he talked about the Scimitar giving itself over to blasphemy. That doesn't sound like a man at peace with this horror show. I think you'll find he arrived the old-fashioned way."

"I can hack the immigration records," said Tommy.

Isobel shook her head. "Both Luca and the werewolf had passports on them, presumably so they could go home the 'old-fashioned' way. No doubt they've already falsified records to facilitate that."

"Assuming they planned on going home? It hasn't gone well for them so far. They haven't the first clue how to use their new abilities."

"Shock troops," mused Colin. "To test our strengths and defences. The real assault is still to come."

"So, what does that make Luca?" Brett asked.

"Part of a disgraced family who refused to back the scheme," Isobel said. "That's one way to punish the father, send the boy to an almost certain death."

"Except Luca *isn't* Salvatore's son."

"Oh? Oh!"

"How's he doing, anyway?" Brett asked. Nice to know I could count on my boy for a little compassion in this nightmare.

"Surprisingly well, given some ups and downs. As for the others, I think it would be a mistake to dismiss them all as 'shock troops. The daemons that attacked us weren't so incompetent with their new abilities.

"You think they're getting stronger with each attack?" Isobel asked.

"I'd speculate that the first few—Luca, possibly the werewolf woman—were coerced or strongarmed into being part of this. Or were just stupid enough to volunteer."

"Interesting thought," Iain began. "However—"

"How do you reason that?" Colin asked.

"Because if you're about to send a strike force through a highly unpredictable gateway between realities, you don't risk your most formidable or loyal soldiers on the front line."

"If I can have everybody's attent—"

"Not so smart to tip us off… unless they're so confident they'll win that they want us to know judgement is at hand."

"Confident they'll win?" Peter asked. "Shit. How many are they sending?"

"Fourteen," Iain finally got out. "They've sent fourt… No. Fifteen, now. Fifteen."

Now, he had the room's undivided attention.

"You know this how?" Colin asked.

"I'm picking up fifteen minds either in the house or on the grounds, not counting— Move!"

Brett dived out of the way as Iain grabbed hold of what seemed like thin air, then wrestled some unseen force to the ground. Peter was on his feet in a flash, handing the Shaper a knife. A great scream erupted as Iain thrust it down into the unseen assailant with a sickening squelch. The space just above the floor began flickering with bluish light, and I watched with fascination as the creature materialised into a small, wiry woman, completely unclothed save the tiny ribbon that secured her blonde hair away from her face. Within seconds, the light had faded, leaving only the corpse. So, that was what it looked like when a Cloak Walker died.

"Fourteen, now?" Isobel asked.

Iain shook his head. "She was new. Must have materialised less than a second before I grabbed her."

"You mean they can just appear anywhere they bloody well please?"

"That's what we've been telling you for the past half hour," Iain answered, not caring at all that he was chastising Bryce right under Colin's nose.

"Where are they?" I asked before the Blood Shade could call him out. Or tear out his arm. Whichever Colin deemed more fitting.

The Shaper shook his head. "They're moving too quickly. Three… no, four in the main hall… I can't track them, sorry. But I can tell you they're not human. At least, not anymore."

"Is there another way out?" Isobel asked.

"Several," Colin admitted. "But there are objects in this house we cannot leave to the Scimitar's curiosity."

"Colin, we may not have a choice," I said. "Those aren't just trained human assassins out there. There's no guarantee we can beat them."

A loud crash came from outside the room. Could they have found us so quickly?

"If you're going to stay and fight, do it soon," Iain said. "Another one just dropped in outside."

"Are there any weapons in the house?" I asked.

"In our room," Bryce said. "Mostly guns, but I think we've got some iron ammo, maybe some silver."

"Fine," said Colin. "We'll keep them distracted. You and Tommy get up there and get as much as you can. Genevieve, I want to know exactly how many are in the garden and what their movements are. The last thing we need is the cavalry rushing in."

I nodded in agreement, though I didn't at all like the idea of the Mannequins being left alone without someone to watch their back. "Brett, stay with her."

"I can take care of myself," Genevieve said.

"I know that, and I'm telling you both to take care of each other."

She waited for Colin's assent, then relented.

"What about Pete?" Brett asked.

Colin's oldest Mannequin collected a long sword from behind one of the room's numerous curtains. "Your diversion's going to need all the help it can get." He wielded the blade as elegantly as any master swordsman. I could have sworn he flashed a smile at Brett.

"Are you any clearer on how many there are?" Colin asked, baring his fangs and gently opening a gash down his arm.

"Six in the main hall," Iain said. "What are you doing?"

Five on six. Less than ideal odds, but they would have to do.

"As soon as we leave this room, speed is going to be everything," Colin said as his four Mannequins lowered to their knees to receive him. "We're going to need every physical and mental advantage. All of us."

I nodded, following Colin's lead and offering Brett my now bleeding wrist. I was sure Iain frowned a little, but he understood. Every advantage.

"Then we're all clear on what we're doing?" Colin asked. "No heroics. You four, up the stairs. Bryce and Tommy, weapons. Genevieve and Brett, stand guard and size up the yard. We'll join you when we've finished with them down here, and in case it wasn't clear to all of you, show no mercy. If certain items from this house fall into the Scimitar's hands—"

"Items…?" Iain asked, catching a look from Colin that could have shred a man's soul. "…the nature of which is immaterial right now. Got it."

Peter opened the door onto the short passageway that separated us from the occupied hall. No doubt we'd look quite the parade to any intruder who came upon us. Said intruder's head would look quite fine upon the wall of Colin's trophy room.

With a nod from Iain, I grasped the doorknob and flung the thing open. The body of one intruder glanced off my side as I passed them, putting all supernatural speed behind me. I looked back at the Scimitars, whose surprise gave way to fury as they realised not only had we surrounded them, but that they'd allowed four Mannequins to escape up the stairs. A powerfully built Blood Shade was on me before I could savour

our little victory. A few inches taller and considerably broader than I across the chest, what he lacked in the power of Blood Shade years, he made up for in raw strength and fury. Tightly corded muscles filled out his black t-shirt, just as murder filled his eyes.

"*Maledetto…*" He grinned through newly acquired fangs.

A bit late to be throwing stones in that glasshouse, sweetheart.

A female Blood Shade threw herself at Isobel with a loud shriek, which distracted me long enough for my beefy opponent to land a hard blow across my face. It took several seconds of searing pain to realise I'd been struck by the six-inch curved blade in the Blood Shade's fist. I could feel the gash across my head, and it wasn't healing.

"Watch the weapons!" I called, narrowly diving out of the way of another attack and grabbing the bastard's arm, straining to hold him in stalemate. "They're laced."

Isobel was too preoccupied with her attacker to acknowledge me. Colin meanwhile, was trying to fend off two goblins, each no more than three feet in height, who'd nonetheless set upon him like he was some living climbing gym. Their claws left jagged, bloody red scratches wherever they climbed, and though not laced with the same poison that denied us our natural healing, they made a bloody mess of Colin's shirt and chest as he tried to grab hold. The little beasts evaded his every effort. Why was Peter not helping his master?

Seconds later, a great roar erupted from the far corner of the hall. Even my enemy seemed startled as we turned to see the long elongating snout, powerful limbs, heavy claws, and thick, shrouding fur. Four against five didn't count for a hell of a lot when we were up against a werewolf. As my Blood Shade foe sent me reeling with another punch to the side of the head—no less painful, coming from his unarmed hand—

I hoped we'd last long enough for the werewolf to become a problem.

I caught the Blood Shade's next attempted blow and used his weight to unbalance him, yanking his arm hard toward me. I wrapped my other arm around his neck and swung myself up onto his solid frame. The blade nicked my wrist again, but I had two great advantages, experience and speed, as I dug my fingers into the sockets of his eyes. Ignoring his screams as he doubled over, I slipped off his back and pushed myself away before his flailing could do me more grievous injury. He howled in fury at the daemon that had so thwarted his new, blasphemous form. I'd have to finish him off before his eyes regrew, but his youth at least bought me some time. He wouldn't heal an injury like that so quickly.

I saw Isobel going blow for blow with the other Blood Shade, though she seemed focused on avoiding blows rather than landing any of her own. Of course, we were unarmed. Colin managed to grab one of the goblins by the arm and swing it hard against an ornate door frame, but the wiry little monster didn't skip a beat, coiling itself back up Colin's arm. Hooking its claws into his dark skin, it inched its way back into the fray.

Then, there was Peter, whose many hidden talents now revealed themselves to include swordsmanship as he ducked and rolled, evading blow after blow from his wolfen opponent. The few blows he did land seemed to do little more than irritate the wolf as it swung around for another attack. Just as the two Goblins seemed to accomplish little beyond distracting and annoying Colin, Peter danced around the werewolf like a mosquito that would not be smote, keeping the Scimitars' most powerful weapon off the rest of us. But for how much longer?

I lurched away as my blinded foe threw another punch with his blade in my direction. The movement set my head spinning. I still wasn't healing.

Iain. Where the hell was Iain?

Even in my confusion, I heard Isobel yelp as she fell afoul of her opponent's blade. What now soaked her opened sleeve was no mere trickle of blood. If these holy warriors couldn't finish us off quickly, they'd apparently settle for bleeding us into submission. Swiftly as I could, I leaped upon the back of Isobel's enemy. Perhaps wise to the fate of her comrade, the woman ducked just low enough to flip me over. I landed hard on the floor, opening my eyes just in time to see Isobel block the attacker's blade-wielding hand. I managed to latch onto the Blood Shade's ankle as Isobel landed a swift boot into her chest. The woman went down with an enraged screech, just as I heard another from my blind nemesis. On the other side of the hall, he roared, throwing fists both armed and unarmed in a vain attempt to find a target.

Voices, voices everywhere. But where could I be?

Clear as a bell, I heard Iain's thoughts. Nice to know he'd not abandoned us, though I wished he'd quit playing games!

You're no fun.

"Damn it, Iain! Get out of my head!"

Fine, in that case, I'll get into his.

"What?"

By the time I realised what was happening, the blind Blood Shade was already barrelling toward Colin like a steam train. One of the goblins dived to avoid the mountainous, screaming bulk now flying toward him with empty, bleeding eye sockets. It left the other, perched on Colin's shoulder, too stunned to offer more than a brief scream before the Blood Shade's knife slammed into its throat, decorating the rather dull landscape painting behind it with a spray of arterial blood. Before the Scimitar could realise his mistake, Colin grabbed the other

Goblin, lifted it high above his head and tore it in two. The screams of the blinded thug pierced the air soon after.

His comrade remained focused on Isobel, which made her my next priority. The woman kept her stance defensive, but nonetheless seemed to be circling us, the corners of her mouth teasing a perverse smile as she sized us up. She ignored the last gasps of her colleague, before Colin tossed away what remained of his corpse.

Reylan, she's—

Iain's warning came seconds before the Blood Shade pulled something from her belt and threw it to the floor. A circle of blue flame surrounded her feet, then leapt toward each of us, setting alight any rug, chair, drapery, or artwork it touched. Of course! If the Scimitar had made peace with the blasphemy of embracing their monstrous dormant genes, a little black magick was no stretch.

We pulled ourselves back, narrowly missing the rapidly spreading flame. The wolf howled in frustration as Peter dived through the fire, obviously not wishing to test his dexterity against both the creature and this infernal magick at the same time.

"Crazy bitch," Isobel muttered in disbelief as the grinning female Scimitar disappeared into the flames.

Colin, on the other hand, burst forth right on Peter's heels.

"Iain?" I called. "Iain! Where the hell—"

"Up here!" came the Shaper's now audible response.

I couldn't believe what I was seeing. There was Iain, atop the landing, narrowly dodging flames as they zipped along the railing, lighting all in their path like someone had poured a trail of gasoline. Except there was no such smell. What we now saw was no more or less than black sorcery, and judging by the worry in Iain's eyes, it wasn't of a kind the Shapers either sanctioned, or wanted to be dealing with. I had to reach him. God, I had to reach Brett! Where were the Mannequins?

It wasn't as if the werewolf was about to give us much choice. The four of us bounded up the stairs, regrouping in tight formation with Iain just in time to see the beast try to follow us, only to have the burning staircase collapse under its weight.

"This way!" Colin said, using his coat to ward off licks of flame as he led us to the end of the hall.

"Reylan!"

I recognised Brett's voice immediately, breaking into a stride until I'd reached the doorway from which he'd emerged. The first thing to draw my eye was blood all over floor. The next was Tommy, laying barely conscious in Bryce's arms with half his torso ripped open.

"Jesus Christ," Iain muttered as the rest of the group caught up.

"Out of my way." Colin went to his Mannequin's side. The surface of the bed lay strewn with weapons but none of them had helped Tommy against whatever had done this.

"We didn't see anything," said Brett. "By the time I turned around, Genevieve was screaming and Tommy…"

"Cloak Walker," I muttered. 'Six in the main hall,' Iain had said. Two Blood Shades, two goblins, and the werewolf accounted for only five. How could we have been so stupid? "Watch yourselves. It can't have gone far. Iain?"

"I'm trying. Too many busy minds in this house."

"Bryce," Colin said quietly. "I'm sorry."

I couldn't claim to know Bryce well, but the words brought more pain to the man's eyes than I'd ever thought I'd see. Colin was right. There were limits, even to the bond between Blood Shade and Mannequin, and Tommy's wounds were too severe. Giving Colin's family their privacy, I set about helping Isobel and Brett collect weapons from the bed. "Are there any Scimitars in the garden?"

"Oh yes," Genevieve replied, not turning from her vantage point by the window. In fact, her tone seemed strangely indifferent to Tommy's fate.

"How many?" Isobel asked without looking up.

Rather than answer, Genevieve finally turned to face us, shuffling her feet as though she were sleepwalking. Her ashen brown hair obscured her face.

"Get down!" Iain shouted, snatching up a gun and putting four rounds into Genevieve's chest just as Brett dove out of the firing line.

The Mannequin, or whatever had assumed her form, let out an ear-splitting shriek. Where her human mouth should have been, opened a jagged maw of razor-sharp teeth, while her eyes burned as red as the blood that seeped from her mouth. Blue flames began dancing around the thing's palms with a faint hiss.

If the bullets had slowed her, Colin wasn't about to count on it, throwing himself at his former servant and shoving her through the window with a loud shattering of glass and frame. The creature screamed as it fell, no longer mistakeable as Genevieve, or anything remotely human.

"If that's what I think it is, you've got to—" Before Iain could finish, Colin snatched up a heavy sword from the bed and leapt out the window after the daemon. "Okay, that works too."

There came a loud crash from the hall outside, and the guttural roar that followed sent a chill through each of us, fire or no fire.

"If you guys want to load up, now's the time," said Bryce, tilting his head at the weapons.

Isobel, Peter, and Brett didn't need to be told twice. Iain swapped his emptied gun for another as I strapped two revolvers and a long hunting knife around my waist. Not that guns would fell everything, but at this point, I was willing to seize every advantage.

"I think you'll want this," Iain said, passing Bryce what to my untrained eye looked like an Uzi.

"You read my mind?" the Mannequin asked.

Iain nodded. "You're sure you can cover us?"

Bryce squeezed his dead lover's shoulder. "That thing's in for a world of hurt. Go!"

Brett, Isobel, and Peter leapt out the window after Colin.

"Reylan?" said Iain.

"Just go! I'll push you if I have to!"

The Shaper shook his head and leapt after them. I hesitated just long enough to see the werewolf charge through the open door and cop a spray of hot silver from Bryce's gun. Staying to help the man would have been suicide, but if I couldn't do that, I could at least see Bryce make good on his promise. Judging by the howls and screams that faded as I dove out the window, he put up a damn good fight.

What greeted me as I got to my feet was madness. A monster-driven tempest punctuated by shouts, roars, popping gunshots, and the clink of clashing blades. Isobel deftly fended off two Blood Shades with a long dagger in each hand. Peter brandished his sword with the same elegance he'd used against the werewolf, though this time his foe was unseen—a Cloak Walker, I presumed. I saw Brett, a pistol in each hand and a shining black shotgun on his back, fire off a volley of shots into an enemy I'd barely words to describe—like misshapen goblins with their stunted height and gnashing teeth, yet with limbs thick and heavy, and one long, vicious claw extending from each hand. There were three of them. I thought back to Luca. The unholy side effects of their mad experiment.

Three more of the creatures burst from the bushes. No sooner had I squared my shoulders into an attack posture than three gigantic heads, each one snapping hellfire came after them, catching one of the beasties and hurling it into the air, where another head caught it, chewing it up hungrily with a short scream followed by the splintering of bone.

Good girl, Kali.

The Cerberus chased after the second of its quarry while the third beast sprinted toward me, its own jaws snapping until its head was split apart by gunfire.

"Brett!" I cried too late as a Blood Shade I'd not yet seen leapt onto his back and sank her teeth into his neck. Peter's sword whirled around in seconds, cleaving the creature's head from her shoulders in one fast, bloody movement. Yet the damage to my boy had been done. I threw my arms around his chest and pulled him to relative safety behind a large bush beside the house. Though Brett's wounds put him in little mortal danger, the creature's careless bite coupled with its violent disengagement had lost him a lot of blood. Blood I couldn't afford to share until after my next feed. Until then, he was out of action.

Iain, I thought, not knowing if the Shaper was listening, or quite how his telepathy worked. *Iain, can you hear me? I need help!*

Bit busy right now!

I looked for him in the melee, eventually finding him hunched over, brandishing a handgun of some sort. On the brick walls on either side of him perched two abominations, their feet, the talons of eagles, their wings, long and black as oil, and their faces, still a vague mockery of the humans they'd once been, yet also sharpened into wicked beaks that shrieked as they dove upon their prey. The Shaper threw himself on the ground, raised the gun and shot one out of the air, right before the other landed a nasty gash across his shoulder.

"Reylan, here!" Brett said, handing me his shotgun.

"You've got to be fucking joking."

"You don't know how to use a shotgun?"

A loud screech came from right on top of us. Without thinking I brought the butt of the gun up and clocked the harpy across the head, sending it crashing to the ground. I pinned one of its vile wings beneath my boot, pointed the rifle barrel against its breast, released the safety, cocked it, and fired, sending a spray of blood and feathers across the lawn, my boots, and a startled Brett. Not bad for a first time.

Iain rushed over to us. "Harpies? They have fucking harpies at their beck and call?"

"Never mind that. Can you influence the minds of the Scimitars?"

"Of course."

"Good. Keep yourself and Brett hidden from them as long as it takes to get you both out of here."

"Reylan—"

"I'm not arguing this with either of you! If we don't get out of here, I don't want Patricia left to fight these bastards on her own."

"You want… Wait, you want the House of Magick—"

"To back and defend the Arcadia Trust if we can't. That is, unless they want this entire city under Scimitar control. If we are, as you say, all in this together, then prove it. If the Blood Shades can't hold Sydney, it falls to the Arcadia Trust and you."

The flicker of a smile crossed Iain's lips. "Funny. For a moment, I thought you were concerned about me."

I wrapped my arm around his shoulders and pulled him into a kiss so deep, he'd no time for more sarcasm. "Go to Valia's. Deborah can take care of Brett. Then call me tomorrow night."

It didn't take long for Iain to do his work. No sooner had I turned my back than both men were gone. Were it not for the memory of Iain's kiss, I might have questioned whether they'd been there at all.

I assumed Peter had managed to dispatch his Cloak Walker foe, as I watched him help Colin fight off the creature that had assumed Genevieve's form. Any resemblance it still bore to the Mannequin was purely coincidental as its wicked dance taunted the towering Blood Shade and his nimble servant with bursts of deadly blue flame. Then, there was Isobel, still acquitting herself well against her enemies, but at no point gaining a clear advantage. Just how much longer could she hold them off? I heard Kali's low growls as three new Scimitars whose species I could not yet determine, stepped from the bushes. Those were just the ones we could see. How many more could they send? We were outnumbered, and counting the werewolf I assumed had killed Bryce, we were seriously outgunned.

I unsheathed my own weapons and went to Isobel's aid, just in time to see her land a blow across an enemy's unguarded throat. The sudden victory startled the other Blood Shade, who hesitated long enough for Isobel to run him through with her sword. Worse luck, neither of these was a killing stroke, but the impalement distracted the man long enough for me to thrust one of my own blades into his back and up through his heart. The other kept trying to stem the blood running from his throat. His Blood Shade physiology would soon slow the bleeding by itself, but if he didn't realise that, I wasn't going to tell him.

An odd rustling went through the garden as Isobel and I got out of the thrashing Scimitar's way, as though the wind had picked up some unseen force and now whistled through the leaves. Only there was no wind. The air was as still as the thickest night, save for the smoke that rose through it, and the screams and shouts of the fighting and wounded. I spun around as one piercing scream broke above all others. The man whose throat Isobel had opened fell hard to the ground, only to be dragged into the bushes and out of sight. His comrade, chest and stomach still bleeding from a gaping wound, stood slack-jawed, retreating several steps before a tall shrub blocked his escape. Yet the garden didn't slow its embrace. By the time the man realised what was happening, the vines and tendrils of several plants had staked their claim on his limbs. His every cranial orifice was full of foliage before he could even scream.

Isobel and I retreated to where Colin and Peter were trying to calm all three heads of the madly barking Kali.

"Getting some help from your garden, Colin?" I asked as another shrub devoured the body of the false Genevieve.

"Perhaps, though I wouldn't put much faith in its distinguishing friend from foe."

Whatever the garden's appetite, we had another problem. The flames that had engulfed the hall and upstairs now licked the frames of the outside windows.

"I think we'd best leave," I said.

"Where's Genevieve?" asked Peter. "If that thing replaced her, she's got to be—"

"There's no time." Colin's answer was quiet and final, a contrast to the rawness that crossed Peter's face. To lose all his blood siblings in one night… and to what? A gang of religious thugs playing with powers they couldn't understand.

"Ah, Colin?"

I looked around for the object of Isobel's warning. If any Scimitars remained, I couldn't see them. There was only the garden, blocking any path that didn't take us through the burning halls of Victoria House. Whether it was advancing or just digesting its sizeable meal, I couldn't say.

"Colin, how do we—"

A great shattering of glass above interrupted me. We shielded our eyes from fragments and cinders, opening them in time to see a fully transformed werewolf standing between us and the garden. As the beast let out its great roar, any control we had over Kali was gone as the Cerberus tore from our grasp and threw itself fearlessly upon the wolf. All three heads caught purchase, one on its throat, one on its flank, and the other on its arm. The creature tried madly to shake it loose, but Kali wouldn't yield, forcing the wolf to stagger back on its powerful, but still new and unwieldy hind legs. Still, its uninjured arm was strong. We could only watch as it grabbed the nearest of Kali's heads and dug its claws in. We heard the snapping of bone as it used its grip to toss the rest of the Cerberus away into the garden wall, where it collapsed into the leaves.

Now sure of its footing, the werewolf roared at us again.

"Colin," I muttered, catching a whiff of the beast's hot breath as it drew nearer to us. "Ideas? *Now?*"

We dove out of the way as the wolf lurched toward us. Yet its target didn't seem to be the band of cowering Blood Shades in its path, but rather the window behind us, which shattered, releasing a burst of hot air that threw the beast back with a fearsome bellow.

"This way!" came a voice from inside the house. Brett stood at the front door, his expression frantic as he shied away from angry licks of flame.

"Go on!" I barked at the others, helping Peter through the window. Colin followed, shielding his Mannequin with his jacket as they dashed through the burning hall and out to the safety of the front courtyard.

The werewolf hadn't come at us again. It just stood there, staring at us, as if it wasn't quite sure whether to eat us, swat us against the wall, or… did it recognise us?

"Reylan," Isobel cautioned. "It's not him. We have to go."

"Reylan!" Brett called again. "Come on!"

But what if it was? Rather than kill us, the thing had broken the window behind us, clearing an escape route just as Brett had arrived to help us the rest of the way. Now, despite abundant opportunity to tear us apart, it simply stood there.

"Go," I said to Isobel. "I'll be right behind you, I promise." I had to know. Chances were, my friend was right, but I couldn't leave any doubt. I just couldn't. What I wouldn't have given for Iain's powers in that moment. The wolf and I never broke eye contact as I drew closer, raising my hands in what I hoped it would see was a gesture of trust. This was it. Either Jorgas would recognise his old friend and lover, or I'd have less than a second to duck the swipe of an angry Scimitar wolf's claws.

Instead, the thing bellowed once more, startling me flat on my backside. There was no hunger in the creature's cry, only fury as its massive form began to shrink. I heard the crack of bone and watched the hair and claws recede. Left standing before me was not Jorgas, but a small, frightened man who couldn't have been much older. Standing naked before me, his face and long, dirty blonde hair were caked with blood, his eyes wide with confusion and terror as he took in the burning house and the rapidly encroaching garden.

"Help me," he pleaded in English, squeezing his shoulders. "Please help!"

I moved to grab him but the vines beat me to it, pulling him swiftly into the garden. I watched, helpless to reach him as he screamed and thrashed against the foliage, until it mercifully ripped him apart. I'd be facing the same fate if I waited any longer. I dove through the window and bolted to where Brett stood in the doorway. A hot piece of flaming timber grazed my ankle just as I reached the safety of the threshold. At least we could allay Colin's fears. No way was Victoria House falling into Scimitar hands.

Yet that man, who despite his wolfen form, and his brutal slaughter of Bryce, had given us an escape route, then begged for my help. None of it made sense. He'd been Scimitar, hadn't he?

Hadn't he?

"Get in," said Iain from behind the wheel. "We don't know where the Wound is or how many more of them might come through."

I looked up at the inferno that had engulfed Victoria House. Let them try. If the fire didn't consume them, the garden would.

"Where are we going?" I asked, sliding into the passenger seat. "Where's Colin?"

"He and Peter took another car. As for us, you tell me. Valia's?"

No way was I involving Deborah in this more than she already was. "Paddington." I gave Iain the Trust's address before turning to Isobel, an apology on the tip of my tongue. She simply stared out the window.

"Do you think they'll help?" Brett asked.

"Last time we joined forces, we defeated a god. Doesn't seem like a bad plan to deal with God's fanatics."

"You paid no small price for that victory," Iain reminded me, squeezing my hand.

This time, I did catch Isobel's look.

I shook my head. "They've already killed three members of Colin's family and had more than their share of close calls with us. What choice do we have?"

"Puts our little mate in a pretty tough position," Brett pointed out.

"If you mean Luca, he doesn't owe them a thing. Not after what they've put him through. He's Ross's kin, and if Salvatore taught us anything, it's that there's no love between them and the Scimitar right now."

"Let's hope Luca sees it that way."

"He's right, Reylan," said Iain. "Don't underestimate a desperate man's devotion to his god, especially when it's been coerced."

Coerced? The very word unsettled me. That young wolf… 'Help me.' After observing a century and a half of human behaviour, I knew it had been no trick. From what had he needed escape? The garden, or the Scimitar?

Tell me what happened back there, I thought, squeezing Iain's hand.

"Huh?" he asked. "Did you say something?"

"No," I said, focusing my thoughts again. *Because I don't think either of us want the others listening in, do you?*

This time, he heard me. *What do you mean, what happened? You were there.*

I saw an enraged werewolf open up an escape route as he fumbled an attack on us, only to have Brett waiting, ready to help us at the front door. Besides the fact that I told you to go straight to Valia's, do you know what I saw after the others had escaped?

I didn't need to explain. The memory of the wolf's human face was etched upon my mind, and now, I supposed, upon Iain's as well.

Iain let out a long, slow breath. *I know it's hard not to feel for these people after what you've been through with Luca.*

This isn't about Luca, I snapped back so fast, the words almost came out aloud. *Don't patronise me.*

What I'm saying is, you've seen what happens to the mind of a Scimitar soldier from both sides. It's torture, what these people do to their children.

I'm not convinced the man I watched die was there of his own free will.

That young man killed Bryce. He meant to rip all of you limb from limb and suck the marrow from your bones. Don't doubt that for a second. Count yourself lucky the werewolf mind is so malleable.

I couldn't force myself to look at him, instead keeping my eyes fixed on the road as we neared Paddington. *Did your interference also make him lose the change?*

It's possible, and I'd do it again. I've no compassion for religious zealots, Reylan, and while it's normally one of your most endearing qualities, you'd do well to arrest yours.

For god's sake, man! He wasn't much older than Luca!

They are not Luca! You won't honour your dead friend's memory by going soft on fundamentalist thugs. If you want to help his son, fine! Do that to the best of your ability. But coerced or otherwise, you can't save them all, and I can't save you every time you have a moment's hesitation. Why didn't you run with the others when I gave you the chance?

The truth was, I'd no good explanation, except perhaps blind optimism. My better sense had known it couldn't be him, and yet…

Jorgas really did a number on you, didn't he?

"All right, now's the part where you can get out of my head," I barked without thinking.

Iain's eyes closed as he seemed to swallow his own flash of anger. Perhaps my tone had been cruel, but my relationship with Jorgas was none of the man's business, regardless of what we were pursuing now. Isobel and Brett were wise enough to remain silent.

"I'm sorry, that was uncalled for," I said.

"But fair. I didn't mean to scratch a fresh wound."

After another minute of silence, I could no longer help myself. *Do you think he's all right?*

I thought you wanted me out of your head?

All right, so I'm a great big hypocrite. Do you?

He squeezed my hand again, only now making me realise that despite our tense exchange, I'd not let the man go. *I have a good feeling about it. That's all I can tell you.*

Nothing more was said until we reached the Arcadia Trust. A row of dim lights revealed its faux antebellum fixtures, peering through fresh jacaranda blooms in the front yard.

"Wait," Iain said, not letting go of my hand as I moved to unbuckle myself. "Something's wrong."

We watched the house for any sign substantiating his claim.

"Dude, what is it?" Brett asked.

"Reylan," Isobel cautioned. "He's right."

"Meaning what? Wrong, how?"

My old friend shook her head. "Just a feeling."

"One you shouldn't dismiss." Iain squeezed my hand.

We waited a moment longer, watching the darkened windows of the house for any sign of distress. Any sign of life at all. None came. Not even the sway of a curtain or the flick of a light.

"Well, we can't just sit here," I said at last, unbuckling my belt and opening the door.

"What are you doing?" Brett asked.

"I'll be quick."

An uncomfortable warmth sweetened the air as a breeze swept down the street. Still, as I approached the house, it remained unchanged. I tried to keep my footsteps light on the ancient, almost rotting stairs leading to the building's porch. It didn't matter. I was expected. One of the great wooden doors opened just a little to reveal a familiar pale face, peering out at me from waist height.

"Sophia," I said quietly. "Is Patricia in?"

"She can't see you right now." The words seemed to pain her, her voice almost a mockery of her usual, outspoken and confident self.

"Sophia, it's important. Please, may I come in?"

"I told you, she can't see you."

There was something profoundly wrong in the way the little girl spoke, the way she stood so rigid in the doorway, the way her eyes betrayed none of their usual arrogant spark.

"Is everything all right?" I asked.

Her only answer was the faintest tilt of her head, before a long blade severed it from her neck and let a long stream of blood run down into her dress.

I leapt back as the little body crumpled into a heap in the open doorway, and a long black boot stepped over it. The boot's owner revealed herself as a woman several inches taller than myself with jet black hair, and a steely, no-nonsense expression that made me long for the sight of Patricia at her most officious.

"Well?" she asked, making no effort to hide the bloodstained sword in her hand. "Are you coming in, or not?"

I turned and bolted across the yard, not stopping until I'd reached the car, where Iain already had the engine running. "Get us out of here, now!"

"We saw," he answered. "What the hell?"

"Just *drive*, will you?" said an all too familiar disembodied voice.

"Kelvin?"

"Drive where?" Iain asked, pulling out into the street.

"I'm open to suggestions, pretty boy. Just not here!"

"My place," I said at last. It was a risk. A huge risk, given the Scimitar's proven skill at materialising in our very homes. But what other choice did we have? "Tell Colin we'll meet him there. What the hell is going on, Kelvin? Sophia… Sophia!"

"There's nothing you could have done, pretty boy, and before you ask, Patricia's fine. Giorgios too, last I saw."

"And Luca? Suzette?"

"Hopefully your new pet's got the good sense to stay quiet. The bastards got in while I was out cleaning up *your* bloody mess at the church, though I'm fucked if I know how!"

"I think we know how," said Isobel. "You mean the Scimitars, of course?"

"Yes, the bloody Scimitars! Who else? There must be eight, maybe nine of them in there."

"Do you think they were trying to get Salvatore?" asked Brett. "I mean, they wouldn't know he's dead."

"That still wouldn't make sense," I answered. "He called their scheme blasphemy. They'd see him as a liability, if not an outright traitor."

"I'm afraid your organisation was a target long before you killed one of their soldiers," Iain chipped in. "A mixed alliance of supernatural beings, working together? They want to know more about you. Perhaps use your resources."

"Meaning Patricia's more valuable to them alive," Isobel pointed out.

"One could say the same for the Premature," Iain argued. "From my understanding, that girl was quite the researcher in her own right, *and* she carried all of Elspeth's knowledge."

"Okay mate, you tell me," said Kelvin. "Just who the hell are you and how do you know so much?"

"There'll be time for that later," I said. "If they're willing to kill Sophia so casually, it means they either got what they wanted out of her already, or they place no value on it, *or* they believe they can get it from Giorgios. He's younger and smaller. Perhaps an easier target."

"Yeah, all this is bloody interesting," Kelvin interrupted again. "What I want to know is, how'd they know?"

"What?"

"How'd they know *exactly* when to attack? Right after I got a call from you, as a matter of fact."

"What are you trying to say, mate?" Brett snarled.

"Before you get carried away on conspiracy theories, you should know they attacked Victoria House too. Colin lost three Mannequins. The rest of us barely escaped with our lives."

This revelation seemed to shut the bastard up, if only for a minute.

"Shit," he finally said.

"Reylan," Isobel murmured.

"I know. We need to take the Trust back, tonight."

"We need to do more than that," Iain pointed out. "You don't know how many loyal soldiers they've got lined up ready to do their bidding, or what the hell those soldiers will turn into once they pass through the Wounds. We might have a whole horror show waiting to burst into this city and take control. It'd make sense. A major city like Sydney, so far from House reinforcements? And once they're entrenched—"

"They'll be impossible to remove and can reshape the city into anything they want."

"And possibly cities beyond. How organised are the supernatural factions in Melbourne? Brisbane? Auckland?"

"All right, slow down a bit!" said Kelvin. "Does one of you want to explain what the fuck these freaks are doing and how?"

I took a deep breath as Isobel went over the basics in the simplest terms she could. We had bigger problems than Kelvin being out of the loop.

"Iain," I said quietly. "What time is it?"

CHAPTER THIRTEEN

I missed the nights when the threat of impending daybreak meant a fate no worse than having to settle for a less than appealing companion. How Patricia Bakker had complicated my life since! Now, as we sat around my living room with the curtains safely drawn, we faced the unenviable task of retaking Bakker's home from an army of now supernatural thugs bent on our destruction—in broad daylight.

"What's taking him so long?" asked Kelvin.

"Do you think Colin might have decided it was too near sunrise?" asked Brett. "Gone to ground somewhere light-tight?"

A loud hammering on the door answered him before an uncharacteristically agitated Colin strode into my living room with Peter close behind. "I hope you have a good explanation for why we're here, rather than in a secure, light-tight location less than fifteen minutes before sunrise."

"Colin, you've seen how these people operate. There *are* no secure locations, but protection against the light, I can do."

Giving my home a quick once-over, my former mentor did nothing to hide the look of faint disappointment that crossed his face.

Looks like someone wishes you'd married a doctor or a lawyer.

Now, I really wished Iain would get out of my head.

"What makes you think the Scimitar won't strike here?" Isobel asked.

"It's a risk," I admitted. "But I don't know where else to go on short notice. Besides, we won't be here any longer than we have to be. I want us moving on the Arcadia Trust as soon as the sun sets."

"That leaves the bastards a full day to get reinforcements, not to mention interrogate Patricia, find and kill Giorgios, Luca, and Suzette, and shore up their defenses," said Kelvin. "Not a plan, Reylan!"

"That's if they don't bring Luca back into the fold," Isobel added. "The Scimitar thrives on manipulation, and if they get him back on their side, they'll have one hell of a powerful weapon to use against us."

"Bit of an unpredictable one," said Kelvin.

"Their whole strategy has been wildly unpredictable and reckless. What makes you think they're going to change now?"

Still, it was better than ours. I had no strategy, beyond us surviving the day, at least.

Brett moved discretely to my side. "Can we talk?"

Accepting the proffered escape, I lead my Mannequin to the privacy of my bedroom. "You and Iain were very quiet in there. Do you have something to tell me?"

Brett nodded. "I'm not sure I understand what he means."

"So, he *has* been communicating with you, telepathically?" I'd suspected as much, but what could Iain possibly have to say to Brett that couldn't be said aloud?

"Look, I know he's your friend, but—"

"Never mind that. What did he say?"

"If he's right—"

"Right about *what*, damn it?"

He took a deep breath, never quite meeting my eyes. "Deborah's on her way over."

"Deborah?" My morning just got better and better.

"I'm sorry. I know I should have told you," said Iain, who now stood in the doorway.

My eyes fixed on the priest-come-Shaper-come… whatever the hell he was. "No, you should have *asked* me. World of difference, Iain."

"And you would have said what?"

"Even so," I was fighting to keep my temper. "I don't appreciate you using Brett to—"

"I apologise for the method, but we are almost out of time."

"We *are* out of time! Sunrise is in ten minutes. There's nothing we can do tonight, and by bringing Deborah here, all you've done is put her in danger as well. Why? And why Deborah?"

"Because she may be your only chance to retaking the Trust today."

"You're fucking joking," Brett said. "I'm calling her now. Telling her to go home."

"Wait," I said, not taking my eyes off Iain. "That's a big call, considering you've never met Deborah. Of course, Elspeth did."

A smile crossed the Shaper's face. "Elspeth told me everything. The power that she felt in Deborah is nothing short of extraordinary."

"Huh? Deborah's a Shaper?" Brett asked.

"Not yet. Not by a long shot. But the rudimentary ability and energy is there, running through her like… I don't have time to explain it to you. But we can do this, Reylan. I just need you to trust me. I won't let Deborah come to any harm. You have my word."

I didn't know if I wanted to kiss him or punch him. Or both. Did they have a word for humans who did both? In German, probably. "I suppose we don't have much choice.

But whatever it is you're planning ends the moment I see Deborah in any danger whatsoever. Is that understood?"

"As you wish," he said, after a pause that didn't ease my discomfort in the slightest.

"Ah, gentlemen?" called Isobel from the living room. "Not to put pressure on, but where are we sleeping?"

"We're not." Whether Iain had noticed the death-stare Colin was giving him, and was simply choosing to ignore it, I couldn't say. "Nobody here is sleeping until we get the Scimitars out of the Arcadia Trust."

"What?"

"That's a crispy plan for some of us," said Kelvin.

A sharp knock at the door spared me further explanation.

"Brett, will you please get that?" I said, turning to Iain. "Your show."

I couldn't see Kelvin bristling, but he made sure I could hear it.

"I'll ask one more time, mate," he said. "Who the hell are you?"

"He's the one who's going to get us into the Trust in broad daylight without three of us turning into torches."

"Not me, exactly," Iain said. "Speak of the devil."

"Good morning, Deborah," I said as she entered the room with a sheepish looking Brett close behind.

"Yeah, righto," she said. "Before we start, I just want to point out that it is five-thirty in the fucking morning, and if you were *anybody* else, I would have told Brett where to stick his call."

"I appreciate that, thank you."

"Good. Now, *please* tell me you have coffee."

"He does," Iain answered for me. "And given what we have to discuss, I think coffee would be an excellent idea."

*   *   *

Deborah took one last sip of coffee before putting her mug down in the sink with a metallic thump. Not wishing to overwhelm her with Iain's revelation, we'd taken her to the kitchen, where she now leaned against the bench, ignoring the towering presence of Colin, who'd insisted on being present for our conversation.

"You're taking this remarkably well," I said.

"It's not the first time I've been called a witch."

"I take it you don't believe me?" Iain asked.

"Of course I don't!"

Colin rolled his eyes. "Utter waste of time."

"Deborah, I know it seems far fetched."

"Far fetched? Not so much. Vampires... sorry, *Blood Shades?*" She spat the term out with such contempt I feared Colin would take her head off then and there. "I'll admit, that took some getting used to, but okay. Werewolves? Sure. Witches? Hell, why not? But me? You're telling *me* that I've got some kind of... latent witchy power?"

"Most Shapers live out their entire lives undiscovered," Iain continued. "They might become doctors, or scientists, or artists, or businesspeople, knowing they've got a natural aptitude for something bigger, like they're bound for greatness somehow, and they're right. But it is so much more than that. You said a moment ago that you'd always felt this connection when you touched someone who was hurt, how it always seemed to make them feel better, or how you could relieve a days-long headache just by touching someone's neck."

"Oh, come on! That's not magick! That's just—"

"Give me a better example. The one you're holding back."

Deborah folded her arms, setting her gaze on the empty coffee cup. "I don't know what you're talking about."

"The moment in your life you still can't explain. The one you thought about mentioning before you decided we wouldn't believe it. Except I would believe it, Deborah. So, I think, would Reylan."

Another loud knock at my door broke the silence.

"Bloody hell, you're popular," came Kelvin's disembodied voice.

"Brett?" I called out.

"Got it."

"Mister Raymond?"

Christ! Not now.

"Excuse me," I muttered, returning to the living room determined to get rid of Dorotha as quickly and as gently as possible. "Dorotha, this really isn't a good—"

"Mister Raymond! You not tell me you have so many guests at this hour. This is not one of your special parties, is it? I mean, Miss Isobel is here."

"No, it's not."

"Special parties?" Isobel asked. "Now I feel left out."

I didn't bite. "What can I do for you, Dorotha?"

"Oh, I was hoping that nice Father Grieg was here. Or are you seeing him soon? I wanted to give him this." She lifted the corner of the gigantic plastic container she'd brought in, allowing the smell of fresh, sugary pastries to fill the room.

"That's very kind of you. I'm sure he'll enjoy them. Now, I'm very sorry, Dorotha, I really must—"

"We'll all enjoy them," Brett said, taking Dorotha's arm.

"Ah! You like cinnamon, I hope?" she said as he guided her to the sofa.

I tossed Brett a nod of thanks before returning to the kitchen, where Iain kept Deborah in earnest conversation. But the woman I saw before me, who only moments ago had so casually dismissed her latent power, now seemed on the verge of shaking.

"Your mother," Iain said in a confidential tone. "They gave her two months, or was it three?"

"Look," murmured Deborah. "I don't know what you're trying to do, but don't."

"Iain," I said. "What the hell are you—"

"All I'm doing is asking you to be honest with us, and with yourself," he continued, ignoring me. "The day you sat and read to her? When you'd finished, the nurses told you you'd been reading for six hours. That neither you, nor your mother had responded when it was time for lunch, or when they'd asked you to leave. And that you hadn't turned a single page. Stranger than that, when they ran the next set of tests on your mother, she was looking at a long, healthy life. They didn't discharge her right away, of course. They had to run more tests. Find a rational explanation for this miraculous recovery. They never did, did they?"

"They… they couldn't. I…"

"But you could," Iain said, leaning closer, his voice now a whisper. "Because you felt what's in you, Deborah. What's been in you since you were a child. Unfocused and unpracticed, but it is there."

Deborah's uncertainty gave way to defiance "So, what? Why am I even here?"

"You're here because we need you to put those gifts into practice."

"To what end?"

"To the end of saving all our lives."

My human confidante burst out laughing despite herself, turning her gaze on me. "Where'd you find this guy? I mean, he's cute, but… Hey, what's it actually like, having sex with a mind reader?"

"Deborah," I said. "You should listen to him."

"I am! But really, I want to know. I mean, does he anticipate—"

"Avoiding this won't make it go away, and we are running out of time," said Iain, for the first time showing his own exasperation.

"Father Grieg? I thought it was you! Forgive me, I know you are busy."

"Nice to see you well, my child," the Shaper answered, quickly recovering his composure.

Deborah wasn't having it. "Looks like you guys have got yourselves a witch already."

"Now, look!" I finally barked, hoping Dorotha hadn't heard Deborah's barb. "I'm sorry we're not all getting to know one another under better circumstances. Deborah, I'm sorry to have dragged you into all of this, and Dorotha, I'm sorry to be rude. Hell, I'm sorry either of you even know what the hell we are or what we do!"

"*She knows?*" Dorotha and Deborah said almost at once.

"Yes! Yes! She knows! You know! Some highly irritable nun from Prague, or Amsterdam, or wherever the hell she's from knows! And do you know who else knows? An army of trained assassins, who've murdered several of us and just cut the head off a little girl with no more compunction than you or I might have swatting a fly. So, you will all, I hope, forgive me if I am out of patience! Because if these people get a foothold in this city, they will track down and eliminate each and every person like us, along with any human to whom we're attached. More than that, they're willing to *become* us, everything they've ever despised, in order to accomplish that goal. I can only imagine what that might unleash on the city once their aims are achieved. So, if anyone here is in any way comfortable with that outcome, the door is there. Otherwise, we're solving this problem *today*. Is that perfectly clear to one and all?"

Nothing. Not so much as a smart remark from Kelvin.

"Right answer," I continued. "Now, I'm no expert on any of this, but you are all in my house. That means, while I may not always be right, I am always in charge. If anyone has a problem with that—"

"We know where the door is," Kelvin said. "Don't worry, pretty boy. Not going anywhere."

"Who said that? I hear a voice, but no-one is—"

"Dorotha…" Christ. Where did I even begin? "This is Kelvin. He's just like you, only he can't be seen. Trust me, he's there. Kelvin, this is Dorotha, my—"

"Your tenant. I know."

"You have been spying on me?"

"Dorotha!" I barely managed to keep my voice down, all patience now thoroughly exhausted. "Please don't think I'm insensitive to how this must look. Again, I am truly sorry that you've been dragged into any of it. But for your own safety, please, go home."

From Deborah's bewilderment to Colin's barely contained fury that our natures were already so widely known, I wasn't sure Dorotha would escape the room alive, much less live to tangle with the Scimitars.

"No," the old woman said at last.

"I'm sorry?"

"You ask me to go home? To sit in my chair and pretend like there is nothing wrong? I tell you no, Mister Raymond."

"Dorotha, I'm sorry, but—"

"You keep saying that! 'Sorry, so sorry, everybody is so sorry.' Do you know, any of you, what makes men so sorry?"

Before any of us could answer, she rolled up her sleeve to reveal the faint blue remnants of a tattoo on her forearm, well faded with time, but unmistakably a series of numbers. Now that I thought of it, I'd never seen Dorotha without long sleeves before, even in the heat of summer. She must have been no more than a child.

"You see now, that I understand what you say," she continued. "If these people would destroy you, for… for being what you are, then in any way I can, I will help."

"Very well then, Sister," Iain said. "Could we perhaps trouble you for some candles?"

*　　*　　*

"I feel ridiculous!"

It was hard to argue with Deborah as I sat on the floor, my weight evenly distributed between my knees, holding Isobel and Colin's hands like a troupe of children in school. Slowly circling us counter-clockwise like sharks were Iain and Deborah, while the Mannequins and Dorotha looked on. I could only imagine what was going through Kelvin's mind.

"Focus on me. Listen to my voice. Look into my eyes—"

"Ow!" Deborah barked, tripping.

"Minding the candles," Iain said.

"Fine. Hey, shouldn't those be black?"

"We're not trying to channel Satan."

"Do you think he'd help?"

"No. Now, concentrate."

"What's this supposed to do again?" asked Brett.

"You've also never consciously cast a spell before," Iain said to Deborah. "We need to amplify your abilities as much as possible."

"Right, and why can't you just cast it yourself?"

"Not my quarter," he said with a smile. "Quarters being the four primary disciplines of magick. But you can manipulate the physical and natural world."

"So… we're fucking with the laws of nature?"

"Just as you've been doing your whole life."

"I'm confused," said Brett "Are we supposed to just sit here?"

"Wait."

"Waste of time," Kelvin snapped. "This isn't doing anything!"

"Be quiet!" Dorotha said firmly. "Let them work."

Though I swore I heard Kelvin grumbling, they complied, watching Iain and Deborah move faster and faster, circling us like some demented carousel.

"You look like a theatre sports exercise," said Peter.

"We're going to look a lot more like one in a minute. Dorotha, in lieu of drums, I need you to listen very carefully to the rhythm I'm about to tap out on my leg, then repeat it, understood? All of you, except for the Blood Shades, repeat the rhythm exactly in time with Dorotha."

"This is ridiculous."

"Quiet!" Dorotha hushed Kelvin again, falling silent herself as she listened to Iain's rhythm, a short burst of four claps followed by a single long clap, then another short one. A second later, she echoed him precisely on her own knees, beckoning Brett and Peter to join her, until Kelvin added a fourth set in synch.

"Excellent, keep it going," Iain instructed, his steps breaking into a light canter around my room. "Don't stop until I tell you. Deborah, try to keep up with me."

"Sure," she got out almost stumbling again as she tried to mimic his steps. "You want me to start chanting too?"

"Just repeat the words after me."

None of us spoke as they continued circling. Iain recited a string of utterances in a language I didn't recognise. Deborah did her best to repeat the words without breaking her stride. They continued circling on opposite sides of the ring they'd formed around us. Each time Deborah stuttered or hesitated, Iain urged her on, until her repetitions grew faster and faster, almost matching him until at last, they spoke in unison in an uninterrupted stream of speech.

"My goodness! I feel so strange!"

This time, Kelvin hushed Dorotha as Iain and Deborah's steps and words picked up speed. I too felt the odd sensation, first in my fingertips, then up my arms and across the rest of my skin. Exchanging looks with Isobel and Colin, it didn't take long to realise they were feeling the same sensation. Not a tingling as such. More of a thick, oily presence, sliding up our limbs and across our bodies. Raw, irrational panic seized me as it engulfed my mouth, nose, and eyes. Yet as it wrapped around my head, sealing itself around the small of my back, fear gave way to an odd serenity. Even a sense of security, as though the substance or energy that had enclosed us now clung like a second skin. As the chanting between the Shaper and his apprentice slowed, the three of us let go of each other, trying to get used to the sensation.

"How do you feel?" Iain asked. "You too, Deborah."

"Dizzy," the human admitted as Brett offered her his arm.

"So long as it's not violent nausea, I'm calling that a win. And the three of you?"

"Iain," I got out. "What just happened?"

"This." He grabbed the curtains and threw them open.

I lurched backward in a futile attempt to escape the morning light that streamed through the now naked window. From the corner of my eye, I saw Colin leap to his feet and bound toward Iain, only to stop and stare in amazement as the light bathed our hitherto un-tanned skins, doing no damage whatsoever.

"Well, fuck me," said Kelvin.

"Iain…" I said, barely able to breathe. "What the hell did you just do?"

CHAPTER FOURTEEN

Our plan, such as it was, didn't fill me with confidence, but neither did the nauseating warmth of sunlight on my face. Even wearing a pair of Brett's sunglasses—a bizarre sensation that made me question how humans who wore such accessories remained sane—offered little relief. His assurance that Colin, Isobel, and I looked 'kind of badass' in them had done little to boost my morale.

Still, it could have been worse.

"I feel ridiculous."

I could have been dressed like Brett and Peter.

"Well, you look adorable." Peter grinned, seemingly proud of his disguise and planned diversion as he straightened Brett's black nametag. 'Elder Woods' and 'Elder Hill' did make a pretty fetching pair. Almost as fetching as the nametags' original owners, as I recalled.

"Fine," said Brett. "After today, we never speak of this again."

That's okay. Deborah took photos.

"Jesus," I muttered. "Iain, are you listening?"

Yes, and through no small effort at this distance. Do you want my help or not?

Having established a kinship with each of them, the Shaper had stayed behind to ensure Deborah and Dorotha were safe. If the Scimitar decided to spring any nasty surprises, he was the best early warning system the two humans could have.

Deborah's resting. She and I have a lot to talk about.

The thought of that conversation going on in my absence made me more uncomfortable than I wanted to admit.

I heard that.

"Damn you!" I said aloud, startling Isobel. "Sorry."

"Any chance your psychic mate could let us all in on this conversation?" Kelvin asked. "Since we're the ones about to risk our bloody lives."

I can only communicate telepathically with one of you at a time. Any more than that, we'd risk crossing psychic wires and believe me, that is something you'd rather avoid. But I can read all your emotional states at once. If any of you runs into trouble, I can alert the others and send help.

"Okay, fine," I said, quickly repeating what he'd just told me for the benefit of my passengers.

"So, he's like a conference call on really shitty wi-fi?"

"Kelvin…"

We need to talk about your taste in friends.

I imagined we'd have plenty more to talk about. Deborah, for one.

She's fine. Exhausted, but that's to be expected, pre-Emergence.

Pre-Emergence?

Not something I have time to go into right now, and nothing I'd let a group of non-Shapers witness, to say nothing of the danger it would put you all in.

All right, you've made your point.

I know you're concerned. Deborah's Emergence will come, when she's ready and not before. You have my word.

My grip on the steering wheel tightened. One thing at a time. What on earth had possessed me to drive? I hadn't driven an actual vehicle since we'd lived in Los Angeles, sixty years ago. I was handling it well, considering. I'd tried not to take it personally when Colin had elected to walk. "So, one more time. Brett, Peter, and Kelvin, I'm dropping you two blocks from the Trust, where Colin's meeting us. Kelvin, you're there—"

"To make sure nothing happens to your pets. I know."

"I mean it. We want at least one, ideally more of the Scimitars distracted at the front door for as long as possible. Play the charade as long as you can while Colin, Isobel, and I take care of any guards at the rear and side doors. Hopefully, by the time anyone knows we're there, it won't make a difference."

"What about Luca?" asked Isobel.

"If he's still alive, they've either taken him captive, or he's in the cellar with Suzette. Either way, I can't risk bringing him into the sunlight."

"A shame. He'd be a powerful weapon."

"Isobel."

"All right. Forget I mentioned it."

I soon spied Colin, waiting for us in the shade of a large tree. I dropped off Brett, Peter, and Kelvin as we collected him, then drove around to a side street and pulled into the curb. Even as Colin approached us, Isobel hesitated.

"Are you sure you want to do this?" I asked. "I know Patricia—"

"The alternative is horrifying." She unclipped her seatbelt and opened the door.

"Reylan, are you coming?"

There was no adjusting quickly to the sensation of sunlight on my skin, and Iain had offered no guarantees on how long the effect would last. I did my best to dismiss the churning in my stomach as we made our way to the back of the Trust. The back gate could be accessed via a small laneway, and jumping the fence was no great trial for one of our kind. Still, we had to act fast.

"Besides the front door and the one into the rear courtyard, there's a side entrance at the northern end of the building," Isobel briefed us. "We have to assume both entrances are guarded."

"I can't see two presenting much of a challenge," said Colin.

"The question is how heavily guarded," I said. "There's no point charging in only to find ourselves outnumbered five to one. How many can you smell?"

Isobel frowned. "Hard to say. The garden's not helping. You?"

"The same. Could be one or fifty."

"Then we focus on the exits, and god help any of them who get in our way."

"Agreed," I said. "Though in this case, I'm hoping their god abandoned them long ago."

Colin smiled at that.

"Are you ready?" I asked Isobel.

Two shining blades sprang from the cuffs of her sleeves, their hilts fitting snugly into the palms of her hands. "As soon as you are."

No sooner had I nodded than Isobel was over the fence, charging up the yard with Blood Shade speed. A blade flashed in her hand, opening the hapless sentry's throat before he had time to look up. Grasping at the wound, the man hadn't even a chance to scream. A severe looking woman made the mistake of coming outside to investigate the fuss, only to find one of Isobel's blades in her neck.

While Colin dashed around to the northern entrance, I went to Isobel's side, making sure the two were dead before regaining my feet. Too easy. Far, far too easy.

"Human," I said quietly. "They're only human."

"With no reason to think we'd attack before nightfall, why would they risk their supernatural soldiers?"

"Unless those soldiers are Blood Shades, in which case, they can't."

"Or they're keeping them inside." To my dismay, her eyes fell upon the wine cellar. "Why not?"

"Because I've no idea if he's immune to sunlight."

"If he's a Death Shade, I'm willing to take that risk."

I tightened my fists. About the least productive thing I could think of doing just now was fighting with Isobel. "He's only just got his life back. I can't and won't—" My heart leapt into my throat as she dove upon the cellar door and wrenched it open with preternatural speed and strength. "What do you think you're doing?"

She peered into the pit. "You can relax. He's not here."

"Hello?" came a small voice. "Who's there? Help!"

"Suzette?" I hissed, trying to hush her quiet. "Are you all right? Keep your voice down."

"I… I don't know. They grabbed Luca and took him inside. We couldn't stop them."

"Where are you going?" I asked Isobel, who already had a foot on the ladder.

"To get her out. She's not going to hurt anyone."

Sure enough, we had the girl free and above ground within minutes, though she still looked a little worse for wear.

"Listen to me," I said, keeping my voice low. "I'm going to give you my address. There are people there who'll protect you until we get Luca back."

"Oh, fuck off!" she said under her breath.

"Suzette—"

"No." She slipped form my grasp and looked around the yard, finally wrenching a garden fork from an empty bed of soil and brandishing it. "*We're* getting him back, so you can either tell me where to stab somebody or get out of my way, because you're not forgetting about me again."

"All right," I said, starting to like her. "Stay close. I'm still hoping you won't have to stab—"

The comforting sound of the front doorbell announced the arrival of our diversion. So far, so good.

"Come on," Isobel whispered, slipping through the back door that had spilled the two ill-fated guards.

Suzette and I followed as silently as we were able, hoping to god that Brett and Peter were a convincing enough—

"You!"

I clapped a hand over the man's mouth, recognising the scent immediately. Blood Shade. Against better sense I forced him face first into the sunlight, covering his scream as his skin splintered under the rays. Newly changed Blood Shades began their immortality unusually sensitive to the sun, and this one couldn't have been more than a day or two old. Satisfied he'd properly burn, I lifted my blade and cut his throat for good measure before releasing him, singing my hand in the process.

I overheard Brett and Peter bluff their last promises of the Kingdom of Heaven before shots rang out and a woman screamed on the other side of the building. The good word of Joseph Smith gave way to a furious din at the front door, right before an unseen force knocked me to the floor. I barely managed to push the Cloak Walker off me before Isobel sank both her daggers into its skull. I rolled the corpse away just in time to see another man coming at us with a long sword. Before either Isobel or I could react, Suzette peeked out from behind a door where she'd taken cover and sunk her fork into the man's neck with all her newfound Mannequin strength. She fell back with an expression of disbelief and repulsion.

"Holy fuck! Did I kill him?"

"Look out!" I called, just as a shot stopped another assailant in his tracks. The man barely had time to realise a bullet was lodged in his skull before a machete came down and split it in two. Even a Blood Shade wouldn't recover from that kind of injury in a hurry. Kelvin wrenched out the blade and swiftly separated the bleeding head from its body just to make sure. Both head and body ignited for an instant, then vanished in a puff of ash.

Perhaps we were foolish, bursting into the ballroom with no idea how many would be waiting for us. Patricia and Giorgios were captives, of course, the latter held prisoner by same imposing woman who'd executed Sophia. Licks of blue flame burst from her fingertips, surrounding the Premature like a cage of energy. Also in the room were Colin… and Luca.

"Any closer, Blood Shade—"

"You'll what? Murder him like you did his sister? I thought that was your entire purpose."

"Reylan—"

"Go on," I said. "Our lives mean nothing to you, so do it! Unless you're afraid? Unless you're just like the other sad little Scimitars, who decided to embrace their gifts only to find they couldn't control them. I hope betraying your god was worth it."

"You talk too much," the woman answered, otherwise unmoving. "I assume by your confidence that my guards are dead?"

Brett and Peter burst into the room wielding vicious looking knives, their faces, hair, and crisp white shirts spattered with blood.

"I'd call that a good assumption."

"It's over, Greta," said Patricia, her tone cool and even as ever. "Your army's gone. You've failed. Go home."

"Failed?" the woman asked, her brief confusion spreading into a broad grin. "Oh, Sister. You think *this* was our main objective? You have no idea what's unfolding here. But you will."

"When your reinforcements arrive?" I guessed. "What makes you think we won't dispatch them as quickly as we did the last? You may outnumber us. Hell, you may have abducted and coerced dozens, perhaps hundreds of supernatural children to do your bidding. Twisted them against their own natures—"

"But you can't control them," Isobel finished. "Just as they can't control their own powers. They're wearing supernatural bodies without the slightest idea how to inhabit or wield them."

"Greta," I said. "Look at what so few of us were able to do to the first waves of your 'army.' How many lives will end for this? Even if you were able to overwhelm and destroy us, what then? You'll have abandoned everything the Scimitar believes in and for what? A city the ancient Houses couldn't care less about?"

"Call off your reinforcements, Scimitar," Colin said. "No more blood will be spilled today."

"You're the Haitian," the woman said, her smile unchanged. "The eyes and ears of the Bloodites in Sydney. Why don't I give you something interesting to report?"

I tensed as a Wound began to open behind her, ripples of pink and orange light opening onto an endless darkness beyond.

"Reylan…" Patricia said.

"Try to stop me, and you can say goodbye to this little blood sipper. Besides, don't tell me you're not in the least bit curious."

I tensed for a fight as a man stepped from the Wound.

Iain.

I couldn't speak, even as every set of eyes in the room fell upon me. The screaming accusations within me found fury but no voice. Nor was there any point in throwing myself on him and tearing his throat out with my raw teeth. This man I'd allowed into my home, my mind, my bed… Shaper. Scimitar. *Judas.*

"You're a dead man."

"Reylan—"

"*LIAR!*"

"Before you leap to judgement," Greta continued, "There bears some—"

"What? Explanation?" What was there to explain? He'd tricked us, myself most of all. One of their number, gifted in the magickal arts, hiding in plain sight. He'd even assumed the persona of a bloody priest, just to drive the sick joke home! I stared into his eyes. Far from the eyes of a scornful victor, or remorseful betrayer, they seemed to pity me. It infuriated me all the more.

"I know what you're thinking."

"That would hardly take a bloody mind-reader right now! I swear to whatever hellish god you people worship, if you've harmed Deborah or Dorotha in any way—"

"They are both well out of harm's way" he said. "I gave you my word."

"Right now, your word means fuck all to me."

He sighed, taking an awfully bold step forward. "Why would we harm one of our own? Especially one beginning to show such promise?"

Nobody said a word. One of their own?

"Are our friends in place?" Greta asked.

"Ready and waiting for your word."

There was something about the tilt of Iain's lips. Something about the way he looked at me. I was sure Isobel had noticed it too.

"Let's not keep them waiting any longer," the woman said.

"Reylan?" Patricia asked as the boot of the first Scimitar soldier pierced the barrier.

The full form of a lithe, athletic young man collapsed through the barrier to the ground, coughing and gasping for air. Peter and Brett raised their weapons.

"Wait," I said. Greta still held Giorgios hostage, after all. But something wasn't right.

The man who'd burst through the barrier lifted his head with undisguised contempt. If a supernatural change was to take place, it had not yet done so. When his dark eyes fixed on Luca, his disdain gave way to a scarlet strain of pure murder. If he touched the boy, I would personally make sure he was the last of his brethren to die.

"Renato?" Luca whispered. "Renato!" Before I could stop him, he dove forward and tried to embrace the man, only to be pushed away. The pair littered the rapid-fire Italian that followed with too many idioms and curses for me to follow. But the pain of betrayal on Luca's face said enough as he reached again for his former... comrade? Friend?

Oh.

Reylan.

I turned upon Iain, my contempt no better disguised than Renato's. *One more word out of you—*

Reylan, if you care about that boy, grab him, now!

Another Scimitar emerged from the Wound, just as the first, Renato, belted Luca hard across the mouth. I went to the boy's side, only to see a third intruder join us. I grabbed hold of Luca's shoulders just in time to stop him launching himself at Renato again. For all the lies and misdirection, I believed Iain now. The look he'd given me had been that of a man who knew precisely what he was doing. Colin hissed, fangs bared as a fourth Scimitar emerged from the Wound.

"I wouldn't do that, if I were you, Haitian," said Greta. "These aren't your former slave masters."

"Liar!" Luca screeched, launching himself at Renato so hard I could barely restrain him.

Reylan, you don't have much time.
Time until what? Answer me!

Two more Scimitars had stepped from the Wound. Whether they knew an immediate attack to be suicide, or just wanted to show off their numbers, they fanned out, sizing us up. Renato however remained fixed on Luca, letting forth another stream of slurs. Those I managed to catch included 'perversion,' 'abomination,' 'corrupter,' and finally, 'faggot.'

Not even my Blood Shade strength could hold Luca back. The boy broke free and toppled Renato to the ground, burying his face in the young man's… Oh, shit.

Renato's screams pierced the air. His colleagues pulled Luca away, only to be shaken off with ease by the rapidly transforming Death Shade.

"Reylan!" Patricia called.

"Stay back!"

Another Scimitar emerged from the Wound, only to have Luca fall upon him until his increasingly weakened colleagues dragged him free. At this rate, we had only to stand back and let Luca have his way with the intruders. Joining the fray ourselves would have been suicide.

Renato, meanwhile, clutched his bleeding neck, crying out in pain as he tried to pull himself along the floor toward Iain. The Shaper offered him only the briefest glance before exchanging a look with Greta, who finally released Giorgios from his prison. The boy scampered to Patricia's side.

As the two Shapers withdrew to the far wall, I knew they'd given us far from the whole story. Yet I couldn't take my eyes off Renato. Nor the being that now emerged behind him, its body a tangle of hot white energy strands, held together in mid-air, propelled by six thicker tendrils that extended to the floor. No, seven. It was hard to tell amid the light they cast.

"Reylan?" Patricia said again. "I think we should leave."

"You should listen to her, Blood Shade," said Greta. "This is more than you're ready to handle."

Renato startled as one of the tendrils wrapped around his boot, holding him firm. Another clasped his opposite wrist, dragging him across the floor toward the light creature.

"Help me!" he cried out in English, before repeating his plea in panicked, high-pitched Italian. What aid did he think Luca would give him? The boy had already killed one of the other Scimitars. The rest of the pack weren't looking so hot either.

Three more of the light creatures broke through the Wound, ignoring Renato in favour of the surviving Scimitars. Renato screamed once more as one of his pursuer's tendrils stabbed through his body, exiting just below his bleeding neck. This time, his pleas seemed to register with Luca, as the Death Shade looked up in time to see the thing retreating toward the Wound with Renato in its clutches. It wasn't long before the other Scimitars found themselves skewered with tendrils, each being dragged toward the void.

Greta and Iain's utter passivity said everything. A trap. An elaborate House of Magick scheme to destroy the Scimitars, now coming to grim fruition.

"Everybody out!" I heard the sound of a door being thrown open. Patricia, Giorgios, Brett, and Peter bolted toward it, not looking back. "Isobel, I told you to go!"

"I'm not leaving you."

Neither was Colin. I wasn't going to force the point.

"You know what they are, don't you?" I asked.

"I know you're better off dead than letting them take you."

Luca stared at us, tears in his black, pit-like eyes. He'd understood every word. As the other Scimitars were pulled inside, he grabbed Renato's head and swiftly broke the man's neck. A great howling wind swept through the room as the being dropped the body to the floor, withdrawing its tendrils.

As if in response, an even greater howling, one that seemed composed of a hundred such voices responded from within the Wound. The anguished screams of what sounded like dozens, maybe hundreds of souls followed. The remaining Scimitars. All too human. All being dragged to… what, exactly?

I advanced on Greta. "What the hell did you just do?"

"Destroyed one of the most enduring and dangerous threats to both our Houses. You're welcome."

Staring into her eyes, I loosened my grip. How could I have been so foolish?

"The Scimitar of Light didn't just choose to embrace their monstrous natures, did they? The House of Magick manipulated them. You planned this!"

"When we first learned that the Wounds could be controlled and used as a form of transport, that sowed the seed. All it took was a few good infiltrators, and patience. Eventually, those consumed by blind hate will accept any sin that furthers their cause."

"And when they were ready, you sent them right to our doorstep."

"The Scimitar would never attack us, nor the House of Blood directly. The Arcadia Trust offered a more realistic and tempting target. If they succeeded in eliminating you, Sydney and the rest of your country would be theirs to take."

"Meanwhile, you stood to lose nothing," said Colin, approaching us. "Whether they succeeded or died trying."

"We took care never to stack the odds too high against you. I'm deeply sorry for your losses, but you do understand, it had to look real."

"And now?" I asked.

The Shaper offered us a wan smile. "Now, they pay for their sins."

"Reylan!"

I turned in the direction of Isobel's cry just in time to see the light creature knock Luca off his feet and drag him toward the Wound.

"No!" came the shrill voice of Suzette from the shadows. I watched helplessly as Isobel dove to stop her only to be knocked aside by the creature.

Iain's arms closed around my shoulders before I could go after them myself.

"Let me go, damn you!"

But Iain would not relent. The creature skewered Luca and Suzette with its tendrils, swiftly dragging them both into the Wound before I could break free. All that remained was the dark, shining void of the Wound itself.

I bellowed with rage, grabbing Iain by his jacket and throwing him up against the wall.

Reylan, enough!

My breath heaved as I paused, not loosening my grip. His telepathic words still echoed in my head.

"There was nothing you could have done," he said, aloud this time. "I'm sorry."

Nothing I could have done? I'd done plenty! Bringing Luca here. Failing to kill Suzette when I'd known it would be a mercy. Who knew now what fate awaited them?

"I suggest we close up before those creatures decide to bring their masters additional offerings," Greta said, not taking her eyes off... Isobel. Why was she so intent upon Isobel?

"Agreed." Colin rounded on Greta, lifting her by her throat as if she were weightless. "But I think we should make sure their gods are thoroughly appeased. Isobel?"

Getting to her feet, my old friend fixed all of her attention on the Wound.

"Wait," Iain cried out. "Are you mad? We barely escaped with our lives and you—"

"You listen very carefully to my words, false priest. I'm letting you live only because I want the House of Magick to know exactly what happened here today. I want them to know the exact fate that befell the architect of a plan that killed three members of my family, and most importantly, I want them to know that if they *ever* bring their machinations to this city again, it won't be some human nun who destroys them."

I heard Greta's futile attempts to choke out a scream as the white tendrils emerged from the Wound once more, coming ever closer.

"You understand, it has to look real." Ignoring his captive's screams, Colin tossed her into the creature's writhing grasp. Greta barely had time to call for Iain's help before the thing pulled her into the Wound. Watching with satisfaction. Colin didn't see the tendril around his boot.

"Colin!"

My former mentor landed hard against the wooden floor, lashing out helplessly at the creature before he too was gone.

"No!" Peter rushed into the room, seized with panic. I caught him in my arms just as Brett secured a grip on his shoulders, but the man continued to struggle and wail with despair.

"Peter! Pete, stop!" Brett's assurances did nothing to console the man, even as his struggle weakened. "He's gone, mate. I'm sorry. He's gone."

Satisfied that Peter wasn't going to do anything stupid, I rounded on Iain and threw him up against the wall.

"What the—"

"You listen to me very closely! I've danced to your tune pretty damn well these past few days, but for your sake, there had better be a way to get our people back, or you won't have the chance to tell anyone what happened here today. Is that at all unclear?"

"Get them back? Did you not see what those things do?"

"*Wrong answer!*" I shook him hard again. "You and your comrade seemed quite comfortable bringing those things within inches of taking us all through that damn portal, so don't tell me there's no way to rescue our people or I am going to be very, *very* unhappy!"

"Reylan, I'm sorry, but he's right." The voice of pessimism had not been Iain's, but Isobel's. "You saw what happened. There's nothing to be done once those things latch hold except end it, quickly."

And it was too late for that. I tensed my grip on Iain once more, wanting so much to hit him. To hurl him inside the Wound. Anything I could do to make myself feel better, as if more violence was going to undo this mess. Luca, Suzette, Colin, Sophia, Bryce, Tommy, Genevieve, the Scimitars... How many more would fall victim to this mad scheme? Not Iain. At least, not by my hand.

"We need to close this thing," Patricia said, rejoining us. "I trust one of you knows how?"

Iain and Isobel exchanged a glance before Iain spoke. "That's a more complicated procedure."

"Simplify it, quickly."

Iain grimaced, offering me his hand. "I guess I'd be a fool to ask if you still trusted me?"

I shook my head. "I have far worse things to call you right now. As for trusting you, do I have a choice?"

His hand closed around mine before I could resist. "No."

Patricia calling my name was the last thing I heard before the Shaper pulled me into the Wound.

CHAPTER FIFTEEN

The steady hum of a dozen conversations, underpinned by faint jazz music did nothing to alleviate my splitting headache as I slowly came to. I felt the roughness of cheap curtain on my cheek, as well as the cool timber of a hard seat beneath me. The smell of cigarettes and human perspiration filled my nose...

A familiar smell that now defied all logic and reason.

Slowly righting myself, I scanned the room, not at all trusting what I saw. The dozen or so well-built young men lounging on tattered couches, or leaning across the bar, posturing to offer the best show of their bodies, cheap white singlets hanging from their athletic shoulders, suspenders pulled just far enough apart so as to not spoil the view of well worked chests. Sometimes with a young man on one arm, or both, sometimes in earnest conversation with a well-dressed peer, a decidedly mixed crowd of men mingled among these proud peacocks, exchanging words, lighters, wry smiles, affectionate touches, and just occasionally, open, sensual kisses.

All my senses could not be lying to me, could they? I even recognised the bar, though the name escaped me as I tried in earnest to listen in on one fellow's conversation with one of the singlet-clad boys. German. All of them, speaking German.

Where the hell was I?

"*Entschuldigung*," I attempted to excuse myself into the conversation of two men at the bar.

The pair ignored me as if they'd not heard.

"*Entschuldigung, bitte*," I said, more forcefully. Surely my accent hadn't grown that sloppy? I turned my attention upon the bartender. "*Entschuldigung, mein Herr, bitte.*"

"They won't answer you."

I turned to the familiar voice that addressed me from a darkened corner of the room.

Iain slid from a leather couch until he stood where I could see him. "They're aware enough of your presence not to bump into you, but that's about all."

"What is this? Where the hell are we? I know this place."

He nodded, face as blank as the curtains blocking the windows. "Perhaps it's where you felt most at peace? In any case, it's your mind that's brought us here, so it must have some importance to you."

"Some importance? It's... Berlin, obviously, but... Damn it, *when* are we?"

"I'd have thought that was clear by the window dressing. We're in the Weimar years you look back on so fondly. Except of course, we're not."

I stared at him, incredulous. "What do you mean? Talk sense!"

"You don't remember, do you? We're inside the Wound."

Acute panic ripped through me. "Those things—"

"They didn't bring you here. I did."

My hands were on Iain before he had time to react, shoving him hard into the nearest corner. A few of the patrons lifted their heads at the commotion.

"Keep it down," Iain said, taking hold of the fist I'd wrapped around his collar. "Or you *will* attract somebody's attention, and in this place, that's something you do not want."

"I thought you said they couldn't see or hear?"

"That's not exactly what I said. Look, even if I could answer half your questions about this place, there's no time. If we don't close the Wound, it's going to keep reappearing, and all the Patrons and beings like them will see is an irresistible opportunity to breach that opening."

"And send more of those creatures?"

"Or worse. Never mind the effect this place could have on our corporeal bodies and minds. Now, I know how the House of Magick enabled the Scimitar to open the Wounds, and I know how to collapse them. But you need to come with me. I'd ask if you trust me, but as you said, you don't have a choice."

I looked to the all too real recreation of the bar, to the equally real figures loafing around it, resigned to poverty and prostitution, ambivalent to a world about to come crashing down around their heads. "I take it you know where we need to go?"

"I can get us there. Stay close. Try not to directly engage with anyone you see. They may manifest as people to you, but *nothing* in here is as it appears. You only saw what the Willows—that's what we calling them for lack of a better term—look like once they breach our world. This is a reality much closer to their own. Their powers of illusion and seduction are... Well, you heard what happened to the Scimitars."

"I did. We'll discuss the ethics of that—"

"Later, yes. Though I doubt you'll like what I have to show you much better."

I followed him through the smoky mists of the bar, grateful for the fresh night air of the street. Whatever else could be said of the place, its recreation was flawlessly accurate. Kleiststrasse, precisely as I remembered it before changing political tides had sent us scurrying. Taxis humming their way past the U-Bahn, the faint glow of the Theater am Nollendorfplatz apparent around the end of the block, women in shamelessly indulgent fur coats and men in immaculate evening dress laughed gaily as young men in overcoats scurried between them exchanging shy smiles. I couldn't place the year, or even the time of year. But if this was, as Iain said, a manifestation of where I had felt most 'at peace,' then no wonder I saw no…

Scratch that. There they were, coming out of a bar opposite the theatre. Brownshirts.

"I felt that," Iain said.

"Felt what?"

"Your anxiety just bounced sky high. You're looking at those Nazis through 21st century eyes. If you don't want the wrong kind of attention, act natural. Ignore them, just like you did in 1930."

"We were no great fans of them then."

It wasn't just the brownshirts. The entire place felt wrong. As if every building, car, tree, or person in this illusion carried the faint stench of hopelessness.

"This way," Iain said, taking us down a side street off Motzstrasse, rounding the building and coming to a small door leading to what I assumed was a basement level. Iain ushered me inside what revealed itself to be another bar. It was smaller than the one we'd left, though it was empty, save for a greasy, bored looking bartender reading a newspaper, and a sorrowful record playing in the corner. Ignoring the chanteuse's anguished tale of loneliness, I allowed Iain to lead me through to the back of the bar and down a darkened passage. So dark that even my keen Blood Shade vision lost sight of my feet in front of me.

"Iain?"

"Just stay close."

Only the man's footsteps betrayed his presence in the dark until a dim light taunted us from around a corner up ahead. Upon reaching it, I stopped dead in my tracks. My jaw fell open on the sight of the young man, tied spreadeagled to some strange apparatus, rippling with arcane energy. Lashings of pale blue light leapt across the naked, unconscious body, which seemed thinner than I remembered. Perhaps even malnourished. But there was no mistaking that face, nor those tattoos.

Jorgas.

I closed my eyes, supporting myself on my knees, trying to shake the illusion. It couldn't be real. Iain had said that this entire place was a product of my own imagination, knowledge, and memory. What I saw was not what others saw. In that case, what I saw could surely not be Jorgas, tied to… whatever that thing was.

"Reylan, please. I need your help."

I opened my eyes again, but the apparition refused to budge.

"Give me your hand," the Shaper said.

I let Iain take hold of my wrist and guide me toward the mirage until I felt the familiar, lightly furred skin of my former lover's chest beneath my fingertips.

My god.

"I'm not going to defend it. But we can get him back to—"

A loud crack echoed through the tiny room as my fist collided with the Shaper's jaw. He stumbled backward, barely stabilising himself against the wall before I leapt upon him, grabbing hold and unleashing the full force of the monster that dwelled beneath my human visage.

HEAR ME OUT! Panic heightened his telepathic voice.

I snarled, tightening my grip as the words bellowed inside my head. They only enraged me further.

An odd chill crept into the chamber, which seemed to darken for a second, before returning to its dimly lit state. Had the Shaper's telepathy agitated something within the Wound?

"I know what he means to you and you have every right to be furious. But if we're to have any chance of returning to the mortal world, I need you to do exactly what I tell you. Please?"

Return to the mortal world? I would have been content to strap Iain into the infernal contraption until it tortured him to madness. Though now I had a moment to catch myself, Jorgas didn't seem to be in pain. He just lay there, almost serene in his silence, save for the crackling energies around his body. Even these seemed to leave little or no effect.

"Why?" I asked quietly. "What's he doing here?"

"Making all of this possible. Regulating where the Wounds open and close, helping to mask our presence, allowing people—allowing *us*—to move safely through this realm undetected. There's so much more to werewolves than you know. Not just in their bodies, but in their minds. Supernal energies."

"Energies that could trigger a transformation?"

Iain swallowed. "Even the Scimitars aren't mad enough to disturb the Patrons."

I tensed, then released my fists. "And why *him*?"

Iain regarded me with a sympathy I wasn't sure I liked. "I'm afraid that was mostly about his relationship with you."

"Me?"

"I tried to warn you away. There are factions in the House—powerful factions—that opposed the plan to eliminate the Scimitar. Those same factions wanted the two of you killed for your little liaison. This was their compromise. Understand that to them, what Jorgas had done was… Reylan, I am beyond sorry."

"Spare me. The only reason you're still alive is because we need to get him out."

"I know, and perhaps I deserve that. I'll answer your questions once we're safely home, but we need to get him out of that device, now."

The urgency in his voice chilled me. Getting Jorgas out had never been part of the plan.

"They don't even know you're doing this, do they?"

"At the risk of repeating myself, there's no time! The Scimitars are either in the hands of the Patrons or dead. It's over, meaning Jorgas's usefulness has come to—"

"Fine! What do you need me to do?"

"What you do best. Feed from him."

Strands of energy lashed around my former lover. "Can we even get in there?"

"It's going to hurt like hell. Those discharges aren't electricity. But the pain should last for only a moment. I can protect your mind, but beyond that, let's hope your Blood Shade's constitution is all it's cracked up to be."

"What about your human constitution?"

A sly smile returned to his face. "So, you do care about me?"

"Don't bet on it."

Iain put his hands under my arms and wrapped them around my shoulders. If there were words to describe the feeling of his presence on my mind in that moment, they failed me.

"Ready?"

"Yes, damn it!"

I plunged my teeth into Jorgas's throat, releasing the life-giving stream of blood. Whatever the House of Magick's device had done to his body or his mind, his blood remained as rich, warm, and fulfilling as ever. The blood of a werewolf in human form.

Holy mother of nine shrieking hells!

Iain's warning about the pain proved no exaggeration as a sensation halfway between electricity and molten silver tore at my nerves. It took every scrap of fortitude not to cry out in pain, but I dared not.

Then, just as he'd promised, the pain subsided, and I found myself back in my bedroom, overlooking Jorgas as he slept, safe and sound as I'd ever seen. An illusion, of course, but a chillingly realistic one. I reached out toward the young man's sleeping body, only to see two small pinpricks of blood form on his neck, running into shining red rivulets as their sweet nectar drained into the sheets of my bed. I went to try and stem the bleeding, only for the scene to change. My room was now a dimly lit alley. Not just any alley, but the one in which Jorgas and I had first met. In place of Jorgas lay… Rory. The human I'd seen mortally wounded during one of Jorgas's uncontrolled changes. The human I'd been forced to euthanise.

"Ray?" Even his voice was the same. His legs were stripped almost to the bone, torso eviscerated, blood running down his face. "Help me."

Jorgas now stood beside me, sharing my helplessness and horror. He too remembered Rory.

"Why didn't you help me?"

We both jumped as the man's features gave way to hideous distortion, dark eyes growing wide, his once handsome face splitting into an obscene, bloody maw as skeletal hands lunged for us. Then this image too was gone. Jorgas remained at my side, but far from the horror that had marked his features a moment ago, his expression was now serene. Almost happy as he took his seat in a church pew, something I'd struggled to imagine, even knowing his background. A plump and ruddy looking priest I recognised as Father Isaac O'Baer sat down beside him. I'd met O'Baer only once, but the meeting had revealed just how much the man knew about us, Patricia Bakker, and Jorgas's true nature. That the two seemed so comfortable together did not surprise me. At least, not nearly as much as when the good Father leaned closer to him.

O'Baer's features began to splinter like cracking glass. The lines advanced rapidly, crossing his face like spiderwebs until the illusion fell away in time for Jorgas to claim his kiss—from Iain.

Now, I was furious. Not because some unshakeable instinct within me knew this was a memory, not an illusion, and not because I begrudged Jorgas sex with other people. I watched Iain's last lie of omission explode before my eyes. He'd played me with the greatest precision and skill since before our first encounter. This may have been a place of imagining, but it was also a place of truth. For all Iain's powers over the mind, he couldn't hide here. Had 'O'Baer' been a glamour to cover Iain's true identity? Or was my good Samaritan Shaper a murderer as well?

I hated him. Hated him more than I'd hated anyone. No wonder he'd been so willing to help me rescue Jorgas!

Unless their affection was more than pretence, and Iain genuinely cared for him.

I called Jorgas's name. The two men turned to me and stared, Jorgas with the look of a man bewildered, and Iain with faint bemusement, which then became laughter, though not the laughter of the man I saw. It was the carefree laughter of a young boy. The church's colourful windows shattered to reveal utilitarian panes of glass, pews folded into themselves, forming instead a row of desks, where the same young boy sat, laughing his head off. His soft black hair matched the endless darkness of his eyes, but even they betrayed a twinkle of the joy he released into the room. A joy clearly not shared by the nun teaching the class as she advanced on him with undisguised fury.

"That's enough!" she snapped.

I recognised the voice immediately. "Patricia?"

As the woman turned on me, there was no denying it. Patricia Bakker, much younger, in the full ceremonial penguin robes of her order.

"I'm sorry. Do I know you?" she asked. "What are you doing in— Get off of me at once!"

The boy had risen from his desk and thrown his arms around Bakker's legs, hugging her tight as he beamed with excitement, repeating over and over, "Can't hear you! Can't hear you! Can't hear you!"

"Stop it!" She physically pushed him away. When it became clear the boy would not, Bakker gestured to the door. "Get out, both of you! Now! Get out! Get out!"

"*Get out?*"

I caught my breath as an immense vision of Iain's face erupted from pitch darkness and barked the command, the sight of its pitch-black eyes chilling me. The school was gone. I felt the weight of Jorgas's body collapse into my arms as Iain's presence slipped from my shoulders. I licked closed the wound on Jorgas's neck where I'd bitten him, and held him tight in my arms, kissing his cheeks, his neck, his shoulders, his face, anywhere I could reach.

"Rey… Reylan?"

I hushed him quiet, letting him relax into me. Could he speak? Did he remember me?

"We need to leave," Iain said. "Now, Reylan. We need to go—"

"What did I just see in there? What the hell did you do to him, Shaper? And the little boy Bakker scolded? That was you, wasn't it?"

"There's no time! Jorgas was the only thing keeping the Wounds open to us. They've already begun to close. We need to leave, now."

It seemed futile to argue. For all my rage, he was right. The questions could wait. But oh, there would be questions!

"How do we do that?"

"We find a Wound that's still open. It'll seal up behind us once we go through, so no need to worry about that."

"Swell. How do we find one?"

"That's not as difficult as you might think. To our eye, they usually manifest as doors or gateways of some kind. The bigger they are, the more stable they are. But we need to move quickly. With Jorgas free, any creature that's lurking either in this realm or on its fringes will know there are living, corporeal beings in here, and where to find us."

I nodded, my mind racing. "The Brandenburg Gate."

"What?" Jorgas asked.

"It's the biggest gateway in the city, unless you have another suggestion."

Iain nodded. "It should work. Your problem will be getting there in time and in one piece. Even if you have the benefit of Blood Shade speed, we don't."

"We're not going to use Blood Shade speed," I said, looking at Jorgas.

The werewolf rolled his eyes.

*　　*　　*

I gripped the wolf's fur as impeccably dressed Berliners scrambled to get out of our way. Iain held tight to my waist as Jorgas's wolfen form bounded over taxis, charged beneath the tracks of the U-Bahn and leapt over Landwehr Canal in one bound. Did I need to remind the wolf that even as an 'immortal' being, I could still die—or worse—in this realm? Still, there was something refreshing about releasing the beast in a major city without a care for secrecy or consequence. The sight of humans realising they were no longer top of the food chain brought an arch smile to my lips. I knew from Jorgas's bound and speed that he was enjoying it, and I dared say Iain was as well.

I held tighter as Jorgas hit another burst of speed down an open street, heading right for the woods of Tiergarten. I heard him sniff the air with a tiny snarl, slowing as we reached the forest's edge and weaved inside the trees. My sharpened Blood Shade vision spied a large crowd up ahead, just beyond the edge of the park.

Hundreds of black, grey, and brown uniforms and suits, lit by torchlight, spread out from beneath the gate's glowing arches. Like many others, I'd left Berlin just as Hitler's lunatics had begun to find traction. I recalled seeing a sight like this one—hundreds of souls calling in unison, unified only by anger and hate—only once during my stay. Once was enough. A small man on a makeshift stage beneath the gate itself, barked into a microphone. Not the Fuhrer, but some pretender waiting in the wings for enough of his superiors to 'disappear,' and who knew the rhetoric and bluster to use in the meantime. Would such a gathering have been allowed so openly before the Nazis came to power, with nary a challenger in sight? Something was wrong with this picture, another reminder that this wasn't my Berlin.

"Iain, need I point out this is *not* where I felt most 'at peace?'"

"I know, but I'm afraid that mob isn't just a product of your mind. They're very real, and they're not human."

"Willows?"

"No way to know. They might be creatures whose true form we can't comprehend. But if your mind manifests them as Nazis, I don't want us anywhere near them."

"Maybe so. But we have to reach the gate."

The Nazis cheered once more. Jorgas's fur bristled as a swift breeze crossed it. I turned to face Iain, who nodded at me, not needing telepathy to know what I was thinking. With a light tug on his fur, Jorgas barrelled toward the crowd, the scampering of his paws drowned out by their angry shouts and cries until it was too late. The impact sent the first few sailing like ragdolls into the throng, but Jorgas barely slowed down, charging through grey and brown uniforms, tossing them aside with his massive snout, tearing off the odd arm or leg as needed as the men scattered in panic, unable to process the chaos that had besieged them. Uniforms caught fire as torches dropped in the melee. One man tried throwing his torch at Jorgas only to have it set one of his comrades ablaze. The scent of blood hung thick on the air, but Iain had been right. It smelled bitter, more like petrol, and there was no mistaking it for human blood, though it ran just as freely from the men's wounds. A few gunshots popped through the air, but even the truest bullet would have barely slowed the beast. Not that it stopped me swearing as one grazed my leg. If one of them hit Iain, he wouldn't heal up so easily. Hell, were these bullets at all, as we understood them?

A group of the thugs gathered themselves into a thick phalanx of scowls, torches brandished ahead of them like an angry mob of villagers trying to deflect the beast.

They did no such thing. I smelled singed fur and flesh as Jorgas hit their front-line head on, knocking a man to the ground and extinguishing his torch under a heavy paw. The man screamed until Jorgas tore his throat out and went to work on his closest neighbour, latching hold of that man's midsection and ripping open his stomach. But the Nazis were now so high on rage that even the sight of their comrade's unspooling innards didn't ward them off. A few well-placed chomps and heavy paws laid more of the men low, but they kept coming, eyes wide, mouths screaming curses in a language that no longer resembled German, or anything human.

"Iain?" I held tight as Jorgas caught another of the men's throats in his bloody jaws.

"Their minds aren't of our world, Reylan." He booted another Nazi hard across the face. "There's nothing I can do here."

I had to assume my own telepathic gifts—to beguile, hypnotise, or frighten the hell out of my target—would be equally useless. My gaze fell upon one of the Nazis, a few rows back. Unlike the others, who came at us with wide eyes filled with hatred, this small, balding man stared at us with dark, dead eyes until his skull cracked open to reveal a half dozen long, spindly grey legs.

Jorgas must have seen it as well, as he quickly had the man pinned to the ground with several bleeding gashes down his chest. The thing that had emerged from his skull however, skipped nimbly over Jorgas's snout, evading my attempts to knock it away as it finally found its target.

I grabbed with futility for the thing, only to see it dive upon Iain's shoulder, knocking him off Jorgas's back and into the throng. I cried out to him, trying to steer Jorgas around to help. But the wolf was not accustomed to being steered, and it had no shortage of prey. The thugs swarmed the fallen Shaper, whose cries for help could no longer be heard under the din of the crowd. The man on the stage had started up again, this time more agitated, screaming and pointing at us. No matter how many men Jorgas felled, we'd soon be dead if we stayed here,

Reylan? Reylan!

Where are you? I tried to reach out. If he could just tell us who to kill.

I don't… Help!

Jorgas roared as I yanked on his fur, bringing him around to attack the Nazis who'd swarmed Iain. Though he landed a few well-placed chomps and clawings, it didn't thin them.

Jorgas was bleeding. There was no mistaking the toxic blood of a fully transformed werewolf.

Iain? Damn it! Where are you?

This time, I heard nothing. As Jorgas sent several more Nazis flying, I scanned the crowd, looking for any sign of the Shaper. The snarls of a furious mob greeted me, as they continued to swarm the spot where Iain had fallen. In doing so, they opened a thinly guarded path in their ranks, leading right to their leader—and the gate.

Iain? Iain! Answer me!

Nothing. Not a word.

One of the Nazis grabbed my leg, digging into it with claws too sharp to be human. I kicked him away with no small effort, looking once more at the gate, and our path to freedom.

"Luca…"

Only now did I see the detail of four faces, set in stone within the columns of the gate. With a Blood Shade's sharpened vision, there was no mistaking them. Luca, Suzette, Colin, and… Peter, against all Brett's efforts to keep him safe. Or perhaps he'd seen little point in suffering the brief existence left to him without his master. Now, here they were, all four of them, left to who knew what fate?

"Iain!" I yelled. But if there was a way to find him, or to save Luca, Colin, or the others, I would never find out.

A loud roar from Jorgas scattered more of the mob. I tightened my grip on his back and held on as he charged the stage. The little orator's eyes widened as the werewolf knocked the microphone aside and dived into him, taking all three of us through the gate's arches, where the shouts of the crowd abruptly vanished.

CHAPTER SIXTEEN

I startled as we landed on the cold, wet street, not sure of my surroundings until my eyes adjusted to the dim light emanating from the backs of buildings. Sydney. It looked, sounded, and smelled like Sydney. I lapped at the rain pelting my face. Blood Shades weren't naturally disposed to thirst, but who knew what passing through the Wound—twice—had done to my system?

And there was Jorgas, returned to human form and barely conscious as he lay naked in my arms, but alive. Flopping around on the ground just past our feet was… I'd no fucking idea. The thing emitted a high-pitched whine as it reached out with gangly pink limbs, mouth opening and closing at the centre of what might charitably be called a head. But it didn't belong in this world.

I gently released Jorgas and got to my feet, not taking my eyes off the creature until I'd crushed it beneath my boot with a satisfying squelch. Nazi or nymph, it had no place here.

"Reylan?"

I helped Jorgas to his feet, grateful for the rain that gently pummelled away whatever entrails still clung to his skin. I wiped more of the muck away and took him in my arms. "I've got you. You're safe."

He shivered. "Where's Iain?"

How could I answer that? Honestly, I supposed. "I don't know. The last I saw…"

We stared at each other, and for the first time, I got a good look at his eyes. Anxious. Fearful. Jorgas had cared for Iain. He still did. Perhaps the Shaper had cared for him too.

"He knows a lot more about that place than either of us. If anyone can find a way out, it's him."

Silence. Was I raising false hope?

"Come on," I said, wiping the last of the creatures' blood from his shoulders and pulling Jorgas into me once more. "Let's go home."

He nodded silently, a thousand questions in his eyes as his face drew close to mine.

Questions that could wait.

Also in *The Arcadia Trust* series:

THE BEAST WITHOUT

Reylan is everything a Sydney vampire aspires to be:
wealthy, handsome and independent, carefully feeding off
companions plucked from the gay bars of Oxford Street.

When one of those companions is killed by Jorgas, a hot-
headed young werewolf prowling his streets, Reylan
reluctantly puts his cherished lifestyle of blood and boys on
hold to help a mysterious alliance of supernatural beings
track down the beast. It can't be that hard…not when Jorgas
keeps coming after him.

But there's more to this werewolf than a body count and
a bad attitude. As their relationship grows deeper and more
twisted, Reylan tastes Jorgas's blood, reawakening desires the
vampire had thought long dead. And what evolves between
them may be far more dangerous than some rival predator in
the dark…

THE ORCHARD OF FLESH

Reylan's last assignment for The Arcadia Trust brought a rebellious human servant under his roof, and a volatile werewolf lover named Jorgas into his bed, leaving the self-reliant Blood Shade—known to the outside world as vampires—in no hurry to risk his immortality for them again.

But when a new terror starts disappearing humans from a bad part of town, Reylan must do everything in his power to keep Sydney's supernatural factions from the brink of war. Having an ambitious, meddlesome human in the mix is only going to make things worse…especially when that human is Jorgas's father.

Reylan will need all his determination and cunning to keep the peace under his roof, between the night's power brokers, and in his lover's troubled heart.

Also by Christian Baines:

PUPPET BOY

A school in turmoil over its senior play, a sly career as a teenage gigolo, an unpredictable girlfriend with damage of her own, and a dangerous housebreaker tied up downstairs. Any of these would make a great plot for budding filmmaker Eric's first movie. Unfortunately, they're his real life. When Julien, a handsome wannabe actor, transfers to Eric's class, he's a distraction, a rival, and one complication too many. Yet

Eric can't stop thinking about him. Helped by Eric's girlfriend, Mary, they embark on a project that dangerously crosses the line between filmmaking and reality. As the boys become close, Eric soon wants to cross other lines entirely. Does Julien feel the same way, or is Eric being used on the gleefully twisted path to fame?

SKIN

Kyle, a young newcomer to New Orleans, is haunted by the memory of his first lover, brutally murdered just outside the French Quarter.

Marc, a young Quarter hustler, is haunted by an eccentric spirit that shares his dreams, and by the handsome but vicious lover who shares his bed.

When the barrier between these men comes down, it will prove thinner than the veil between the living and the dead…or between justice and revenge.

www.ingramcontent.com/pod-product-compliance
Lightning Source LLC
Chambersburg PA
CBHW021305190726
48288CB00003B/698